TOMORROW, THE STARS

A SCIENCE FICTION ANTHOLOGY

EDITED AND WITH AN INTRODUCTION BY

Robert A. HEINLEIN

A BERKLEY MEDALLION BOOK
published by
BERKLEY PUBLISHING CORPORATION

For DOROTHY and CLARE

SBN 425–02931–X

BERKLEY MEDALLION BOOKS are published by
Berkley Publishing Corporation
200 Madison Avenue
New York, N.Y. 10016

Berkley Medallion Books ® TM 757,375

Printed in the United States of America

BERKLEY MEDALLION EDITION, JUNE, 1967
TWELFTH PRINTING

PREFACE

The first science-fiction anthology merited a reader's examination as something new; the nineteenth (or fiftieth; the number changes rapidly) cannot plead that justification and needs a reason for being other than the well-known hunger of writers, editors, and publishers.

The purpose of this book is to give you pleasure.

The stories have been selected to entertain, and within the very broad category of "speculative fiction," no other criterion has been used. Our intention has been to bring together good stories, ones which give pleasure on rereading and which have not previously been available in book form. These stories may possibly instruct, mystify, elevate, or inspire; if so, consider such to be bonuses not covered by the purchase price; our single motive is to entertain you.

Science fiction has only recently become popular and is not yet fully respectable. Until the end of World War II it was, in the opinion of most critics, by definition "trash" and so convicted without a hearing. The scientific marvels of World War II—radar, atom bombs, giant rockets—and the rather spectacular success of science-fiction writers in predicting these things combined to cause a widespread postwar interest in speculative fiction, stories about the future, which in time forced the professional critics to notice this stepchild of literature.

And yet one may pause to wonder why the stepchild was so completely ignored before the war. Quite aside from the pulp specialty magazines, many worth-while, deeply thoughtful novels of this genre were available to the critics before World War II, for example, S. Fowler Wright's monumental *The World Below,* or Olaf Stapledon's philosophical novels of the future of our race. And many of the standard literary lions had ventured at least one science-fiction novel. Why should so much of J. B. Priestley's reputation rest on *Angel Pavement* while *The Doomsday Men* is almost unheard of? Why was there a rage for *The Green Hat* while Michael Arlen's *Man's Mortality* made hardly a ripple? The four authors cited cannot possibly be accused of being semiliterate hacks suited only to publication on pulpwood paper and catering to that portion of the public which moves its lips while reading. Why were their serious works in speculative fiction ignored?

I'll chance a guess. The story about the future never has fitted comfortably into the implicitly defined limits of serious literature. In the prose field, "literature" in the stuffy and respectable sense usually meant either the historical novel or certain rather pedestrian types of the contemporary novel. One gathers the impression that it helps for the author to be dead or to have had the good judgment to write his story first in a language less well known than English, but these are not indispensable requirements. Rather ponderous length seems to be part of the unspoken definition, extensive research should be either self-evident or claimed, and dialogue is usually sparse and not too sprightly. A clearly stated regional scene is a help too, especially if it is back country. Such a novel the literary critic can take in his stride, read in one evening, and compose his review while shaving. It either does or does not come up to his standards and he knows why. Either way, it is an accepted type and a serious piece of work.

Science fiction does not fit into this frame; it's a much more exotic art. The critic may find himself shying away from this literary freak. He can judge quickly whether or not it is grammatical and readable, but what about the content? A man who has applied himself seriously to the field of English literature may not have had time to be well-read in geology, nuclear physics, rocket engineering, astrophysics, genetics, cosmogony, cybernetics, chemistry, biophysics, and electronics. Can he afford to recommend this item as a serious and worth-while work? Does the author know what he is talking about—or is the rude fellow pulling one's leg? Perhaps his "science" is of the Sunday-supplement variety, in which case one would not wish to recommend it. But how is one to *know?*

The dilemma is quite real, for there are many stories around which bear the same close superficial resemblance to honest science fiction that a lead quarter does to a product of the Denver mint. The critic is hardly to be blamed if he chooses to pass up extravagant stories of the future in favor of the tried and true.

Science fiction is even less prepared to compete for attention in the most modern of the ultra-literary school. Science-fiction heroes are almost always likable, rarely psychotic (the mad scientist has had his day), and they almost never fall in love with their sisters or their fathers' wives or mistresses. The writers of science fiction without exception favor clear, lucid, grammatical sentences; I do not guarantee against an occasional split infinitive, but they never write in a Joycean or neo-Freudian mishmash. As you can see, the fiction of the future is much too old-fashioned to win even a passing nod from the *avant-garde* school critics. Perhaps it is just as well.

Let me add that the skilled practitioners (no other sort are represented in this volume) have learned not to lard their stories with obscure and polysyllabic technical terms and have learned how to define in context such few special terms as may be indispensable to following the story. They have even given up the long-cherished practice of assigning to natives of other planets names consisting mainly of throat-rasping gutturals. I must admit that sparsely dressed and exceedingly nubile young ladies still appear on the covers of some of the specialist magazines, but they are rarely to be found now in the stories inside those same magazines; their persistence on the covers is simply a part of the same phenomenon to be found in cigarette, automobile, and deodorant ads.

Literature or not, science fiction is here to stay; it will not be crowded out even by the new Plunging-Neckline school of the historical novel, nor by the four-letter-word school of the contemporary novel. Youths who build hot-rods are not dismayed by spaceships; in their adult years they will build such ships. In the meantime they will read stories of interplanetary travel—and they are being joined by their entire families. The future rushes at us apace, faster than sound, approaching the speed of light; the healthy-minded are aware of our headlong plunge into a strange and different, possibly terrifying, future and see nothing improper in speculating about the shape of tomorrow.

Science fiction is sometimes miscalled "escape literature," a mistake arising from a profound misconception of its nature and caused by identifying it with fantasy. Science fiction and fantasy are as different as Karl Marx and Groucho Marx. Fantasy is constructed either by denying the real world *in toto* or at least by making a prime basis of the story one or more admittedly false premise—fairies, talking mules, trips through a looking glass, vampires, seacoast Bohemia, Mickey Mouse. But science fiction, *no matter how fantastic its content may seem,* always accepts all of the real world and the entire body of human knowledge about the real world as the framework for the fictional speculation. Since the field of human knowledge concerning the real world, its natural laws, events, and phenomena, is much too large for any one brain, every science-fiction author is bound to make some slips, but here it is the intention that counts: the author's purpose is not to escape from reality but to explore seriously the complex and amazing manifold of possibilities which lie unrevealed in the future of our race—to explore them in the light of what we *do* know *now.*

If such is escape literature, then so is an insurance policy. (There is only one story here, "I'm Scared," by Jack Finney, which could possibly be called "escape literature"—but it provides no escape for the reader. Better skip it.)

All of the stories herein are honest science fiction, but there is another type of story masquerading as science fiction which circulates like the lead quarters mentioned earlier. Call it "pseudo-scientific fantasy." The writers thereof are either too ignorant or too careless to do the painstaking work required to produce honest speculation. Much of it gets printed, unfortunately, since all editors cannot be expected to be erudite in all fields of knowledge. Nor do you find it only in the pulp magazines with the pretty bare-skinned ladies and the bug-eyed monsters on the covers; it is as likely to pop up in the most respected slick-paper magazines or between the boards of dignified trade-book houses. Such stories may be rife with spaceships, ray guns, and mutant monsters, but they are marked by a crude disregard for established fact. However, knowledge of the world about us and of the scientific facts which describe its functioning is rather widespread these days; the effect of such barbarisms on the reader who does happen to know that the facts are being manhandled is much like that which would arise from the reading of a "historical" novel which asserted that Henry VIII was the son of Queen Elizabeth, or a war story in which the writer was under the impression that corporals were senior to master sergeants. It is to be hoped that, as the public increases in sophistication in these matters, such writers will find it necessary to go back to working for a living. In the meantime, such slips as you may find in this book are the honest mistakes of honest workmen; I think I can vouch that such errors as exist do not invalidate the stories in which they appear.

Science fiction is not fantasy, but it can certainly be fantastic—and be assured that the more fantastic it is, the more wild, the more extravagant it sounds, it is that much more likely to be a reasonably correct extrapolation of what our real future will be. Regard the difference between the 1900 horse-and-buggy and the 1950 faster-than-sound plane. Our fictional prophecies almost certainly err on the side of conservatism. In this book you will find stories of space travel (of course!), a gambol in the fourth dimension, telekinesis, robots, intelligent plants, strange nonhuman creatures from the other side of the galaxy, and invasions from Mars. The Wonderful Land of Oz has not more to offer—and none of it is fantasy.

Did I hear someone describe robots as fantasy? I myself find humanoid robots hard to believe in, but who am I to set my prejudices against the facts? I put it to you that a B-36 in flight is a fair example of a robot activated by a controlling human brain. I submit further that it is a longer step from the covered wagon to the B-36 than it is from present cybernetic machines to Dr. Asimov's "positronic robots." But can a machine have consciousness, life, volition? We don't know, because we do not as yet know what any of those things are. Meanwhile, robotics is a legitimate field for speculation.

Time travel? We don't understand the nature of time; it is much too early to say that time travel is impossible. Telekinesis? Refer to the abstruse reports pouring out of Duke University and elsewhere, then resolve never again to bet on dice. The control of mass by the human mind is as factually established as yesterday's sunrise. (Tomorrow's sunrise is, of course, only a high probability.) For the impact that telekinesis may have on your grandchildren— or on *you*—see "The Barnhouse Effect" herewith. Space travel? Go down to White Sands, watch them throw one of the big ones away, and be convinced. Space travel is about to move from speculative fiction to contemporary fiction and news story, and some of us are a wee bit wistful about it. How can we dream up wonderful new Martians when the *National Geographic* starts running photographs of real ones?

One story is included here almost as a period piece— "Rainmaker." When first published shortly after World War II this piece was science fiction; now the commercial trade of rainmaking has reached the point where lawsuits dealing with it clutter the courts. Technology has overtaken prophecy. But a good story is not ruined thereby; "Rainmaker" is still fun to read. Besides, it is clinching demonstration of the vast difference between pseudo-scientific fantasy and the real article. But it is the fact that "Rainmaker" was and remains a pleasure to read that controlled its inclusion here; we the editors are strongly convinced that science-fiction pieces should be *stories,* warm and human, not thinly disguised engineering reports. On that note this essay will close in order that you may get on with the real purpose of this book, the reading of stories about people who might be your grandchildren, facing new problems in this wildly fantastic universe. Each story has been read and reread by each of five editors—and enjoyed each time; we expect that you will enjoy them too.

My thanks to the other four—Truman Talley, Judith Merril, Fred Pohl, and Walter Bradbury.

ROBERT A. HEINLEIN

Colorado Springs

CONTENTS

I'M SCARED

by Jack Finney

I'm very badly scared, not so much for myself—I'm a gray-haired man of sixty-six, after all—but for you and everyone else who has not yet lived out his life. For I believe that certain dangerous things have recently begun to happen in the world. They are noticed here and there, idly discussed, then dismissed and forgotten. Yet I am convinced that unless these occurrences are recognized for what they are, the world will be plunged into a nightmare. Judge for yourself.

One evening last winter I came home from a chess club to which I belong. I'm a widower; I live alone in a small but comfortable three-room apartment overlooking Fifth Avenue. It was still fairly early, and I switched on a lamp beside my leather easy chair, picked up a murder mystery I'd been reading, and turned on the radio; I did not, I'm sorry to say, notice which station it was tuned to.

The tubes warmed, and the music of an accordion—faint at first, then louder—came from the loud-speaker. Since it was good music for reading, I adjusted the volume control and began to read.

Now I want to be absolutely factual and accurate about this, and I do not claim that I paid close attention to the radio. But I do know that presently the music stopped and an audience applauded. Then a man's voice, chuckling and pleased with the applause, said, "All right, all right," but the applause continued for several more seconds. During that time the voice once more chuckled appreciatively, then firmly repeated, "All right," and the applause died down. "That was Alec Somebody-or-other," the radio voice said, and I went back to my book.

But I soon became aware of this middle-aged voice again; perhaps a change of tone as he turned to a new subject caught my attention. "And now, Miss Ruth Greeley," he was saying, "of Trenton, New Jersey. Miss Greeley is a pianist; that right?" A girl's voice, timid and barely audible, said, "That's right, Major Bowes." The man's voice—and now I recognized his familiar singsong delivery—and, "And what are you going to play?"

The girl replied, "'La Paloma.'" The man repeated it after her, as an announcement: "'La Paloma.'" There was a pause, then an introductory chord sounded from a piano, and I resumed my reading.

As the girl played, I was half aware that her style was mechanical, her rhythm defective; perhaps she was nervous. Then my attention was fully aroused once more by a gong which sounded suddenly. For a few notes more the girl continued to play falteringly, not sure what to do. The gong sounded jarringly again, the playing abruptly stopped and there was a restless murmur from the audience. "All right, all right," said the familiar voice, and I realized I'd been expecting this, knowing it would say just that. The audience quieted, and the voice began, "Now——"

The radio went dead. For the smallest fraction of a second no sound issued from it but its own mechanical hum. Then a completely different program came from the loudspeaker; the recorded voices of Bing Crosby and his son were singing the concluding bars of "Sam's Song," a favorite of mine. So I returned once more to my reading, wondering vaguely what had happened to the other program, but not actually thinking about it until I finished my book and began to get ready for bed.

Then, undressing in my bedroom, I remembered that Major Bowes was dead. Years had passed, half a decade, since that dry chuckle and familiar, "All right, all right," had been heard in the nation's living rooms.

Well, what does one do when the apparently impossible occurs? It simply made a good story to tell friends, and more than once I was asked if I'd recently heard Moran and Mack, a pair of radio comedians popular some twenty-five years ago, or Floyd Gibbons, an old-time news broadcaster. And there were other joking references to my crystal radio set.

But one man—this was at a lodge meeting the following Thursday—listened to my story with utter seriousness, and when I had finished he told me a queer little story of his own. He is a thoughtful, intelligent man, and as I listened I was not frightened, but puzzled at what seemed to be a connecting link, a common denominator, beween this story and the odd behavior of my radio. Since I am retired and have plenty of time, I took the trouble, the following day, of making a two-hour train trip to Connecticut in order to verify the story firsthand. I took detailed notes, and the story appears in my files now as follows:

Case 2. Louis Trachnor, coal and wood dealer, R.F.D. 1, Danbury, Connecticut, aged fifty-four.

On July 20, 1950, Mr. Trachnor told me, he walked out on the front porch of his house about six o'clock in the morning. Running from the eaves of his house to the floor of the porch was a streak of gray paint, still damp. "It was about the width of an eight-inch brush," Mr. Trachnor told me, "and it looked like hell, because the house was white. I figured some kids did it in the night for a joke, but if they did, they had to get a ladder up to the eaves and you wouldn't figure they'd go to that much trouble. It wasn't smeared, either; it was a careful job, a nice even stripe straight down the front of the house."

Mr. Trachnor got a ladder and cleaned off the gray paint with turpentine.

In October of that same year Mr. Trachnor painted his house. "The white hadn't held up so good, so I painted it gray. I got to the front last and finished about five one Saturday afternoon. Next morning when I came out I saw a streak of white right down the front of the house. I figured it was the damn kids again, because it was the same place as before. But when I looked close, I saw it wasn't new paint; it was the old white I'd painted over. Somebody had done a nice careful job of cleaning off the new paint in a long stripe about eight inches wide right down from the eaves! Now who the hell would go to that trouble? I just can't figure it out."

Do you see the link between this story and mine? Suppose for a moment that something had happened, on each occasion, to disturb briefly the orderly progress of time. That seemed to have happened in my case; for a matter of some seconds I apparently heard a radio broadcast that had been made years before. Suppose, then, that no one had touched Mr. Trachnor's house but himself; that he

had painted his house in October, but that through some
fantastic mix-up in time, a portion of that paint appeared on
his house the previous summer. Since he had cleaned the
paint off at that time, a broad stripe of new gray paint was
missing *after* he painted his house in the fall.

I would be lying, however, if I said I really believed this. It
was merely an intriguing speculation, and I told both these
little stories to friends, simply as curious anecdotes. I am a
sociable person, see a good many people, and occasionally I
heard other odd stories in response to mine.

Someone would nod and say, "Reminds me of something
I heard recently———" and I would have one more to add to
my collection. A man on Long Island received a telephone
call from his sister in New York one Friday evening. She
insists that she did not make this call until the following
Monday, three days later. At the Forty-fifth Street branch of
the Chase National Bank, I was shown a check deposited
the day before it was written. A letter was delivered on East
Sixty-eighth Street in New York City, just seventeen minutes after it was dropped into a mailbox on the main street of
Green River, Wyoming.

And so on, and so on; my stories were now in demand at
parties, and I told myself that collecting and verifying them
was a hobby. But the day I heard Julia Eisenberg's story, I
knew it was no longer that.

*Case 17. Julia Eisenberg, office worker, New York City,
aged thirty-one.*

Miss Eisenberg lives in a small walk-up apartment in
Greenwich Village. I talked to her there after a chess-club
friend who lives in her neighborhood had repeated to me a
somewhat garbled version of her story, which was told to
him by the doorman of the building he lives in.

In October 1947, about eleven at night, Miss Eisenberg
left her apartment to walk to the drugstore for toothpaste.
On her way back, not far from her apartment, a large black-
and-white dog ran up to her and put his front paws on her
chest.

"I made the mistake of petting, him," Miss Eisenberg
told me, "and from then on he simply wouldn't leave. When
I went into the lobby of my building, I actually had to push
him away to get the door closed. I felt sorry for him, poor
hound, and a little guilty, because he was still sitting at the
door an hour later when I looked out my front window."

This dog remained in the neighborhood for three days, discovering and greeting Miss Eisenberg with wild affection each time she appeared on the street. "When I'd get on the bus in the morning to go to work, he'd sit on the curb looking after me in the most mournful way, poor thing. I wanted to take him in, but I knew he'd never go home then, and I was afraid whoever owned him would be sorry to lose him. No one in the neighborhood knew whom he belonged to, and finally he disappeared."

Two years later a friend gave Miss Eisenberg a three-week-old puppy. "My apartment is really too small for a dog, but he was such a darling I couldn't resist. Well, he grew up into a nice big dog who ate more than I did."

Since the neighborhood was quiet, and the dog well behaved, Miss Eisenberg usually unleashed him when she walked him at night, for he never strayed far. "One night—I'd last seen him sniffing around in the dark a few doors down—I called to him and he didn't come back. And he never did; I never saw him again.

"Now our street is a solid wall of brownstone buildings on both sides, with locked doors and no areaways. He *couldn't* have disappeared like that, he just *couldn't*. But he did."

Miss Eisenberg hunted for her dog for many days afterward, inquired of neighbors, put ads in the papers, but she never found him. "Then one night I was getting ready for bed; I happened to glance out the front window down at the street, and suddenly I remembered something I'd forgotten all about. I remembered the dog I'd chased away over two years before." Miss Eisenberg looked at me for a moment, then she said flatly, "It was the same dog. If you own a dog you know him, you can't be mistaken, and I tell you it was the same dog. Whether it makes sense or not, my dog was lost—I chased him away—two years before he was born."

She began to cry silently, the tears running down her face. "Maybe you think I'm crazy, or a little lonely and overly sentimental about a dog. But you're wrong." She brushed at her tears with a handkerchief. "I'm a well-balanced person, as much as anyone is these days, at least, and I tell you I *know* what happened."

It was at that moment, sitting in Miss Eisenberg's neat, shabby living room, that I realized fully that the consequences of these odd little incidents could be something more than merely intriguing; that they might, quite possibly, be tragic. It was in that moment that I began to be afraid.

I have spent the last eleven months discovering and tracking down these strange occurrences, and I am astonished and frightened at how many there are. I am astonished and frightened at how much more frequently they are happening now, and—I hardly know how to express this—at their increasing power to tear human lives tragically apart. This is an example, selected almost at random, of the increasing strength of—whatever it is that is happening in the world.

Case 34. Paul V. Kerch, accountant, the Bronx, aged thirty-one.

On a bright clear Sunday afternoon, I met an unsmiling family of three at their Bronx apartment: Mr. Kerch, a chunky, darkly good-looking young man; his wife, a pleasant-faced dark-haired woman in her late twenties, whose attractiveness was marred by circles under her eyes; and their son, a nice-looking boy of six or seven. After introductions, the boy was sent to his room at the back of the house to play.

"All right," Mr. Kerch said wearily then, and walked toward a bookcase, "let's get at it. You said on the phone that you know the story in general." It was half a question, half a statement.

"Yes," I said.

He took a book from the top shelf and removed some photographs from it. "There are the pictures." He sat down on the davenport beside me, with the photographs in his hand. "I own a pretty good camera. I'm a fair amateur photographer, and I have a darkroom setup in the kitchen; do my own developing. Two weeks ago we went down to Central Park." His voice was a tired monotone, as though this was a story he'd repeated many times, aloud and in his own mind. "It was nice, like today, and the kid's grand-mothers have been pestering us for pictures, so I took a whole roll of films, pictures of all of us. My camera can be set up and focused and it will snap the picture automatically a few seconds later, giving me time to get around in front of it and get in the picture myself."

There was a tired, hopeless look in his eyes as he handed me all but one of the photographs. "These are the first ones I took," he said. The photographs were all fairly large, perhaps seven by three and a half inches, and I examined them closely.

They were ordinary enough, very sharp and detailed, and each showed the family of three in various smiling poses. Mr. Kerch wore a light business suit, his wife had on a dark dress and a cloth coat, and the boy wore a dark suit with knee-length pants. In the background stood a tree with bare branches. I glanced up at Mr. Kerch, signifying that I had finished my study of the photographs.

"The last picture," he said, holding it in his hand ready to give to me, "I took exactly like the others. We agreed on the pose, I set the camera, walked around in front, and joined my family. Monday night I developed the whole roll. This is what came out on the last negative." He handed me the photograph.

For an instant it seemed to me like merely one more photograph in the group; then I saw the difference. Mr. Kerch looked much the same, bareheaded and grinning broadly, but he wore an entirely different suit. The boy, standing beside him, wore long pants, was a good three inches taller, obviously older, but equally obviously the same boy. The woman was an entirely different person. Dressed smartly, her light hair catching the sun, she was very pretty and attractive. She was smiling into the camera and holding Mr. Kerch's hand.

I looked up at him. "Who is this?"

Wearily, Mr. Kerch shook his head. "I don't know," he said suddenly, then exploded: "I don't *know!* I've never seen her in my life!" He turned to look at his wife, but she would not return his glance, and he turned back to me, shrugging. "Well, there you have it," he said. "The whole story." And he stood up, thrusting both hands into his trouser pockets, and began to pace about the room, glancing often at his wife, talking to *her* actually, though he addressed his words to me. "So who is she? How could the camera have snapped that picture? I've never seen that woman in my life!"

I glanced at the photograph again, then bent closer. "The trees here are in full bloom," I said. Behind the solemn-faced boy, the grinning man and smiling woman, the trees of Central Park were in full summer leaf.

Mr. Kerch nodded. "I know," he said bitterly. "And you

know what *she* says?" he burst out, glaring at his wife. "She says that *is* my wife in the photograph, my *new* wife a couple of years from now! God!" He snapped both hands down on his head. "The ideas a woman can get!"

"What do you mean?" I glanced at Mrs. Kerch, but she ignored me, remaining silent, her lips tight.

Kerch shrugged hopelessly. "She says that photograph shows how things will be a couple of years from now. She'll be dead or"——he hesitated, then said the word bitterly—— "divorced, and I'll have our son and be married to the woman in the picture."

We both looked at Mrs. Kerch, waiting until she was obliged to speak.

"Well, if it isn't so," she said, shrugging a shoulder, "then tell me what that picture does mean."

Neither of us could answer that, and a few minutes later I left. There was nothing much I could say to the Kerches; certainly I couldn't mention my conviction that, whatever the explanation of the last photograph, their married life was over. . . .

Case 72. Lieutenant Alfred Eichler, New York Police Department, aged thirty-three.

In the late evening of January 9, 1951, two policemen found a revolver lying just off a gravel path near an East Side entrance to Central Park. The gun was examined for fingerprints at the police laboratory and several were found. One bullet had been fired from the revolver and the police fired another which was studied and classified by a ballistics expert. The fingerprints were checked and found in police files; they were those of a minor hoodlum with a record of assault.

A routine order to pick him up was sent out. A detective called at the roominghouse where he was known to live, but he was out, and since no unsolved shootings had occurred recently, no intensive search for him was made that night.

The following evening a man was shot and killed in Central Park with the same gun. This was proved ballistically past all question of error. It was soon learned that the murdered man had been quarreling with a friend in a nearby tavern. The two men, both drunk, had left the tavern together. And the second man was the hoodlum whose gun had been found the previous night, and which was still locked in a police safe.

As Lieutenant Eichler said to me, "It's impossible that
the dead man was killed with that same gun, but he was.
Don't ask me how, though, and if anybody thinks we'd go
into court with a case like that, they're crazy."

*Case 111. Captain Hubert V. Rihm, New York Police
Department, retired, aged sixty-six.*

I met Captain Rihm by appointment one morning in
Stuyvesant Park, a patch of greenery, wood benches, and
asphalt surrounded by the city, on lower Second Avenue.
"You want to hear about the Fentz case, do you?" he said,
after we had introduced ourselves and found an empty
bench. "All right, I'll tell you. I don't like to talk about it—it
bothers me—but I'd like to see what you think." He was a
big, rather heavy man, with a red, tough face, and he wore
an old police jacket and uniform cap with the insignia
removed.

"I was up at City Mortuary," he began as I took out my
notebook and pencil, "at Bellevue, about twelve one night,
drinking coffee with one of the interns. This was in June of
1950, just before I retired, and I was in Missing Persons.
They brought this guy in and he was a funny-looking
character. Had a beard. A young guy, maybe thirty, but he
wore regular muttonchop whiskers, and his clothes were
funny-looking. Now I was thirty years on the force and I've
seen a lot of queer guys killed on the streets. We found an
Arab once, in full regalia, and it took us a week to find out
who he was. So it wasn't just the way the guy looked that
bothered me; it was the stuff we found in his pockets."

Captain Rihm turned on the bench to see if he'd caught
my interest, then continued. "There was about a dollar in
change in the dead guy's pocket, and one of the boys picked
up a nickel and showed it to me. Now you've seen plenty of
nickels, the new ones with Jefferson's picture, the buffalo
nickels they made before that, and once in a while you still
even see the old Liberty-head nickels; they quit making
them before the first world war. But this one was even older
than that. It had a shield on the front, a United States shield,
and a big five on the back; I used to see that kind when I was
a boy. And the funny thing was, that old nickel looked new;
what coin dealers call 'mint condition,' like it was made the
day before yesterday. The date on that nickel was 1876, and
there wasn't a coin in his pocket dated any later."

Captain Rihm looked at me questioningly. "Well," I said,

glancing up from my notebook, "that could happen."

"Sure it could," he answered in a satisfied tone, "but all the pennies he had were Indian-head pennies. Now when did you see one of them last? There was even a silver three-cent piece; looked like an old-style dime, only smaller. And the bills in his wallet, every one of them, were old-time bills, the big kind."

Captain Rihm leaned forward and spat on the patch, a needle jet of tobacco juice and an expression of a policeman's annoyed contempt for anything deviating from an orderly norm.

"Over seventy bucks in cash, and not a federal reserve note in the lot. There were two yellow-back tens. Remember them? They were payable in gold. The rest were old national-bank notes; you remember them too. Issued direct by local banks, personally signed by the bank president; that kind used to be counterfeited a lot.

"Well," Captain Rihm continued, leaning back on the bench and crossing his knees, "there was a bill in his pocket from a livery stable on Lexington Avenue; three dollars for feeding and stabling his horse and washing a carriage. There was a brass slug in his pocket good for a five-cent beer at some saloon. There was a letter postmarked Philadelphia, June 1876, with an old-style two-cent stamp, and a bunch of cards in his wallet. The cards had his name and address on them, and so did the letter."

"Oh," I said, a little surprised, "you identified him right away, then?"

"Sure. Rudolph Fentz, some address on Fifth Avenue—I forget the exact number—in New York City. No problem at all." Captain Rihm leaned forward and spat again. "Only that address wasn't a residence. It's a store, and it has been for years, and nobody there ever heard of any Rudolph Fentz, and there's no such name in the phone book either. Nobody ever called or made any inquiries about the guy, and Washington didn't have his prints. There was a tailor's name in his coat, a lower Broadway address, but nobody there ever heard of this tailor."

"What was so strange about his clothes?"

The captain said, "Well, did you ever know anyone who wore a pair of pants with big black-and-white checks, cut very narrow, no cuffs, and pressed without a crease?"

I had to think for a moment. "Yes," I said then, "my

father, when he was a very young man, before he was married; I've seen old photographs."

"Sure," said Captain Rihm, "and he probably wore a short sort of cutaway coat with two cloth-covered buttons at the back, a vest with lapels, a tall silk hat, a big, black oversize bow tie on a turned-up stiff collar, and button shoes."

"That's how this man was dressed?"

"Like seventy-five years ago! And him no more than thirty years old. There was a label in his hat, a Twenty-third Street hat store that went out of business around the turn of the century. Now what do you make out of a thing like that?"

"Well," I said carefully, "there's nothing much you can make of it. Apparently someone went to a lot of trouble to dress up in an antique style—the coins and bills I assume he could buy at a coin dealer's—and then he got himself killed in a traffic accident."

"Got himself killed is right. Eleven-fifteen at night in Times Square—the theaters letting out, busiest time and place in the world—and this guy shows up in the middle of the street, gawking and looking around at the cars and up at the signs like he'd never seen them before. The cop on duty noticed him, so you can see how he must have been acting. The lights change, the traffic starts up, with him in the middle of the street, and instead of waiting, the damn fool, he turns and tries to make it back to the sidewalk. A cab got him and he was dead when he hit."

For a moment Captain Rihm sat chewing his tobacco and staring angrily at a young woman pushing a baby carriage, though I'm sure he didn't see her. The young mother looked at him in surprise as she passed, and the captain continued:

"Nothing you can make out of a thing like that. We found out nothing. I started checking through our file of old phone books, just as routine, but without much hope, because they only go back so far. But in the 1939 summer edition I found a Rudolph Fentz, Jr., somewhere on East Fifty-second Street. He'd moved away in '42, though, the building super told me, and was a man in his sixties besides, retired from business; used to work in a bank a few blocks away, the super thought. I found the bank where he'd worked, and they told me he'd retired in '40, and had been dead for five years; his widow was living in Florida with a sister.

"I wrote to the widow, but there was only one thing she could tell us, and that was no good. I never even reported it, not officially, anyway. Her husband's father had disappeared when her husband was a boy maybe two years old. He went out for a walk around ten one night—his wife thought cigar smoke smelled up the curtains, so he used to take a little stroll before he went to bed, and smoke a cigar—and he didn't come back, and was never seen or heard of again. The family spent a good deal of money trying to locate him, but they never did. This was in the middle 1870s some time; the old lady wasn't sure of the exact date. Her husband hadn't ever said too much about it.

"And that's all," said Captain Rihm. "Once I put in one of my afternoons off hunting through a bunch of old police records. And I finally found the Missing Persons file for 1876, and Rudolph Fentz was listed, all right. There wasn't much of a description, and no fingerprints, of course. I'd give a year of my life, even now, and maybe sleep better nights, if they'd had his fingerprints. He was listed as twenty-nine years old, wearing full muttonchop whiskers, a tall silk hat, dark coat and checked pants. That's about all it said. Didn't say what kind of tie or vest or if his shoes were the button kind. His name was Rudolph Fentz and he lived at this address on Fifth Avenue; it must have been a residence then. Final disposition of case: not located.

"Now, I hate that case," Captain Rihm said quietly. "I hate it and I wish I'd never heard of it. What do you think?" he demanded suddenly, angrily. "You think this guy walked off into thin air in 1876, and showed up again in 1950?"

I shrugged noncommittally, and the captain took it to mean no.

"No, of course not," he said. "Of *course* not—but give me some other explanation."

I could go on. I could give you several hundred such cases. A sixteen-year-old girl walked out of her bedroom one morning, carrying her clothes in her hand because they were too big for her and she was quite obviously eleven years old again. And there are other occurrences too horrible for print. All of them have happened in the New York City area alone, all within the last few years; and I suspect thousands more have occurred, and are occurring, all over the world. I could go on, but the point is this: What is happening, and *why*? I believe that I know.

Haven't you noticed, too, on the part of nearly everyone you know, a growing rebellion against the *present?* And an increasing longing for the past? I have. Never before in all my long life have I heard so many people wish that they lived "at the turn of the century," or "when life was simpler," or "worth living," or "when you could bring children into the world and count on the future," or simply "in the good old days." People didn't talk that way when I was young! The present was a glorious time! But they talk that way now.

For the first time in man's history, man is desperate to escape the present. Our newsstands are jammed with escape literature, the very name of which is significant. Entire magazines are devoted to fantastic stories of escape—to other times, past and future, to other worlds and planets—escape to anywhere but here and now. Even our larger magazines, book publishers, and Hollywood are beginning to meet the rising demand for this kind of escape. Yes, there is a craving in the world like a thirst, a terrible mass pressure that you can almost feel, of millions of minds struggling against the barriers of time. I am utterly convinced that this terrible mass pressure of millions of minds is already, slightly but definitely, affecting time itself. In the moments when this happens—when the almost universal longing to escape is greatest—my incidents occur. Man is disturbing the clock of time, and I am afraid it will break. When it does, I leave to your imagination the last few hours of madness that will be left to us; all the countless moments that now make up our lives suddenly ripped apart and chaotically tangled in time.

Well, I have lived most of my life; I can be robbed of only a few more years. But it seems too bad—this universal craving to escape what could be a rich, productive, happy world. We live on a planet well able to provide a decent life for every soul on it, which is all ninety-nine of a hundred human beings ask. Why in the world can't we have it?

THE SILLY SEASON

by C. M. Kornbluth

It was a hot summer afternoon in the Omaha bureau of the World Wireless Press Service, and the control bureau in New York kept nagging me for copy. But since it was a hot summer afternoon, there was no copy. A wrap-up of local baseball had cleared about an hour ago, and that was that. Nothing but baseball happens in the summer. During the dog days, politicians are in the Maine woods fishing and boozing, burglars are too tired to burgle, and wives think it over and decide not to decapitate their husbands.

I pawed through some press releases. One sloppy stencil-duplicated sheet began: "Did you know that the lemonade way to summer comfort and health has been endorsed by leading physiotherapists from Maine to California? The Federated Lemon-Growers Association revealed today that a survey of 2,500 physiotherapists in 57 cities of more than 25,000 population disclosed that 87 per cent of them drink lemonade at least once a day between June and September, and that another 72 per cent not only drink the cooling and healthful beverage but actually prescribe it . . ."

Another note tapped out on the news circuit printer from New York: "960M-HW KICKER? ND SNST-NY."

That was New York saying they needed a bright and sparkling little news item immediately—"soonest." I went to the east-bound printer and punched out: "96NY-UPCMNG FU MINS-OM."

The lemonade handout was hopeless; I dug into the stack again. The State University summer course was inviting the governor to attend its summer conference on aims and approaches in adult secondary education. The Agricultural College wanted me to warn farmers that white-skinned hogs should be kept from the direct rays of the summer sun. The manager of a fifth-rate local pug sent a write-up of his boy and a couple of working press passes to his next bout in the Omaha Arena. The Schwartz and White Bandage Company contributed a glossy eight-by-ten of a blonde in a bathing suit improvised from two S & W Redi-Dressings.

Accompanying text: "Pert starlet Miff McCoy is ready for any seaside emergency. That's not only a darling swim suit she has on—it's two standard all-purpose Redi-Dressing bandages made by the Schwartz and White Bandage Company of Omaha. If a broken rib results from too-strenuous beach athletics, Miff's dress can supply the dressing." Yeah. The rest of the stack wasn't even that good. I dumped them all in the circular file, and began to rack my brains in spite of the heat.

I'd have to fake one, I decided. Unfortunately, there had been no big running silly-season story so far this summer— no flying saucers, or monsters in the Florida Everglades, or chloroform bandits terrifying the city. If there had, I could have hopped on and faked a "with." As it was, I'd have to fake a "lead," which is harder and riskier.

The flying saucers? I couldn't revive them; they'd been forgotten for years, except by newsmen. The giant turtle of Lake Huron had been quiet for years too. If I started a chloroform bandit scare, every old maid in the state would back me up by swearing she heard the bandit trying to break in and smelled chloroform—but the cops wouldn't like it. Strange messages from space received at the state university's radar lab? That might do it. I put a sheet of copy paper in the typewriter and sat, glaring at it and hating the silly season.

There was a slight reprieve—the Western Union tie-line printer by the desk dinged at me, and its sickly-yellow bulb lit up. I tapped out: "WW GA PLS," and the machine began to eject yellow, gummed tape which told me this:

WU CO62-DPR COLLECT—FT HICKS ARK AUG 22 105P—WORLD-WIRELESS OMAHA— TOWN MARSHAL PINKNEY CRAWLES DIED MYSTERIOUS CIRCUMSTANCES FISHTRIP-PING OZARK HAMLET RUSH CITY TODAY. RUSHERS PHONED HICKSERS "BURNED DEATH SHINING DOMES AP-PEARED YESTERWEEK." JEEPING BODY

HICKSWARD. QUERIED RUSH CONSTABLE P. C. ALLENBY LEARNING "SEVEN GLASSY DOMES EACH HOUSESIZE CLEARING MILE SOUTH TOWN. RUSHERS UNTOUCHED, UNAPPROACHED. CRAWLES WARNED BUT TOUCHED AND DIED BURNS." NOTE DESK— RUSH FONECALL 1.85. SHALL I UPFOLLOW?— BENSON—FISHTRIPPING RUSHERS HICKSERS YESTERWEEK JEEPING HICKSWARD HOUSESIZE 1.85 428P CLR . . .

It was just what the doctor ordered. I typed an acknowledgment for the message and pounded out a story, fast. I punched it and started the tape waggling through the eastbound transmitter before New York could send any more irked notes. The news circuit printer from New York clucked and began relaying my story immediately:

WW72 (KICKER)
   FORT HICKS, ARKANSAS, AUG 22—(WW)— MYSTERIOUS DEATH TODAY STRUCK DOWN A LAW ENFORCEMENT OFFICER IN A TINY OZARK MOUNTAIN HAMLET. MARSHAL PINKNEY CRAWLES OF FORT HICKS, AR- KANSAS, DIED OF BURNS WHILE ON A FISHING TRIP TO THE LITTLE VILLAGE OF RUSH CITY. TERRIFIED NATIVES OF RUSH CITY BLAMED THE TRAGEDY ON WHAT THEY CALLED "SHINING DOMES." THEY SAID THE SO-CALLED DOMES APPEARED IN A CLEARING LAST WEEK ONE MILE SOUTH OF TOWN. THERE ARE SEVEN OF THE MYSTERIOUS OBJECTS—EACH ONE THE SIZE OF A HOUSE. THE INHABITANTS OF RUSH CITY DID NOT DARE APPROACH THEM. THEY WARNED THE VISITING MARSHAL CRAWLES—BUT HE DID NOT HEED THEIR WARNING. RUSH CITY'S CONSTABLE P. C. ALLENBY WAS A WITNESS TO THE TRAGEDY. SAID HE: "THERE ISN'T MUCH TO TELL. MARSHAL CRAWLES JUST WALKED UP TO ONE OF THE DOMES AND PUT HIS HAND ON IT. THERE WAS A BIG

FLASH, AND WHEN I COULD SEE AGAIN, HE
WAS BURNED TO DEATH." CONSTABLE
ALLENBY IS RETURNING THE BODY OF
MARSHAL CRAWLES TO FORT HICKS.
602P220M

That, I thought, should hold them for a while. I
remembered Benson's "note desk" and put through a long-
distance call to Fort Hicks, person to person. The Omaha
operator asked for Fort Hicks information, but there wasn't
any. The Fort Hicks operator asked whom she wanted.
Omaha finally admitted that we wanted to talk to Mr.
Edwin C. Benson. Fort Hicks figured out loud and then
decided that Ed was probably at the police station, and I got
Benson. He had a pleasant voice, not particularly back-
woods Arkansas. I gave him some of the old oil about a fine
dispatch and a good, conscientious job, and so on. He took
it with plenty of dry reserve, which was odd. Our rural
stringers always ate that kind of stuff up. Where, I asked,
was he from?

"Fort Hicks," he told me, "but I've moved around. I did
the courthouse beat in Little Rock"—I nearly laughed out
loud at that, but the laugh died as he went on—"rewrite for
the A.P. in New Orleans, got to be bureau chief there but I
didn't like wire-service work. Got an opening on the
Chicago *Trib* desk. That didn't last—they sent me to head
up their Washington bureau. There I switched to the New
York *Times*. They made me a war correspondent and I got
hurt—back to Fort Hicks. I do some magazine writing now.
Did you want a follow-up on the Rush City story?"

"Sure," I told him weakly. "Give it a real ride—use your
own judgment. Do you think it's a fake?"

"I saw Pink's body a little while ago at the undertaker's
parlor, and I had a talk with Allenby, from Rush City. Pink
got burned, all right, and Allenby didn't make his story up.
Maybe somebody else did—he's pretty dumb—but as far as
I can tell, this is the real thing. I'll keep the copy coming.
Don't forget about that dollar eighty-five phone call, will
you?"

I told him I wouldn't, and hung up. Mr. Edwin C. Benson
had handed me quite a jolt. I wondered how badly he had
been hurt that he had been forced to abandon a brilliant
news career and bury himself in the Ozarks.

Then there came a call from God, the board chairman of World Wireless. He was fishing in Canada, as all good board chairmen do during the silly season, but he had caught a news broadcast which used my Rush City story. He had a mobile phone in his trailer, and it was but the work of a moment to ring Omaha and louse up my carefully planned vacation schedules and rotations of night shifts. He wanted me to go down to Rush City and cover the story personally. I said yes and began trying to round up the rest of the staff. My night editor was sobered up by his wife and delivered to the bureau in fair shape. A telegrapher on vacation was reached at his summer resort and talked into checking out. I got a taxi company on the phone and told them to have a cross-country cab on the roof in an hour. I specified their best driver, and told them to give him maps of Arkansas.

Meanwhile, two "with domes" dispatches arrived from Benson and got moved on the wire. I monitored a couple of newscasts; the second one carried a story by another wire service on the domes—a pickup of our stuff, but they'd have their own men on the scene fast enough. I filled in the night editor, and went up to the roof for the cab.

The driver took off in the teeth of a gathering thunderstorm. We had to rise above it, and by the time we could get down to the sight-pilotage altitude, we were lost. We circled most of the night until the driver picked up a beacon he had on his charts at about 3:30 A.M. We landed at Fort Hicks as day was breaking, not on speaking terms.

The Fort Hicks field clerk told me where Benson lived, and I walked there. It was a white frame house. A quiet, middle-aged woman let me in. She was his widowed sister, Mrs. McHenry. She got me some coffee and told me she had been up all night waiting for Edwin to come back from Rush City. He had started out about 8:00 P.M., and it was only a two-hour trip by car. She was worried. I tried to pump her about her brother, but she'd only say that he was the bright one of the family. She didn't want to talk about his work as war correspondent. She did show me some of his magazine stuff—boy-and-girl stories in national weeklies. He seemed to sell one every couple of months.

We had arrived at a conversational stalemate when her brother walked in, and I discovered why his news career had been interrupted. He was blind. Aside from a long,

puckered brown scar that ran from his left temple back over
his ear and onto the nape of his neck, he was a pleasant-
looking fellow in his mid-forties.

"Who is it, Vera?" he asked.

"It's Mr. Williams, the gentleman who called you from
Omaha today—I mean yesterday."

"How do you do, Williams. Don't get up," he added,
hearing, I suppose, the chair squeak as I leaned forward to
rise.

"You were so *long,* Edwin," his sister said with relief and
reproach.

"That young jackass Howie—my chauffeur for the
night"—he added an aside to me—"got lost going there and
coming back. But I did spend more time than I'd planned
at Rush City." He sat down, facing me. "Williams, there is
some difference of opinion about the shining domes. The
Rush City people say that they exist, and I say they don't."

His sister brought him a cup of coffee.

"What happened, exactly?" I asked.

"That Allenby took me and a few other hardy citizens to
see them. They told me just what they looked like. Seven
hemispheres in a big clearing, glassy, looming up like
houses, reflecting the gleam of the headlights. But they
weren't there. Not to me, and not to any blind man. I know
when I'm standing in front of a house or anything else that
big. I can feel a little tension on the skin of my face. It works
unconsciously, but the mechanism is thoroughly understood.

"The blind get—because they have to—an aural picture
of the world. We hear a little hiss of air that means we're at
the corner of a building; we hear and feel big, turbulent air
currents that mean we're coming to a busy street. Some of
the boys can thread their way through an obstacle course
and never touch a single obstruction. I'm not that good,
maybe because I haven't been blind as long as they have,
but by hell, I know when there are seven objects the size of
houses in front of me, and there just were no such things in
the clearing at Rush City."

"Well"—I shrugged—"there goes a fine piece of silly-
season journalism. What kind of a gag are the Rush City
people trying to pull, and why?"

"No kind of gag. My driver saw the domes too—and
don't forget the late marshal. Pink not only saw them but

touched them. All I know is that people see them and I don't. If they exist, they have a kind of existence like nothing else I've ever met."

"I'll go up there myself," I decided.

"Best thing," said Benson. "I don't know what to make of it. You can take our car." He gave me directions and I gave him a schedule of deadlines. We wanted the coroner's verdict, due today, an eyewitness story—his driver would do for that—some background stuff on the area, and a few statements from local officials.

I took his car and got to Rush City in two hours. It was an unpainted collection of dog-trot homes, set down in the big pine forest that covers all that rolling Ozark country. There was a general store that had the place's only phone. I suspected it had been kept busy by the wire services and a few enterprising newspapers. A state trooper in a flashy uniform was lounging against a fly-specked tobacco counter when I got there.

"I'm Sam Williams, from World Wireless," I said. "You come to have a look at the domes?"

"World Wireless broke that story, didn't they?" he asked me, with a look I couldn't figure out.

"We did. Our Fort Hicks stringer wired it to us."

The phone rang, and the trooper answered it. It seemed to have been a call he had placed with the governor's office.

"No, sir," he said over the phone. "No, sir. They're all sticking to the story, but I didn't see anything. I mean, they don't see them any more, but they say they were there, and now they aren't any more." A couple more "No, sirs" and he hung up.

"When did that happen?" I asked.

"About a half hour ago. I just came from there on my bike to report."

The phone rang again, and I grabbed it. It was Benson, asking for me. I told him to phone a flash and bulletin to Omaha on the disappearance and then took off to find Constable Allenby. He was a stage reuben with a nickel-plated badge and a six-shooter. He cheerfully climbed into the car and guided me to the clearing.

There was a definite little path worn between Rush City and the clearing by now, but there was a disappointment at the end of it. The clearing was empty. A few small boys sticking carefully to its fringes told wildly contradictory stories about the disappearance of the domes, and I jotted down some 'kind of dispatch out of the most spectacular versions. I remember it involved flashes of blue fire and a smell like sulphur candles. That was all there was to it.

I drove Allenby back. By then a mobile unit from a TV network had arrived. I said hello, waited for an A.P. man to finish a dispatch on the phone, and then dictated my lead direct to Omaha. The hamlet was beginning to fill up with newsmen from the wire services, the big papers, the radio and TV nets and the newsreels. Much good they'd get out of it. The story was over—I thought. I had some coffee at the general store's two-table restaurant corner and drove back to Fort Hicks.

Benson was tirelessly interviewing by phone and firing off copy to Omaha. I told him he could begin to ease off, thanked him for his fine work, paid him for his gas, said good-by and picked up my taxi at the field. Quite a bill for waiting had been run up.

I listened to the radio as we were flying back to Omaha, and wasn't at all surprised. After baseball, the shining domes were top news. Shining domes had been seen in twelve states. Some vibrated with a strange sound. They came in all colors and sizes. One had strange writing on it. One was transparent, and there were big green men and women inside. I caught a women's midmorning quiz show, and the M.C. kept gagging about the domes. One crack I remember was a switch on the "pointed-head" joke. He made it "dome-shaped head," and the ladies in the audience laughed until they nearly burst.

We stopped in Little Rock for gas, and I picked up a couple of afternoon papers. The domes got banner heads on both of them. One carried the World Wireless lead, and had slapped in the bulletin on the disappearance of the domes. The other paper wasn't a World Wireless client, but between its other services and "special correspondents"— phone calls to the general store at Rush City—it had kept practically abreast of us. Both papers had shining-dome cartoons on their editorial pages, hastily drawn and slapped in. One paper, anti-Administration, showed the President cautiously reaching out a finger to touch the dome of the Capitol, which was rendered as a shining dome and labeled: "Shining Dome of Congressional Immunity to Executive

Dictatorship." A little man labeled "Mr. and Mrs. Plain, Self-Respecting Citizens of the United States of America" was in one corner of the cartoon saying: "CAREFUL, MR. PRESIDENT! REMEMBER WHAT HAPPENED TO PINKNEY CRAWLES!!"

The other paper, pro-Administration, showed a shining dome that had the President's face. A band of fat little men in Prince Albert coats, string ties, and broad-brimmed hats labeled "Congressional Smear Artist and Hatchet-men" were creeping up on the dome with the President's face, their hands reached out as if to strangle. Above the cartoon a cut line said: "WHO'S GOING TO GET HURT?"

We landed at Omaha, and I checked into the office. Things were clicking right along. The clients were happily gobbling up our dome copy and sending wires asking for more. I dug into the morgue for the "Flying Disk" folder, and the "Huron Turtle" and the "Bayou Vampire" and a few others even further back. I spread out the old clippings and tried to shuffle and arrange them into some kind of underlying sense. I picked up the latest dispatch to come out of the tie-line printer from Western Union. It was from our man in Owosso, Michigan, and told how Mrs. Lettie Overholtzer, age sixty-one, saw a shining dome in her own kitchen at midnight. It grew like a soup bubble until it was as big as her refrigerator, and then disappeared.

I went over to the desk man and told him: "Let's have a downhold on stuff like Lettie Overholtzer. We can move a sprinkling of it, but I don't want to run this into the ground. Those things might turn up again, and then we wouldn't have any room left to play around with them. We'll have everybody's credulity used up."

He looked mildly surprised. "You mean," he asked, "there really *was* something there?"

"I don't know. Maybe. I didn't see anything myself, and the only man down there I trust can't make up his mind. Anyhow, hold it down as far as the clients let us."

I went home to get some sleep. When I went back to work, I found the clients hadn't let us work the downhold after all. Nobody at the other wire services seemed to believe seriously that there had been anything out of the ordinary at Rush City, so they merrily pumped out solemn stories like the Lettie Overholtzer item, and wirefoto maps of locations where domes were reported, and tabulations of number of domes reported.

We had to string along. Our Washington bureau badgered the Pentagon and the A.E.C. into issuing statements, and there was a race between a navy and an air force investigating mission to see who could get to Rush City first. After they got there there was a race to see who could get the first report out. The Air Force won that contest. Before the week was out, "Domies" had appeared. They were hats for juveniles—shining-dome skull-caps molded from a transparent plastic. We had to ride with it. I'd started the mania, but it was out of hand and a long time dying down.

The World Series, the best in years, finally killed off the domes. By an unspoken agreement among the services, we simply stopped running stories every time a hysterical woman thought she saw a dome or wanted to get her name in the paper. And of course when there was no longer publicity to be had for the asking, people stopped seeing domes. There was no percentage in it. Brooklyn won the series, international tension climbed as the thermometer dropped, burglars began burgling again, and a bulky folder labeled "Domes, Shining," went into our morgue. The shining domes were history, and earnest graduate students in psychology would shortly begin to bother us with requests to borrow that folder.

The only thing that had come of it, I thought, was that we had somehow got through another summer without too much idle wire time, and that Ed Benson and I had struck up a casual correspondence.

A newsman's strange and weary year wore on. Baseball gave way to football. An off-year election kept us on the run. Christmas loomed ahead, with its feature stories and its kickers about Santa Claus, Indiana. Christmas passed, and we began to clear jolly stories about New Year hang-overs, and tabulate the great stories of the year. New Year's Day, a ghastly rat-race of covering 103 bowl games. Record snowfalls in the Great Plains and Rockies. Spring floods in Ohio and the Columbia River Valley. Twenty-one tasty Lenten menus, and Holy Week around the world. Baseball again, daylight-saving time, Mother's Day, Derby Day, the Preakness, and the Belmont Stakes.

It was about then that a disturbing letter arrived from Benson. I was concerned not about its subject matter but because I thought no sane man would write such a thing. It seemed to me that Benson was slipping his trolley. All he said was that he expected a repeat performance of the domes, or of something like the domes. He said "they" probably found the tryout a smashing success and would continue according to plan. I replied cautiously, which amused him.

He wrote back: "I wouldn't put myself out on a limb like this if I had anything to lose by it, but you know my station in life. It was just an intelligent guess, based on a study of power politics and Aesop's fables. And if it does happen, you'll find it a trifle harder to put me over, won't you?"

I guessed he was kidding me, but I wasn't certain. When people begin to talk about "them" and what "they" are doing, it's a bad sign. But, guess or not, something pretty much like domes did turn up in late July, during a crushing heat wave.

This time it was big black spheres rolling across the countryside. The spheres were seen by a Baptist congregation in central Kansas which had met in a prairie to pray for rain. About eighty Baptists took their Bible oaths that they saw large black spheres some ten feet high rolling along the prairie. They had passed within five yards of one man. The rest had run from them as soon as they could take in the fact that they really were there.

World Wireless didn't break that story, but we got on it fast enough as soon as we were tipped. Being now the recognized silly-season authority in the W. W. Central Division, I took off for Kansas.

It was much the way it had been in Arkansas. The Baptists really thought they had seen the things—with one exception. The exception was an old gentleman with a patriarchal beard. He had been the one man who hadn't run, the man the objects passed nearest to. He was blind. He told me with a great deal of heat that he would have known all about it, blind or not, if any large spheres had rolled within five yards of him—or twenty-five, for that matter.

Old Mr. Emerson didn't go into the matter of air currents and turbulence, as Benson had. With him, it was all well below the surface. He took the position that the Lord had removed his sight, and in return had given him another sense which would do for emergency use.

"You just try me out, son!" he piped angrily. "You come stand over here, wait awhile and put your hand up in front of my face. I'll tell you when you do it, no matter how quiet you are!" He did it, too, three times, and then took me out into the main street of his little prairie town. There were several wagons drawn up before the grain elevator, and he put on a show for me by threading his way around and between them without touching once.

That—and Benson—seemed to prove that whatever the things were, they had some connection with the domes. I filed a thoughtful dispatch on the blind-man angle, and got back to Omaha to find that it had been cleared through our desk but killed in New York before relay.

We tried to give the black spheres the usual ride, but it didn't last as long. The political cartoonists tired of it sooner, and fewer old maids saw them. People got to jeering at them as newspaper hysteria, and a couple of highbrow magazines ran articles on "the irresponsible press." Only the radio comedians tried to milk the new mania as usual, but they were disconcerted to find their ratings falling. A network edict went out to kill all sphere gags. People were getting sick of them.

"It makes sense," Benson wrote to me. "An occasional exercise of the sense of wonder is refreshing, but it can't last forever. That plus the ingrained American cynicism toward all sources of public information has worked against the black spheres being greeted with the same naïve delight with which the domes were received. Nevertheless, I predict—and I'll thank you to remember that my predictions have been right so far 100 per cent of the time—that next summer will see another mystery comparable to the domes and the black things. And I also predict that the new phenomenon will be imperceptible to any blind person in the immediate vicinity, if there should be any."

If, of course, he was wrong this time, it would only cut his average down to 50 per cent. I managed to wait out the year—the same interminable round I felt I could do in my sleep. Staffers got ulcers and resigned, staffers got tired and were fired, libel suits were filed and settled, one of our desk men got a Nieman Fellowship and went to Harvard, one of our telegraphers got his working hand mashed in a car door and jumped from a bridge but lived with a broken back.

In mid-August, when the weather bureau had been correctly predicting "fair and warmer" for sixteen straight days, it turned up. It wasn't anything on whose nature a blind man could provide a negative check, but it had what I had come to think of as "their" trademark.

A summer seminar was meeting outdoors, because of the frightful heat, at our own State University. Twelve trained schoolteachers testified that a series of perfectly circular pits opened up in the grass before them, one directly under the education professor teaching the seminar. They testified further that the professor, with an astonished look and a heart-rending cry, plummeted down into that perfectly circular pit. They testified further that the pits remained there for some thirty seconds and then suddenly were there no longer. The scorched summer grass was back where it had been, the pits were gone and so was the professor.

I interviewed every one of them. They weren't yokels, but intelligent men and women, all with masters' degrees, working toward their doctorates during the summers. They agreed closely on their stories, as I would expect trained and capable persons to do.

The police, however, did not expect agreement, being used to dealing with the lower I.Q. brackets. They arrested the twelve on some technical charge—"obstructing peace officers in the performance of their duties," I believe—and were going to beat the living hell out of them when an attorney arrived with twelve writs of habeas corpus. The cops' unvoiced suspicion was that the teachers had conspired to murder their professor, but nobody ever tried to explain why they'd do a thing like that.

The cops' reaction was typical of the way the public took it. Newspapers—which had reveled wildly in the shining domes story and less so in the black spheres story—were cautious. Some went overboard and gave the black pits a ride, in the old style, but they didn't pick up any sales that way. People declared that the press was insulting their intelligence, and also that they were bored with marvels.

The few papers who had played up the pits were soundly spanked in very dignified editorials printed by other sheets which played down the pits.

At World Wireless we sent out a memo to all stringers: "File no more enterpriser dispatches on black-pit story. Mail queries should be sent to regional desk if a new angle breaks in your territory." We got about ten mail queries, mostly from journalism students acting as string men, and we turned them all down. All the older hands got the pitch, and didn't bother to file it to us when the town drunk or the village old maid loudly reported that she saw a pit open up on High Street across from the drugstore. They knew it was probably untrue, and that, furthermore, nobody cared.

I wrote Benson about all this, and humbly asked him what his prediction for next summer was. He replied, obviously having the time of his life, that there would be at least one more summer phenomenon like the last three, and possibly two more—but none after that.

It's so easy now to reconstruct, with our bitterly earned knowledge!

Any youngster could whisper now of Benson: "Why, the damned fool! Couldn't anybody with the brains of a louse see that they wouldn't keep it up for two years?" One did whisper that to me the other day, when I told this story to him. And I whispered back that, far from being a damned fool, Benson was the one person on the face of the Earth, as far as I knew, who had bridged with logic the widely separated phenomena with which this reminiscence deals.

Another year passed. I gained three pounds, drank too much, rowed incessantly with my staff and got a tidy raise. A telegrapher took a swing at me midway through the office Christmas party, and I fired him. My wife and kids didn't arrive in April when I expected them. I phoned Florida, and she gave me some excuse or other about missing the plane. After a few more missed planes and a few more phone calls, she got around to telling me that she didn't *want* to come back. That was okay with me. In my own intuitive way I knew that the upcoming season was more important than who stayed married to whom.

In July a dispatch arrived by wire while a new man was working the night desk. It was from Hood River, Oregon. Our stringer there reported that more than one hundred "green capsules" about fifty yards long had appeared in and around an apple orchard. The new desk man was not so new that he did not recall the downhold policy on silly-season items. He killed it, but left it on the spoke for my amused inspection in the morning. I suppose exactly the same thing happened in every wire service newsroom in the region. I

rolled in at 10:30 and riffled through the stuff on the spike.
When I saw the "green capsules" dispatch I tried to phone
Portland, but couldn't get a connection. Then the phone
buzzed and a correspondent of ours in Seattle began to yell
at me, but the line went dead.

I shrugged and phoned Benson, in Fort Hicks. He was at
the police station and asked me: "Is this it?"

"It is," I told him. I read him the telegram from Hood
River and told him about the line trouble in Seattle.

"So," he said wonderingly, "I called the turn, didn't I?"

"Called what turn?"

"On the invaders. I don't know who they are—but it's the
story of the boy who cried wolf. Only this time the wolves
realized——" Then the phone went dead.

But he was right.

The people of the world were the sheep.

We newsmen—radio, TV, press and wire services—were
the boy, who should have been ready to sound the alarm.

But the cunning wolves had tricked us into sounding the
alarm so many times that the villagers were weary, and
would not come when there was real peril.

The wolves who were then burning their way through the
Ozarks, utterly without opposition—the wolves were the
Martians under whose yoke and lash we now endure our
miserable existences.

THE REPORT ON THE BARNHOUSE EFFECT

by Kurt Vonnegut, Jr.

Let me begin by saying that I don't know any more
about where Professor Arthur Barnhouse is hiding than
anyone else does. Save for one short, enigmatic message,
left in my mailbox on Christmas Eve, I have not heard from
him since his disappearance a year and half ago.

What's more, readers of this article will be disappointed

if they expect to learn how *they* can bring about the so-called "Barnhouse Effect." If I were able and willing to give away that secret, I would certainly be something more important than a psychology instructor.

I have been urged to write this report because I did research under the professor's direction and because I was the first to learn of his astonishing discovery. But while I was his student I was never entrusted with knowledge of how the mental forces could be released and directed. He was unwilling to trust anyone with that information.

I would like to point out that the term "Barnhouse Effect" is a creation of the popular press, and was never used by Professor Barnhouse. The name he chose for the phenomenon was *"dynamopsychism,"* or *force of the mind*.

I cannot believe that there is a civilized person yet to be convinced that such a force exists, what with its destructive effects on display in every national capital. I think humanity has always had an inkling that this sort of force does exist. It has been common knowledge that some people are luckier than others with inanimate objects like dice. What Professor Barnhouse did was to show that such "luck" was a measurable force, which in his case could be enormous.

By my calculations, the professor was about fifty-five times more powerful than a Nagasaki-type atomic bomb at the time he went into hiding. He was not bluffing when, on the eve of "Operation Brainstorm," he told General Honus Barker: "Sitting here at the dinner table, I'm pretty sure I can flatten anything on earth—from Joe Louis to the Great Wall of China."

There is an understandable tendency to look upon Professor Barnhouse as a supernatural visitation. The First Church of Barnhouse in Los Angeles has a congregation numbering in the thousands. He is godlike in neither appearance nor intellect. The man who disarms the world is single, shorter than the average American male, stout, and averse to exercise. His I.Q. is 143, which is good but certainly not sensational. He is quite mortal, about to celebrate his fortieth birthday, and in good health. If he is alone now, the isolation won't bother him too much. He was quiet and shy when I knew him, and seemed to find more companionship in books and music than in his associations at the college.

Neither he nor his powers fall outside the sphere of

Nature. His dynamopsychic radiations are subject to many known physical laws that apply in the field of radio. Hardly a person has not now heard the snarl of "Barnhouse static" on his home receiver. Contrary to what one might expect, the radiations are affected by sunspots and variations in the ionosphere.

However, his radiations differ from ordinary broadcast waves in several important ways. Their total energy can be brought to bear on any single point the professor chooses, and that energy is undiminished by distance. As a weapon, then, dynamopsychism has an impressive advantage over bacteria and atomic bombs, beyond the fact that it costs nothing to use: it enables the professor to single out critical individuals and objects instead of slaughtering whole populations in the process of maintaining international equilibrium.

As General Honus Barker told the House Military Affairs Committee: "Until someone finds Barnhouse, there is no defense against the Barnhouse Effect." Efforts to "jam" or block the radiations have failed. Premier Slezak could have saved himself the fantastic expense of his "Barnhouse-proof" shelter. Despite the shelter's twelve-foot-thick lead armor, the premier has been floored twice while in it.

There is talk of screening the population for men potentially as powerful dynamopsychically as the professor. Senator Warren Foust demanded funds for this purpose last month, with the passionate declaration: "He who rules the Barnhouse Effect rules the world!" Commissioner Kropotnik said much the same thing, so another costly armaments race, with a new twist, has begun.

This race at least has its comical aspects. The world's best gamblers are being coddled by governments like so many nuclear physicists. There may be several hundred persons with dynamopsychic talent on earth, myself included, but without knowledge of the professor's technique, they can never be anything but dice-table despots. With the secret, it would probably take them ten years to become dangerous weapons. It took the professor that long. He who rules the Barnhouse Effect is Barnhouse and will be for some time.

Popularly, the "Age of Barnhouse" is said to have begun a year and a half ago, on the day of Operation Brainstorm.

That was when dynamopsychism became significant politically. Actually, the phenomenon was discovered in May 1942, shortly after the professor turned down a direct commission in the Army and enlisted as an artillery private. Like X-rays and vulcanized rubber, dynamopsychism was discovered by accident.

From time to time Private Barnhouse was invited to take part in games of chance by his barracks mates. He knew nothing about the games, and usually begged off. But one evening, out of social grace, he agreed to shoot craps. It was a terrible or wonderful thing that he played, depending upon whether or not you like the world as it now is.

"Shoot sevens, Pop," someone said.

So "Pop" shot sevens—ten in a row to bankrupt the barracks. He retired to his bunk and, as a mathematical exercise, calculated the odds against his feat on the back of a laundry slip. His chances of doing it, he found, were one in almost ten million! Bewildered, he borrowed a pair of dice from the man in the bunk next to his. He tried to roll sevens again, but got only the usual assortment of numbers. He lay back for a moment, then resumed his toying with the dice. He rolled ten more sevens in a row.

He might have dismissed the phenomenon with a low whistle. But instead the professor mulled over the circumstances surrounding his two lucky streaks. There was one single factor in common: on both occasions, *the same thought train had flashed through his mind just before he threw the dice*. It was that thought train which aligned the professor's brain cells into what has since become the most powerful weapon on earth.

The soldier in the next bunk gave dynamopsychism its first token of respect. In an understatement certain to bring wry smiles to the faces of the world's dejected demagogues, the soldier said, "You're hotter'n a two-dollar pistol, Pop." Professor Barnhouse was all of that. The dice that did his bidding weighed but a few grams, so the forces involved were minute; but the unmistakable fact that there were such forces was earth-shaking.

Professional caution kept him from revealing his discovery immediately. He wanted more facts and a body of theory to go with them. Later, when the atomic bomb was dropped on Hiroshima, it was fear that made him hold his peace. At no time were his experiments, as Premier Slezak called them, "a bourgeois plot to shackle the true democracies of the world." The professor didn't know where they were leading.

In time he came to recognize another startling feature of dynamopsychism: *its strength increased with use*. Within six months he was able to govern dice thrown by men the length of a barracks distant. By the time of his discharge in 1945, he could knock bricks loose from chimneys three miles away.

Charges that Professor Barnhouse could have won the last war in a minute, but did not care to do so, are perfectly senseless. When the war ended, he had the range and power of a 37-millimeter cannon, perhaps—certainly no more. His dynamopsychic powers graduated from the small-arms class only after his discharge and return to Wyandotte College.

I enrolled in the Wyandotte graduate school two years after the professor had rejoined the faculty. By chance, he was assigned as my thesis adviser. I was unhappy about the assignment, for the professor was, in the eyes of both colleagues and students, a somewhat ridiculous figure. He missed classes or had lapses of memory during lectures. When I arrived, in fact, his shortcomings had passed from the ridiculous to the intolerable.

"We're assigning you to Barnhouse as a sort temporary thing," the dean of social studies told me. He looked apologetic and perplexed. "Brilliant man, Barnhouse, I guess. Difficult to know since his return, perhaps, but his work before the war brought a great deal of credit to our little school."

When I reported to the professor's laboratory for the first time, what I saw was more distressing than the gossip. Every surface in the room was covered with dust; books and apparatus had not been disturbed for months. The professor sat napping at his desk when I entered. The only signs of recent activity were three overflowing ash trays, a pair of scissors, and a morning paper with several items clipped from its front page.

As he raised his head to look at me, I saw that his eyes were clouded with fatigue. "Hi," he said, "just can't seem to get my sleeping done at night." He lighted a cigarette, his hands trembling slightly. "You the young man I'm supposed to help with a thesis?"

"Yes, sir," I said. In minutes he converted my misgivings to alarm.

"You an overseas veteran?" he asked.

"Yes, sir."

"Not much left over there, is there?" He frowned. "Enjoy the last war?"

"No, sir."

"Look like another war to you?"

"Kind of, sir."

"What can be done about it?"

I shrugged. "Looks pretty hopeless."

He peered at me intently. "Know anything about international law, the U.N., and all that?"

"Only what I pick up from the papers."

"Same here," he sighed. He showed me a fat scrapbook, packed with newspaper clippings. "Never used to pay any attention to international politics. Now I study politics the way I used to study rats in mazes. Everybody tells me the same thing—'Looks hopeless.'"

"Nothing short of a miracle——" I began.

"Believe in magic?" he asked sharply. The professor fished two dice from his vest pocket. "I will try to roll twos," he said. He rolled twos three times in a row. "One chance in about 47,000 of that happening. There's a miracle for you." He beamed for an instant, then brought the interview to an end, remarking that he had a class which had begun ten minutes ago.

He was not quick to take me into his confidence, and he said no more about his trick with the dice. I assumed they were loaded, and forgot about them. He set me the task of watching male rats cross electrified metal strips to get to food or female rats—an experiment that had been done to everyone's satisfaction in the 1930s. As though the pointlessness of my work were not bad enough, the professor annoyed me further with irrelevant questions. His favorites were: "Think we should have dropped the atomic bomb on Hiroshima?" and "Think every new piece of scientific information is a good thing for humanity?"

However, I did not feel put upon for long. "Give those poor animals a holiday," he said one morning, after I had been with him only a month. "I wish you'd help me look into a more interesting problem—namely, my sanity."

I returned the rats to their cages.

"What you must do is simple," he said, speaking softly. "Watch the inkwell on my desk. If you see nothing happen to it, say so, and I'll go quietly—relieved, I might add—to the nearest sanitarium."

I nodded uncertainly.

He locked the laboratory door and drew the blinds, so that we were in twilight for a moment. "I'm odd, I know," he said. "It's fear of myself that's made me odd."

"I've found you somewhat eccentric, perhaps, but certainly not——"

"If nothing happens to that inkwell, 'crazy as a bedbug' is the only description of me that will do," he interrupted, turning on the overhead lights. His eyes narrowed. "To give you an idea of how crazy, I'll tell you what's been running through my mind when I should have been sleeping. I think maybe I can save the world. I think maybe I can make every nation a *have* nation, and do away with war for good. I think maybe I can clear roads through jungles, irrigate deserts, build dams overnight."

"Yes, sir."

"Watch the inkwell!"

Dutifully and fearfully I watched. A high-pitched humming seemed to come from the inkwell; then it began to vibrate alarmingly, and finally to bound about the top of the desk, making two noisy circuits. It stopped, hummed again, glowed red, then popped in splinters with a blue-green flash.

Perhaps my hair stood on end. The professor laughed gently. "Magnets?" I managed to say at last.

"Wish to Heaven it were magnets," he murmured. It was then that he told me of dynamopsychism. He knew only that there was such a force; he could not explain it. "It's me and me alone—and it's awful."

"I'd say it was amazing and wonderful!" I cried.

"If all I could do was make inkwells dance, I'd be tickled silly with the whole business." He shrugged disconsolately. "But I'm no toy, my boy. If you like, we can drive around the neighborhood, and I'll show you what I mean." He told me about pulverized boulders, shattered oaks, and abandoned farm buildings demolished within a fifty-mile radius of the campus. "Did every bit of it sitting right here, just thinking—not even thinking hard."

He scratched his head nervously. "I have never dared to concentrate as hard as I can for fear of the damage I might

do. I'm to the point where a mere whim is a block-buster."
There was a depressing pause. "Up until a few days ago,
I've thought it best to keep my secret for fear of what use it
might be put to," he continued. "Now I realize that I haven't
any more right to it than a man has a right to own an atomic
bomb."

He fumbled through a heap of papers. "This says about
all that needs to be said, I think." He handed me a draft of a
letter to the Secretary of State.

> *Dear Sir:*
>   *I have discovered a new force which costs nothing to
> use, and which is probably more important than atomic
> energy. I should like to see it used most effectively in
> the cause of peace, and am, therefore, requesting your
> advice as to how this might best be done.*
>   *Yours truly,*
>   *A. Barnhouse*

"I have no idea what will happen next," said the
professor.

There followed three months of perpetual nightmare,
wherein the nation's political and military great came at all
hours to watch the professor's tricks with fascination.

We were quartered in an old mansion near Charlottes-
ville, Virginia, to which we had been whisked five days
after the letter was mailed. Surrounded by barbed wire and
twenty guards, we were labeled "Project Wishing Well,"
and were classified as Top Secret.

For companionship we had General Honus Barker and
the State Department's William K. Cuthrell. For the
professor's talk of peace-through-plenty they had indulgent
smiles and much discourse on practical measures and
realistic thinking. So treated, the professor, who had at first
been almost meek, progressed in a matter of weeks toward
stubbornness.

He had agreed to reveal the thought train by means of
which he aligned his mind into a dynamopsychic transmitter. But under Cuthrell's and Barker's nagging to do so, he
began to hedge. At first he declared that the information
could be passed on simply by word of mouth. Later he said
that it would have to be written up in a long report. Finally,
at dinner one night, just after General Barker had read the

secret orders for Operation Brainstorm, the professor announced, "The report may take as long as five years to write." He looked fiercely at the general. "Maybe twenty."

The dismay occasioned by this flat announcement was offset somewhat by the exciting anticipation of Operation Brainstorm. The general was in a holiday mood. "The target ships are on their way to the Caroline Islands at this very moment," he declared ecstatically. "One hundred and twenty of them! At the same time, ten V-2s are being readied for firing in New Mexico, and fifty radio-controlled jet bombers are being equipped for a mock attack on the Aleutians. Just think of it!" Happily he reviewed his orders. "At exactly 1100 hours next Wednesday, I will give you the order to *concentrate;* and you, Professor, will think as hard as you can about sinking target ships, destroying the V-2s before they hit the ground, and knocking down the bombers before they reach the Aleutians! Think you can handle it?"

The professor turned gray and closed his eyes. "As I told you before, my friend, I don't know what I can do." He added bitterly, "As for this Operation Brainstorm, I was never consulted about it, and it strikes me as childish and insanely expensive."

General Barker bridled. "Sir," he said, "your field is psychology, and I wouldn't presume to give you advice in that field. Mine is national defense. I have had thirty years of experience and success, Professor, and I'll ask you not to criticize my judgment."

The professor appealed to Mr. Cuthrell. "Look," he pleaded, "isn't it war and military matters we're all trying to get rid of? Wouldn't it be a whole lot more significant and lots cheaper for me to try moving cloud masses into drought areas, and things like that? I admit I know next to nothing about international politics, but it seems reasonable to suppose that nobody would want to fight wars if there were enough of everything to go around. Mr. Cuthrell, I'd like to try running generators where there isn't any coal or water power, irrigating deserts, and so on. Why, you could figure out what each country needs to make the most of its resources, and I could give it to them without costing American taxpayers a penny."

"Eternal vigilance is the price of freedom," said the general heavily.

Mr. Cuthrell threw the general a look of mild distaste.

"Unfortunately, the general is right in his own way," he said. "I wish to Heaven the world were ready for ideals like yours, but it simply isn't. We aren't surrounded by brothers, but by enemies. It isn't a lack of food or resources that has us on the brink of war—it's a struggle for power. Who's going to be in charge of the world, our kind of people or theirs?"

The professor nodded in reluctant agreement and arose from the table. "I beg your pardon, gentlemen. You are, after all, better qualified to judge what is best for the country. I'll do whatever you say." He turned to me. "Don't forget to wind the restricted clock and put the confidential cat out," he said gloomily, and ascended the stairs to his bedroom.

For reasons of national security, Operation Brainstorm was carried on without the knowledge of the American citizenry, which was footing the bill. The observers, technicians, and military men involved in the activity knew that a test was under way—a test of what, they had no idea. Only thirty-seven key men, myself included, knew what was afoot.

In Virginia the day for Operation Brainstorm was unseasonably cool. Inside, a log fire crackled in the fireplace, and the flames were reflected in the polished metal cabinets that lined the living room. All that remained of the room's lovely old furniture was a Victorian love seat, set squarely in the center of the floor, facing three television receivers. One long bench had been brought in for the ten of us privileged to watch. The television screens showed, from left to right, the stretch of desert which was the rocket target, the guinea-pig fleet, and a section of the Aleutian sky through which the radio-controlled bomber formation would roar.

Ninety minutes before H-hour the radios announced that the rockets were ready, that the observation ships had backed away to what was thought to be a safe distance, and that the bombers were on their way. The small Virginia audience lined up on the bench in order of rank, smoked a great deal, and said little. Professor Barnhouse was in his bedroom. General Barker bustled about the house like a woman preparing Thanksgiving dinner for twenty.

At ten minutes before H-hour the general came in, shepherding the professor before him. The professor was comfortably attired in sneakers, gray flannels, a blue sweater, and a white shirt open at the neck. The two of them sat side by side on the love seat. The general was rigid and perspiring; the professor was cheerful. He looked at each of the screens, lighted a cigarette and settled back, comfortable and cool.

"Bombers sighted!" cried the Aleutian observers.

"Rockets away!" barked the New Mexico radio operator.

All of us looked quickly at the big electric clock over the mantel, while the professor, a half-smile on his face, continued to watch the television sets. In hollow tones, the general counted away the seconds remaining. "Five . . . four . . . three . . . two . . . one. . . . *Concentrate!*"

Professor Barnhouse closed his eyes, pursed his lips, and stroked his temples. He held the position for a minute. The television images were scrambled, and the radio signals were drowned in the din of Barnhouse static. The professor sighed, opened his eyes and smiled confidently.

"Did you give it everything you had?" asked the general dubiously.

"I was wide open," the professor replied.

The television images pulled themselves together, and mingled cries of amazement came over the radios tuned to the observers. The Aleutian sky was streaked with the smoke trails of bombers screaming down in flames. Simultaneously, there appeared high over the rocket target a cluster of white puffs, followed by faint thunder.

General Barker shook his head happily. "By George!" he crowed. "Well, sir, by George, by George, by George!"

"Look!" shouted the admiral seated next to me. "The fleet—it wasn't touched!"

"The guns seem to be drooping," said Mr. Cuthrell.

We left the bench and clustered about the television sets to examine the damage more closely. What Mr. Cuthrell had said was true. The ships' guns curved downward, their muzzles resting on the steel decks. We in Virginia were making such a hullabaloo that it was impossible to hear the radio reports. We were so engrossed, in fact, that we didn't miss the professor until two short snarls of Barnhouse static shocked us into sudden silence. The radios went dead.

We looked around apprehensively. The professor was gone. A harassed guard threw open the front door from the outside to yell that the professor had escaped. He brandished his pistol in the direction of the gates, which hung open, limp and twisted. In the distance a speeding government station wagon topped a ridge and dropped from sight into the valley beyond. The air was filled with choking smoke, for every vehicle on the grounds was ablaze. Pursuit was impossible.

"What in God's name got into him?" bellowed the general.

Mr. Cuthrell, who had rushed out onto the front porch, now slouched back into the room, reading a penciled note as he came. He thrust the note into my hands. "The good man left this billet-doux under the door knocker. Perhaps our young friend here will be kind enough to read it to you gentlemen while I take a restful walk through the woods."

> *"Gentlemen* [I read aloud],
>   *As the first superweapon with a conscience, I am removing myself from your national defense stockpile. Setting a new precedent in the behavior of ordnance, I have humane reasons for going off.*
>
>   *A. Barnhouse."*

Since that day, of course, the professor has been systematically destroying the world's armaments, until there is now little with which to equip an army other than rocks and sharp sticks. His activities haven't exactly resulted in peace, but have, rather, precipitated a bloodless and entertaining sort of war that might be called the "War of the Tattletales." Every nation is flooded with enemy agents whose sole mission is to locate military equipment, which is promptly wrecked when it is brought to the professor's attention in the press.

Just as every day brings news of more armaments pulverized by dynamopsychism, so has it brought rumors of the professor's whereabouts. During last week alone, three publications carried articles proving variously that he was hiding in an Inca ruin in the Andes, in the sewers of Paris, and in the unexplored chambers of Carlsbad Caverns. Knowing the man, I am inclined to regard such hiding places as unnecessarily romantic and uncomfortable. While there are numerous persons eager to kill him, there must be millions who would care for him and hide him. I like to think that he is in the home of such a person.

One thing is certain: At this writing, Professor Barnhouse is not dead. Barnhouse static jammed broadcasts not ten minutes ago. In the eighteen months since his disappearance, he has been reported dead some half-dozen times. Each report has stemmed from the death of an unidentified man resembling the professor, during a period free of the static. The first three reports were followed at once by renewed talk of rearmament and recourse to war. The saber rattlers have learned how imprudent premature celebrations of the professor's demise can be.

Many a stouthearted patriot has found himself prone in the tangled bunting and timbers of a smashed reviewing stand, seconds after having announced that the archtyranny of Barnhouse was at an end. But those who would make war if they could, in every country in the world, wait in sullen silence for what must come—the passing of Professor Barnhouse.

To ask how much longer the professor will live is to ask how much longer we must wait for the blessings of another world war. He is of short-lived stock: his mother lived to be fifty-three, his father to be forty-nine; and the life spans of his grandparents on both sides were of the same order. He might be expected to live, then, for perhaps fifteen years more, if he can remain hidden from his enemies. When one considers the number and vigor of these enemies, however, fifteen years seems an extraordinary length of time, which might better be revised to fifteen days, hours, or minutes.

The professor knows that he cannot live much longer. I say this because of the message left in my mailbox on Christmas Eve. Unsigned, typewritten on a soiled scrap of paper, the note consisted of ten sentences. The first nine of these, each a bewildering tangle of psychological jargon and references to obscure texts, made no sense to me at first reading. The tenth, unlike the rest, was simply constructed and contained no large words—but its irrational content made it the most puzzling and bizarre sentence of all. I nearly threw the note away, thinking it a colleague's warped notion of a practical joke. For some reason, though, I added it to the clutter on top of my desk, which included, among other mementos, the professor's dice.

It took me several weeks to realize that the message really meant something, that the first nine sentences, when unsnarled, could be taken as instructions. The tenth still told me nothing. It was only last night that I discovered how it fitted in with the rest. The sentence appeared in my thoughts last night while I was toying absently with the professor's dice.

I promised to have this report on its way to the publishers today. In view of what has happened, I am obliged to break that promise, or release the report incomplete. The delay will not be a long one, for one of the few blessings accorded a bachelor like myself is the ability to move quickly from one abode to another, or from one way of life to another. What property I want to take with me can be packed in a few hours. Fortunately, I am not without substantial private means, which may take as long as a week to realize in liquid and anonymous form. When this is done, I shall mail the report.

I have just returned from a visit to my doctor, who tells me my health is excellent. I am young, and with any luck at all, I shall live to a ripe old age indeed, for my family on both sides is noted for longevity.

Briefly, I propose to vanish.

Sooner or later, Professor Barnhouse must die. But long before then I shall be ready. So, to the saber rattlers of today—and even, I hope, of tomorrow—I say: Be advised. Barnhouse will die. But not the Barnhouse Effect.

Last night I tried once more to follow the oblique instructions on the scrap of paper. I took the professor's dice, and then, with the last, nightmarish sentence flitting through my mind, I rolled fifty consecutive sevens.

Good-by.

THE TOURIST TRADE

by Bob Tucker

Judy had climbed to her place at the breakfast table that morning and announced the presence of a ghost in her room the previous night, a good-looking man ghost who had

Copyright, 1950, by Wilson Tucker, reprinted by permission of the author and his agent, Frederik Pohl.

courteously asked if she were having a nice time.

And Judy's mother, being a sensible, sane American citizen, said nonsense, child, there is no such thing as a ghost.

"Well, then," Judy demanded. "who was the man in my bedroom last night, huh?"

Mother looked up from the toast, startled.

"A man, baby?"

"Yes, Mama. A good-looking man, gooder-looking even than Daddy, and he had on a brown uniform-like, only it wasn't a soldier's uniform of course but just a uniform."

"A man—with a uniform?"

"Yes, Mama. A nice man, you know."

"No," Mama contradicted, "I don't know. Are you *sure* you saw a man in your room last night?"

"Sure, Mama. He was a ghost, a man ghost."

"*Oh*, Judy! Those ghosts again. I've asked you time and again to stop that! There is no such thing as a ghost."

"Well, maybe not, Mama, but this man come riding in right through my wall on a sort of motor scooter, and he stood up and made a speech like that man said at the museum, and he asked me if I was having a nice time."

"All that? Judy!"

"Yes, Mama. And I told him yes and he said, That's nice, and he sat down again and rode the scooter right across my room and went right through my other wall."

"Judy, stop it! You were dreaming."

"Yes, Mama. The motor scooter didn't make any noise, though, and he had a uniform on."

"All right, baby. Forget it, darling."

Judy didn't forget it; she filed the matter away in whatever storage cabinet children have for accumulating knowledge and experiences temporarily unclassifiable. She filed the matter away, somewhat, until that evening and a new bedtime. Scarcely fifteen minutes after climbing the stairs to bed, she was back down again.

Daddy was hunched in a chair reading a whodunit, fighting off the interfering noise of the radio. Mama was listening to the radio and haphazardly working on a jigsaw puzzle. Judy paused in the doorway of the living room, her pajamas still unmussed, a robe trailing in one hand.

"*Now* what do you want, baby? You should have been asleep ten minutes ago."

"That man ghost is back again."

"Now, Judy! Don't start that again."

"Well, Mama, he is, and on top of that he's got some people with him this time, and they're all riding in——"

"Judy!"

"Yes, Mama?"

"*Up to bed.*"

"Yes, Mama." The girl turned and slowly climbed the steps. The last of her trailing footsteps sounded on the stairs and presently the bedroom door slammed in its characteristic manner. Her mother sighed and looked across the room for help.

"Donald, you've got to *do* something. That child has ghosts on her mind; all I hear is ghosts, ghosts, ghosts. I'm worried about it. Do you think she's been listening to the radio too much?"

Donald wearily raised his eyes from the book. "All kids go through that. Forget about it. She's just imaginative, that's all."

"But *such* an imagination! It isn't healthy."

"Oh, bosh. Keep it up and she'll grow up to be an actress, or a writer or something. Listen——" He paused as the sound of Judy's bedroom door opening came to them. The approaching footsteps padded slowly down the stairs.

Judy paused timidly in the doorway, glancing from one parent to the other.

"It's getting late, Judy." Daddy spoke up. "Those ghosts again?"

"Yes, Daddy."

"Won't let you sleep, I suppose?"

"No, Daddy."

"How many of them, do you think?"

Judy beamed. "Four of them—no, five I guess, counting the woman stuck in the wall, only she's kinda fuzzy and you can't see her very good. And the man in the uniform."

"Oh, a uniform, eh? And what's *he* doing?"

"He's showing my room to the rest of them and he drives the scooter everybody rides in and he's telling them about my furniture and my dolls and things. Daddy, he don't like it very much."

"Now, really!" Louise broke in.

"Wait a minute, Louise, I'll handle this." He turned his attention to his daughter. "He didn't like your furniture, eh,

Judy? How do you know that?"

"I could tell by the way he talked, Daddy. He said it was Millerya or something, and he waved his hand and looked down his nose like you do when you don't like something. Like it wasn't much good, you know."

"Sure I know. Millerya, huh? Well, that's too bad. *We* like it, and if he doesn't, he can just lump it, isn't that what you say? What are they going to do next?"

"He wanted to know if there was anybody living in the house besides me."

"Oh, he did, eh? Well, you should have told him we were down here."

"I did, Daddy. And the man in the uniform said for me to come down and tell you they were here."

"I see." He nodded wisely and prepared to wrap it up. "Well, I hate to disappoint your ghost, Judy, but neither your mother nor I feels like climbing the stairs to meet him right now. Will you tell him that for me."

"Sure thing, Daddy."

"All right. Good night, Judy."

Judy climbed the stairs at a brisk trot and the bedroom door slammed in its usual fashion. It was opened again and Judy trotted back down just as briskly. She put her head into the living room.

"Daddy?"

"Uh—what?" He came up from the depths of the book.

"The ghost says you had better come up there or else."

"Indeed! Or else what?"

"Or else he'll report you."

Donald slammed the book to the floor. Judy jumped in alarm.

"Well, Daddy, he did. He did!" the girl cried.

"Judy—you get right back up those stairs and tell that ghost I'm *not* coming up to meet him. Not until he plays 'Yankee Doodle' on the saxophone. Get that?"

"Yes, Daddy."

"All right then, get moving. And good night!"

"Good night, Daddy." The young feet retraced the path up the stairs and the young hands gave the bedroom door a thumping slam. After that the silence from the second floor was a welcome thing.

"There," Donald said in triumph. "I told you I'd handle her. Tact. That's all it takes, tact." He dropped into the overstuffed chair and sought his place in the mystery novel.

From Judy's bedroom came the loud, blaring sound of a saxophone tearing through "Yankee Doodle."

Donald jumped from the chair and hurled the book across the room, narrowly missing a vase. Removing his belt from his trousers in one angry jerk, he sped for the stairs and bounded upward, two steps at a time. His wife shut her eyes and tried to shut her ears after the bedroom door opened and slammed shut again. The blaring of the saxophone ceased. Nervously, she twiddled a piece of the jigsaw puzzle in her fingers and waited for the blows to fall.

Instead, Donald came down the steps and paused in the doorway.

"Louise——"

"Yes, Donald?"

"The ghost wants you to come up there too."

"Donald!"

"But he insists. He said he wanted to exhibit the whole blamed family, and for you to get up there toot-sweet or he'd report us all. Better come along, Louise."

And he turned to mount the staircase.

"Ah, at last," the uniformed gentleman exclaimed. He turned to address the people waiting behind him, all seated in a low motor conveyance.

"This is a complete family unit of the twentieth century," he announced with evident satisfaction. "They spring from a race of aborigines inhabiting the North American continent from about the fifteenth century through the thirty-third. At the stage of their development you see here, they lived together as a closely knit family unit in dwelling places they called *houses,* which is a type of building containing many small cells similar to this one. Usually each member of the unit slept in a separate cell, but they lived together in the remainder of those making up the *house.*

"Notice the male. At this early stage of history he has already assumed the place of head of his family unit and is fond of exhibiting various mental and physical characteristics to identify himself as the leader, or chief. Look closely at his face and you will see hair, or fuzz, growing. This was known as a *beard* and was permitted to grow to assert independence. These early men were extremely stubborn, as you noted a moment ago when it was necessary to use a musical instrument of the twentieth century to summon him from his cell."

"Go away," Donald said to the uniformed man, "you're bothering us."

"Earlier in the rise of their race, as you will soon see when we move along to the next stop, the aborigines had not yet learned the use of tools and were of course unable to erect buildings such as this one. During that distant period they lived in natural caves, squatting over continual fires for protection from the elements, for warmth, and for cooking. During the present period you see here they had found a means of moving the fires indoors for both warmth and cooking, and also developed a few primitive instruments to assist them in eating. Holding raw food in the fingers has almost vanished in the year before you."

"Well, I like that!" Louise exclaimed.

"G'wan, beat it," Donald chimed in. "It's the kid's bedtime. Shove off."

"This race," the smartly uniformed man continued, "were called Indians, or Americans, the two terms being interchangeable. Sections, or tribes, existed among them and each tribe adopted the name of some patron saint, protective god, or robber baron to whom they paid monetary and honorary tribute. Their tribes sometimes bore colorful names like Ohio, Dogpatch; Jones, Republican; and so forth."

"You're a radical!" Donald exclaimed. "Now get out of here or I'll put the dog on you!"

"Not too much is known of their social cultures, because the various tribes were always warring upon each other, making historical surveys hazardous and the gathering of information extremely difficult. We will make one more stop in this era to observe a gathering of the wise men of the tribes, and there you will see laws and customs being enacted, taxes collected, and so forth. Afterward, we shall move a bit farther along for a quick glimpse of this family's forefathers, and perhaps if we are fortunate we shall see them hunting in the forests with primitive weapons. During this stage of the tour I must remind you to keep your protective shields closed at all times, for occasionally stray bolts from their weapons may drop among us." He paused and turned to move a small lever.

The conveyance began to move across the room, drawing

the misty lady from the confines of the wall to give her a solid, human appearance. The uniformed man cast a glance over his shoulder.

"And so we say good-by to the colorful, romantic twentieth century with its many tribes, its primitive peoples, and its quaint customs." He turned to stare at Donald, directing a low-voiced order at the dumfounded man. "And see that you get here on time after this, chum. No more of that silly saxophone business."

The conveyance wheeled across the room and vanished into the opposite wall, the lady in the rear seat turning for a last amused look at the quaint mill-era furniture. Her face faded and the visitors were gone.

"Donald——" his wife quavered.

"They can't do that to me!" Donald roared. "I'm a taxpayer! I'll see my precinct committeeman about this!"

"Wasn't he a nice man, Daddy?"

Daddy correctly reasoned that the nice, uniformed man and his strange conveyance of ghostly passengers would be back on the following night. He readied himself accordingly.

A few minutes before Judy's usual bedtime the vehicle nosed through one wall of the bedroom and the uniformed guide could be seen rising from his seat, preparatory to spouting his lecture on the twentieth-century family unit. As he solidified he glanced about the room, noting the absence of Donald's wife and child.

"Come, come now," he said with displeasure. "Bring in the remainder of your family. We have a nice crowd today."

"I've got a surprise for you," Donald replied softly.

"Indeed?" said the guide. "What?"

"This!" Donald cried, and brought from behind him a double-barreled shotgun. He raised the weapon and fired both barrels at the crowded car. Plaster fountained from the opposite wall and the bedroom window crashed down in shards.

The guide shook his head. "For shame! Please call the family"—he reached behind him to pick up a saxophone—"or must I perform another tune?

"This," he said to the watching tourists, "is a male of the twentieth century. You have just witnessed a primitive fireworks display used by these people to welcome visitors to their land or to celebrate special holidays dedicated to their gods. It would be a generous gesture on our part to show this man we appreciate the display he has prepared for us. Early peoples, you know, thrive on flattery and attention." He broke into polite applause and the tourists seated behind him took it up. Someone pitched a few coins.

Donald hurled the gun to the floor and stamped on it.

"The twentieth-century man is now beginning his dance of welcome, a tribal ritual which has come down to him from the campfires of his ancestors who roamed the forests still hundreds of years away. I hold in my hand a musical instrument of this age called a saxophone, and presently I will blow a little tune which will summon his mate and child from the nether regions of the building in which they dwell . . ."

Donald kept trying. On the following night he laboriously strung a length of hose from the second-floor bathroom to the bedroom, and as the visitors emerged from the wall—a rather thin crowd this particular trip—he attempted to douse them with a strong stream of water. The water squirted through the visitors and splashed down the cracked wall on the opposite side of the room.

"This," said the guide, "is a twentieth-century male. He is welcoming us to his dwelling place with a water ritual designed to wash away the evil spirits which he fears may hamper our coming. When he has thoroughly cleansed the walls of his dwelling and made the unit safe for us, he will begin his dance of welcome and we will be expected to show our appreciation by applause or small gifts and coins. Afterward, by making notes on this instrument in my hand, the remainder of his family will approach. Now, note the quaint furniture of the——"

In an aside as he was leaving, the guide confided to Donald, "Keep it up, chum. You put on the best show on my entire run. We're getting good word-of-mouth advertising."

Donald kept it up. He tried stink bombs, which succeeded only in forcing him and his family out of the house; he brought in a radio, a phonograph, several automobile horns and a borrowed siren in an effort to drive away the tourists from the future by a sheer wall of noise, and succeeded only in blasting his own eardrums; he turned a swarm of bees loose in the room and wound up with numerous stings; he was forcefully prevented by his wife from piling the furniture and the bedding in the room's center and setting fire to it as the guide and his conveyance appeared through the wall.

"This is a man of the twentieth century. He is preparing to welcome us by setting fire to those numerous small red objects you see lying about the floor of the dwelling unit. Presently the red objects will explode with a tremendous repercussion, driving away evil spirits lurking here—he believes—and making our visit a safe one. Now, please note . . ."

A red-eyed haggard man stood on a street corner, leaning dazedly against the lamppost. His wife had left him and returned to her mother, declaring that she and their child would return to that horrible house when—and only when—he had rid Judy's room of those horrible visitations once and for all. He hadn't reported for work for over a week and his job was in danger; he hadn't slept for the same length of time and his health was in similar jeopardy. His friends avoided him, believing he had fallen into the clutches of the demon rum. All in all, he was a sad specimen of twentieth-century man. And he was on the verge of ending it all when the bus went by.

Someone babbling in a loud voice caught his attention, and he glanced up, cringing instinctively at the sight of a rubberneck bus wheeling along the street. Sick at heart, he turned his back to discover passers-by gazing curiously at the bus.

Donald opened his eyes wide.

The low-bodied motor conveyance made its nightly appearance through the wall, and Donald saw the guide rising from his seat to address the tourists behind him. Donald folded his arms and waited. The entire vehicle, well crowded, came into view and stopped.

The uniformed guide looked at him inquiringly.

"Pretty quiet around here, chum. Can't you whip up something?"

"I certainly can, mister," Donald told him. "Just you wait right here." He crossed to the bedroom door and flung it open, jumping back to avoid the mob. "Here they are, folks," he shouted, "as advertised." Holding out his hat, he admitted the crowd into the room, watching carefully to see that each dropped a coin into the receptacle.

"Real, genuine ghosts, folks! The only haunted house in Libertyville! Each night and every night on the hour this ghostly crew rides out of that wall yonder and parades across the room. Step right up to them, folks; try to touch them; try to feel them. You can't! Come right in and meet my ghosts."

The small bedroom was suddenly filled with awed, milling people crowding forward to gaze at the ghostly conveyance. Curious hands reached out to touch the future tourists, only to grasp the empty air. Flashbulbs popped as newspaper photographers snapped what they hoped would be pictures of the visitation. A representative of the American Ethereal Society pinched his glasses to his nose and held a lighted match to the ghostly guide's natty uniform, testing to see if flaming gauze netting would reveal a trickery. The guide stared at the flashbulbs, slightly taken aback.

"Come now," he said, "this will be reported."

"He talks, he walks, he plays a saxophone!" Donald shouted above the din. "A real, genuine ghost, folks. Step right up and take a look at the real article!"

"Where in hell did they come from?" a reporter wanted to know, brazenly pushing two fingers into and through the disapproving face of the guide. "I'm damned if they scare me!"

"He's a legend connected with the house," Donald explained glibly. "According to the story, this fellow in the uniform was an eccentric inventor who used to live here, but he finally killed himself. The story says he was a 4-F but he wore that uniform to ease his conscience; he always claimed to be inventing war machines for the Government. See all those people behind him?"

Necks craned to look at the tourists.

"They were *murdered!*" Donald whispered hoarsely. "According to the legend, this crazy inventor murdered them all and sealed their bodies up in the wall. And now, every night he lines up all the ghosts on this crazy machine he imagines he invented and rides them through the walls."

A fresh onslaught of people in the doorway drew his attention. Snatching up the hatful of jingling coins, Donald fought his way to the door.

"Step right in, folks. The ghosts are here! Come right in

and meet genuine ghosts in the only haunted house in town!
Each night and every night . . ."

Donald's wife and child returned home the following
week end. Judy was installed in a new bedroom, and in due
time developed an intense interest in Hopalong Cassidy.

RAINMAKER

by John Reese

The phone clanged at exactly 3:53 A.M. Bill
Lawson groaned and took it groggily on his back, keeping
his eyes shut and his bare arm under the covers. It would be
blazing hot by noon, late June being what it is in southern
California, but there was a sharp, mountainish chill abroad
now.

"H'lo, Lawson speakin'," he mumbled, sure of a wrong
number.

A girl operator said, "One minute, Bill. Mr. Beck is
calling, but he's on another line." He found himself cut off.
He sat up and groped for his slippers and a cigarette,
wondering why he felt so depressed.

It came to him after a minute, as he clung to the dead line.
He had danced at the Palladium with Patty Vernier until
two o'clock. From Hollywood to Patty's home in Studio
City was a fast thirty-minute drive. Studio City lay in the
San Fernando Valley, northwest of Los Angeles. Bill lived
in Temple City, in the San Gabriel Valley, northeast of Los
Angeles. From her home to his adequate but lonely
bachelor residence was a fast hour's drive through Burbank,
Glendale, Pasadena, and San Gabriel.

In other words, he had been asleep at least twenty
minutes, not enough to say he had "slept on" his problem.
He knew his mind was not subtle—that he had made Patty
mad, or hurt her, or something. "No girl likes to be taken for

granted." That's what she said. He was only trying to say
that he trusted her, believed her . . .

"Hiyah, Bill!" came the drowsy-cheery voice of Sid Beck,
night operator at the California State Weather Service
Station at Pomona, thirty miles up the San Gabriel Valley.
"Want a big fat rain?"

"At this hour?" Bill moaned.

"Why not? I need it personally. Got some zinnias in bad
shape, Bill. Hang on a minute—other phone—expecting
the blimp to check in over Inglewood."

Again Bill was cut off. He stood up and switched on the
ceiling light and studied the big meteorological map of
southern California on the wall over his bed.

Things had changed a lot since scientists first seeded
clouds with pellets of dry ice, making them discharge their
moisture in the form of artificial rain, twenty-odd years ago.
Bill was a kid of eight when he watched a little cub plane
make three passes at a cirro-cumulus formation over a grass
fire in the Santa Monica Mountains, just about the time the
Japanese surrendered—some time in the middle forties,
anyway.

It didn't work, and the fire burned itself out, but the kid of
eight knew what he wanted to be when he grew up. A
rainmaker. Now, at twenty-eight, William Lawson had held
California Precipitation Permit No. 1 for six years, ever
since the state started granting them under the Supreme
Court decision.

The permit meant he was a skilled airplane pilot. It
meant he had two years of college meteorology. It meant he
could tell you at any given time what crops were in what
growing stages, and where. It meant he could tell you,
without looking at the charts, each of the two dozen two-
day to five-day periods during the hot, dry southern
California summer when a rain would do a lot of good for
everyone and harm to no one. Charts? He had written most
of them himself.

He was a pioneer, and now it was a business, same as any
other. Who owned the clouds? Riparian law, governing
streams and watersheds, had gone aloft, and Bill's name
was on most of the litigation that took it there—generally as
defendant. He had been sued for making it rain and sued for
not making it rain. He had been the first man ever enjoined
by a Federal District Court from making it rain, in "City of

San Diego vs. Lawson, Coachella Date Growers Association, et al."

Won that one, too, when it rained anyway. "Respondent is not God," said the unanimous Supreme Court decision. "He does not create rain, on the evidence. Neither has he violated divine or natural law, since it rained anyway. It appears, rather, that he acts in strict accordance with such law, and that the injunction should have been directed against the Creator, rather than respondent. It is therefore vacated, since it is beyond the power of man to write or enforce any law which supersedes or attempts the illusion of superseding divine or natural law."

Sid Beck came back on the line as Bill scratched himself and studied his charts and maps. "Blimp, all right, confirming that the mass appears to be detached. Big black cold front, probably high density, moving in from the Pacific bank over White's Point on a six-mile southerly wind," Sid said.

"Put my name on it." Bill yawned. "I'll start calling clients."

He hung up and tried to focus his eyes on the bedside telephone directory and his mind on his business. He kept seeing Patty's angry pink face and angry brown eyes. Nikano, the aged Japanese who kept house for him, brought in black coffee without being told. Bill dialed the Rosemead Airport and told them to warm her up.

"Now, let's see; McQueen, McQueen."

The phone rang again. It was Jerry Rudd this time, and no way to start a day. Jerry was a millionaire perishable-crop and citrus-farm operator who rubbed Bill the wrong way. He lived in a hundred-thousand-dollar house in Toluca Lake, less than a mile from Patty Vernier and her mother, in the San Fernando Valley. Unfortunately, his intentions were honorable. He wanted to take Patty—and her mother—on a honeymoon cruise through Panama to Florida and Havana on his three-hundred-thousand-dollar yacht.

It started when Patty said, "Mama's all in favor of it." Bill howled at this treachery because he had always been fair to Mrs. Vernier. One word led to another, and pretty soon Patty's eyes were snapping as she said, "Well, you certainly take a lot for granted, including me! Maybe I'd better think the whole thing over." She did not hand him his diamond, but she came close to it.

"Now what do you want?" Bill growled at the cause of his troubles.

Jerry laughed his infectious laugh. Even at four in the morning he was the personality kid, a dangerous adversary with or without money and a yacht.

"Just had a call about a detached cold mass from my man down at Newport," Jerry said. "He tells me that——"

"Your what down at where?" Bill interrupted, making him say it.

"The skipper of my boat. He tells me they're fogged in, and Pomona says you're already on notice. Peas, spinach, and citrus can all use——"

"Nothing doing!" Bill cut in. "You got the last one over there, and it's our turn out here. Besides, the State Highway Department is detouring twenty-five thousand cars a day through an unpaved stubble field on the Sepulveda tunnel near you."

"I've already put in a call for the governor on that," Jerry said serenely.

"Put in your call to the people driving those twenty-five thousand cars, Jerry. I don't want to make everybody sore at me, even if the governor is your pal. Now don't argue. Irrigate and be damned to you! I won't do it."

He took pleasure in hanging up. He called the operator and got two numbers at once, to settle it in one three-way conversation. Roy McQueen, at Duarte, headed the San Gabriel Valley Early Tomato Crop Association; Ollie Niehouse, at Azusa, the San Gabriel Grape Growers. They promised to check their executive committees and call him back.

He got their calls on his auto telephone en route to the airport. Go to it, they said. Some of the tomato men had already started to irrigate, but thousands of feet of precious water could still be saved.

His plane was already ticking away on the apron of the runway. It was an old but serviceable two-engine job. He loaded his six discharge ports with pellets of dry ice from the freezing cabinet, and it was exactly 4:36 when he took off and spiraled upward in a bad temper.

Usually he got a kick out of going up at this hour of the day and watching it make or break below him. At forty-five hundred feet he could see hints of sun through the light high haze to the east. Below him was only a dense gray blanket. Good stuff, but it gave him no pleasure. "No girl likes to be taken for granted." Ye gods, he only wanted to tell her he knew she wasn't the mercenary type, to be swept off her feet by . . .

His phone buzzed two longs, a short, two longs. He lifted the instrument, switched the automatic pilot on for a tight circle, and leaned back against the cushions to muffle the engine roar.

"Lawson."

"Sid again. Where are you, Bill? Can't get anything informative from the ground because everything's fogged in. Keep me posted."

"Over Alhambra." Bill looked out of his window. "Too broad a movement for me to catch local shifts yet, but she's black and big, and looks sopping wet. I think I'll go out to sea and come in with it. How's it out Pomona way?"

"Clear as a bell. That's what worries me—nothing seems to be moving this way yet. Got one call that shows a possible wind shift up Whittier Narrows, but that's all. Bill, herd it this way."

"W'y shore!" Bill said.

He hung up, took the controls away from the automatic, and gunned southward. The misty gray blanket began to slope downward. He knew when he passed over Los Angeles Harbor, at San Pedro, by instruments only. To mariners, this was fog. To real-estate salesmen, it was a "nice morning haze." To meteorologists, it was a detached cold mass. To Bill, it was a big batch of sopping-wet stuff that meant up to thirty-five hundred dollars in his kitty if it went where he wanted it to go and he got there at the same time.

At two hundred and ten miles an hour he went twenty miles to sea and suddenly saw the ocean below him. He called Sid.

"Completely detached from the Pacific bank and clear as a bell here. I'm coming in with it now and try to catch the local currents."

"Fine, fine!" said Sid, drawing new lines on his map.

It was three minutes after five when he crossed White's Point again. The blanket below him was more black than gray now, and Bill had seen enough like it to recognize its definite northward movement. The big mass of cold, moisture-laden marine air—a cloud on the ground—was pushing up against the mountains which ringed the coastal plain, seeking an outlet eastward tó the desert.

Bill cut his engines and headed straight north toward downtown Los Angeles. His mind kept struggling with personal problems—Patty and her mother, Jerry Rudd and his yacht—but his eyes saw everything below him. The cold mass was more like a herd of sheep than anything else.

To his right, although he couldn't see it, lay Whittier Narrows, a defile through low hills, leading to Orange County. The contour of the surface had set up a slight draft through the Narrows, exactly like a chimney. Some of the cold mass was already splitting off, moving eastward. But not enough of it to worry him; he notified Sid, so Sid could notify precipitation fliers in Anaheim and Fullerton. He flew on.

Down under that gray blanket lay the most heavily populated districts of Los Angeles County, and ahead lay the mountains. It was like flying toward a tall, arc-shaped fence with three gates in it. The left one was Cahuenga Pass, connecting Hollywood with the San Fernando Valley. Straight ahead was Arroyo Seco, leading to Pasadena and the foothill communities. To the right was Coyote Pass, opening into the San Gabriel Valley.

If the sheep didn't take the right-hand gate, all this precious, black, sopping-wet stuff—millions of gallons of water—would be wasted. The cold mass would be warmed by the sun and lose its density. It would pour out over the desert beyond the mountains and, diluted by hot, dry, desert air, lose its identity as a rain mass altogether.

Let's see what she looks like over Cahuenga, he murmured to himself. Cahuenga was the deepest pass in the highest part of the mountain barrier. He swung left.

His plane pitched as he crossed Cahuenga at low level. It stopped pitching and he knew he was over Studio City and Toluca Lake, the first of the San Fernando Valley communities. Down there, Patty was sleeping peacefully. Down there, Jerry Rudd was sitting at his telephone, calling his yacht skipper for news, his farm managers to give them orders, the governor for permission to soak a high-priced State Highway Department job.

Why did he keep thinking of Patty? "Of course a girl is flattered to be asked to honeymoon on a yacht. You just don't understand, Bill." Had he been too brusque? He was sure in his own mind that Jerry was crazy about Pat chiefly because she was the one thing his money couldn't buy—so far. Maybe he hadn't been very tactful . . .

Thinking of her, so close down there, made him miserable. He grabbed for the phone before he could change his mind, and asked for her number. Mrs. Vernier answered, a little shortly. He didn't exactly blame her for preferring a millionaire as a son-in-law. He just wished she would keep her nose out of his business.

"She's asleep and I don't like to call her—not after you kept her out so late," Mrs. Vernier said firmly. "This is my wash day and Heaven knows I've got plenty to do, but if you insist——"

He insisted, and in a few minutes he heard Patty's sleepy voice. "Bill! What's the matter? Where in the world are you?"

Her voice faded as he went away from one telephone relay station. It came in clearly as he approached another.

"Right now," he said, "I'm making a portside swing over Northridge." She didn't say anything, and he felt ashamed for having wakened her at this hour. "I just called to apologize."

"For what?" she said coolly, after a slight hesitation.

"For whatever I did that was wrong. For thinking one way and talking another, baby. I'm a slob, but I thought I'd feel better if I told you I was sorry. Now go back to sleep."

"Bill! Is that all you called me for?"

"That's all," he said bleakly.

"You'd better go home and get some more sleep yourself. You sound lightheaded."

"You can say that again, honey. Good-by."

He hung up. Well, he hadn't done any good, apparently, but he did feel better. It was up to her now.

The phone rang again. It was Roy McQueen, at Duarte, in a bad mood.

"What's the matter with you, Bill? The sun came up bright as a dollar here this morning. Gonna be hot as blazes. I had three calls already, should they turn water into the ditches. I thought you said you had a cold mass over us."

"Not over you yet, Roy. Hold on a minute and let's look." He turned southward again, running up a phone bill while McQueen, down there in Duarte, breathed impatiently into his ear. Halfway to the harbor, he turned

and came back again. Now he could see a strong, definite
movement through Cahuenga, light stirrings up the Arroyo
Seco and Coyote Pass. Arroyo Seco didn't worry him, but
Cahuenga did. "Don't be in too big a hurry about irrigating,
Roy," he said. "Give me another hour."

"If we burn up," McQueen threatened, "I'll levy on your
bond, so help me!"

"You won't burn up," Bill comforted him, against his
own dismal better judgment. "She's all over Alhambra,
Monterey Park, Temple City, part of Arcadia. It'll get to
you pretty quick."

But after Roy hung up, he turned back over Hollywood
and shook his head. The shift was definitely through
Cahuenga now. Should he try to stop it or should he peddle
it to Rudd and his peas and spinach and citrus people? The
San Gabriel folks had this one coming, and Bill wanted
them to have it. But maybe it wasn't going to move out
through Coyote Pass at all. Maybe it would be a lot better to
let the San Fernando Valley have it, rather than take a
chance on losing the whole mass.

He decided to settle it on a personal basis, rather than on
its merits. Nuts to Jerry Rudd! He felt better than ever, now
that he had ignobly given in to his own worst nature.

"I'm going to try to set up local precipitation in Cahuenga
and establish an inert cold front there that will stop the flow
through the pass," he told Sid Beck. "Get hold of your
ground contacts there and let me know what I'm doing.
Coming in now."

He went out over the San Fernando Valley and came
back in over Cahuenga Pass, tripping the trigger on his No.
1 magazine as he felt the air over the pass go bumpy under
him. Carbon dioxide exhausted by the pellets themselves
had built up a heavy pressure in the magazine. Two shots
did it. He heard them hissing through the discharge ports
and peeled off just as Mount Hollywood's ugly crown
loomed in his face. He went over Hollywood on his side,
straightened out and spiraled upward to watch. There was a
turbulence down there now, where the pass was supposed to
be, instead of a smooth, swift flow.

Sid Beck called him. "Got symptoms of a good job.
Raining like the dickens over Hollywood Bowl and a nice
shower as far as Lockheed Airport," Sid reported. "How's
she look from up there?"

"Well," Bill said dubiously, "she slowed down through Cahuenga and I think it's moving a little stronger up Arroyo Seco, but nothing doing in Coyote Pass yet. Still clear in Pomona?"

"Still clear."

"All I can do is wait and watch now."

The mass was exactly like a herd of sheep. He had clubbed a few of them in the head as they tried to stream through Cahuenga. They were milling around down there now, wishing they could get out, but lacking sense enough to head for the other gates. A small hole in the mass appeared just beyond Cahuenga. He could see parts of Griffith Park clearly.

This was the gate he had closed, the barrier he had set up. His dry-ice pellets had condensed the moisture there, exactly as cold sweat collects on a water jug on a hot day. Rain had fallen in an area not more than a mile square. The cold mass not only wasn't cold in that spot any more, it wasn't even a mass. The even flow, the draft of the Cahuenga flue, the pell-mell sheep surge through the gate had been disrupted.

Sometimes a man could do it and sometimes he couldn't. Bill circled over downtown Los Angeles. That was good stuff down there, sopping wet, blacker than ever, now that it was being jammed up against the mountain barrier. Wind seemed to have shifted from the south, perhaps a point or two to the southwest.

He called Sid again. "Anything from ground contacts?"

"Windsock at Lockheed turned the circle, but all they got was a shower. How's it look up there? I had a call from McQueen, Bill. They're getting a little haze at Duarte, but he's anxious."

"I'll try it again, Sid," Bill decided, watching the hole over Griffith Park close up again. "She's starting to flow through Cahuenga again, dammit."

"Put a string on it and lead it this way."

He went out over the San Fernando Valley and came in over the pass again, tripping his No. 2 magazine, higher in the pass this time. The vents were still hissing pellets as he roared over Hollywood. He took his finger off the button and went up and laughed to watch it boil down there.

Men had been using Cahuenga Pass for more than a hundred years. Not more than five or six times had it rained

hard there in the arid month of June. In less than twenty
minutes he had made it rain hard twice. Hollywood was getting a good soaking; he didn't need Sid's call to tell him that.

For a minute or two he forgot all about Patty. Sometimes
a man could set up his own local cold front, and sometimes
he couldn't. A man could, this morning. Cahuenga was
closed, for all practical purposes.

"Sid! Got a good, strong movement through Coyote
now," he said jubilantly. "For gosh sakes, keep me posted.
Sun's up and the glare makes everything look alike. Heading
out your way and may make my pass coming in."

He couldn't see Duarte and Puente as he roared up the
San Gabriel Valley, but Pomona had only a light veil and
Fontana and Claremont were fairly clear. He went up to six
thousand feet and lurked there twenty minutes, with the
automatic pilot taking him in a wide circle, with the
telephone clamped to his ear.

Sid gave him the ground-contact reports as they came in,
as fast as his telephone operator could handle them, "Solid
over Arcadia, got that high-density look. San Dimas solid.
Covina solid. Not so hot at Spadra—sun can make a
shadow there. Coyote Pass, seven-and-three-tenths-mile
wind. Still blocked in Cahuenga, but Lockheed windsock
shifted again and maybe flow is about to resume. Solid over
Spadra now—guess it was a pocket. Solid where Base Line
Avenue branches off Foothill Boulevard. Bill, she's good all
the way out here. You know as much about it as I do now."

"I'm going in," Bill said. "Check me." He started down
the north side of the valley, along the San Gabriel and Sierra
Madre mountains, at exactly 6:34, tripping his No. 1 and 2
magazines to clean them out, hitting No. 3 when he ran out.

The air went bumpy and he knew he was over San
Marino. He went up, circling Pasadena without seeding the
black mass there, because they didn't want rain. He could
still see a turbulence over Cahuenga, but the flow had
resumed again.

It didn't matter now, though. The rest of it could go out
over San Fernando Valley, and welcome to it! He turned
back and tripped his No. 4 trigger over Alhambra. The
magazine emptied as he crossed Pomona. He turned toward
Los Angeles again and swept the south side of the valley
with No. 5, and as his pellets ran out over Coyote Pass, he

began to get ground-contact effect reports from Sid.

"Santa Fe dam, nice shower and still coming. Stiff, cold wind. At-a-boy, Bill! Them's symptoms what are symptoms! El Monte airport, soaked. Pomona College, three sixteenths of an inch already, no anemometer reading, but it looks like about six miles an hour out of my window. Puddingstone reservoir, soaked. Arrow Highway at Sierra Way, good shower still going. Fontana, Federal rabbit-husbandry experiment station, nice soaking. Alhambra, corner Garfield and Mission and corner Atlantic and Main, soaked. The west end of the valley got most of it, but us hicks seem to be getting plenty too."

Bill was suddenly tired. Herding the wind, milking the clouds, gave him as much of a kick as it had when he was eight years old and watched a little cub try the fantastic trick over a grass fire. But when it was over, it was over. He had had twenty minutes' sleep after a quarrel with his girl.

"Why did I bother to apologize?" he grumbled to himself. "A man only makes a fool of himself when he does that."

He was over Rosemead Airport, but his own rain was still raining there and it was an excuse for not going in. He crossed Los Angeles and Hollywood and Cahuenga Pass, and gave Sid his last observations. Not that he had to, but he liked to do his share in filling out Sid's maps. The fact that his sweep brought him over Patty Vernier's house was strictly coincidence.

A lot of good stuff had collected over the San Fernando Valley—not heavily, but in patches, thanks to those two disturbing cold barriers he had precipitated. Studio City, where Patty lived, was obscured. On impulse, he slanted down and crossed her house at three hundred feet, both engines roaring.

At this level, he could see clearly. There was Jerry Rudd's big red convertible, parked familiarly in the driveway. There was Mrs. Vernier, hanging out her washing, and Jerry was helping her. Jerry was very democratic at all times, of course. What fun a millionaire had, helping his inferiors with their chores! Bill gritted his teeth.

"Me," he said, "up here working my head off, and him down there in white flannels, hanging up the old lady's lace tablecloth. Any time I ever tell a girl I'm sorry again, I hope I——"

His phone buzzed his signal. He jerked it off the hook and yelled, "Hello!" He expected Roy McQueen, but it was Patty.

"Bill, you fool! Is that you buzzing the house? My gosh, if Jerry reports you and you lose your license——"

"This is a precipitation plane," he cut in, "and I've got a right to take observations where I please, honey. Quite a clubby little scene in the back yard! I see you're wide awake enough now with that jerk out there helping with the laundry."

"Why, Bill!" she caroled. "I believe you're jealous!"

"You're cockeyed right I am. I always treated your old lady square and I always gave Jerry a break, and this is what I get."

"Bill," she said firmly, "I'd like to tease you some more, but you said you were sorry and I'm just as good a man as you are, any day. I already told Jerry he could jump in the lake. The reason I'm awake is that I couldn't go back to sleep after you called. That was nice of you, Bill. Little things like that are what mean so much to a woman. If you—— Where are you, Bill?"

"Right here. Got too far away from relay. You mean that, honey?"

"I sure do mean that, honey!"

"Mama can't influence you?"

"Well," Patty said, "she never could, very much."

He was at twenty-four hundred feet now, looking down at a medium-to-thick concentration that reached from Studio City to Van Nuys.

"Look, honey," he said, "I've got to start getting along with your mother again sometime, but she can use a little lesson. Do me a favor. Tell Jerry I'm going to take care of his peas and spinach and citrus, will you?"

He heard her call Jerry, but he hung up before Jerry could get to the phone. The deal was made. Jerry had already told him he wanted moisture, and he'd have to pay for what he got. The courts had said so.

He went back to Van Nuys, turned, and tripped the trigger of his last magazine as he crossed the valley toward Cahuenga Pass, slowly. He went up and stayed there awhile, chuckling and ignoring the frantic buzzing of his phone. Patty had a sense of humor. Patty would see the joke. Patty was on his side again! He felt good. He'd get some sleep and call her later in the day, and they'd laugh together over how it looked from down there.

From up here, it looked good. He had hit it hard, and what moisture there was in the formation came down hard and sudden. It cleared up enough, in ten minutes, for him to see plainly through his binoculars.

That was Mrs. Vernier, in person, galloping toward the house with the last of her starched white linens, getting them in, of course, just as the rain stopped. She'd have to starch them again—perhaps even wash them again. He hoped.

That was Jerry Rudd, in sodden white flannels, letting Mrs. Vernier rescue her own wash, while he set a new record getting the top up on his convertible. He was quite a boy at hanging out laundry, but not so good at getting it in. Bill might have some explaining to do to Mrs. Vernier, but so would Jerry. After all, he ordered the precipitation!

He saw someone come to the front porch, where Mrs. Vernier and Jerry couldn't see. It was a smallish figure in a pinkish chenille robe, and its hands were locked over its head in the prize-fighter's victory gesture.

Bill rocked his wings to show her he saw her. Then, yawning and smiling, he headed back to Rosemead Airport and put her down. It was just 7:42 when he cut the engines and climbed out in front of his own hangar. He had a feeling it had been a nice day's work.

ABSALOM

by Henry Kuttner

At dusk Joel Locke came home from the university where he held the chair of psychonamics. He came quietly into the house, by a side door, and stood listening, a tall, tight-lipped man of forty with a faintly sardonic mouth and cool gray eyes. He could hear the precipitron humming. That meant that Abigail Schuler, the housekeeper, was busy with her duties. Locke smiled slightly and turned toward a panel in the wall that opened at his approach.

The small elevator took him noiselessly upstairs.

There, he moved with curious stealth. He went directly to a door at the end of the hall and paused before it, his head bent, his eyes unfocused. He heard nothing. Presently he opened the door and stepped into the room.

Instantly the feeling of unsureness jolted back, freezing him where he stood. He made no sign, though his mouth tightened. He forced himself to remain quiet as he glanced around.

It could have been the room of a normal twenty-year-old, not a boy of eight. Tennis racquets were heaped in a disorderly fashion against a pile of book records. The thiaminizer was turned on, and Locke automatically clicked the switch over. Abruptly he turned. The televisor screen was blank, yet he could have sworn that eyes had been watching him from it.

This wasn't the first time it had happened.

After a while Locke turned again and squatted to examine the book reels. He picked out one labeled "BRIAFF ON ENTROPIC LOGIC" and turned the cylinder over in his hands, scowling. Then he replaced it and went out of the room, with a last, considering look at the televisor.

Downstairs Abigail Schuler was fingering the Mastermaid switchboard. Her prim mouth was as tight as the severe bun of gray-shot hair at the back of her neck.

"Good evening," Locke said. "Where's Absalom?"

"Out playing, Brother Locke," the housekeeper said formally. "You're home early. I haven't finished the living room yet."

"Well, turn on the ions and let 'em play," Locke said. "It won't take long. I've got some papers to correct, anyway."

He started out, but Abigail coughed significantly.

"Well?"

"He's looking peaked."

"Then outdoor exercise is what he needs," Locke said shortly. "I'm going to send him to a summer camp."

"Brother Locke," Abigail said, "I don't see why you don't let him go to Baja California. He's set his heart on it. You let him study all the hard subjects he wanted before. Now you put your foot down. It's none of my affair, but I can tell he's pining."

"He'd pine worse if I said yes. I've my reasons for not wanting him to study entropic logic. Do you know what it involves?"

"I don't—you know I don't. I'm not an educated woman, Brother Locke. But Absalom is bright as a button."

Locke made an impatient gesture.

"You have a genius for understatement," he said. "Bright as a button!"

Then he shrugged and moved to the window, looking down at the play court below, where his eight-year-old son played handball. Absalom did not look up. He seemed engrossed in his game. But Locke, watching, felt a cool, stealthy terror steal through his mind, and behind his back his hands clenched together.

A boy who looked ten, whose maturity level was twenty, and yet who was still a child of eight. Not easy to handle. There were many parents just now with the same problem—something was happening to the graph curve that charted the percentage of child geniuses born in recent times. Something had begun to stir lazily far back in the brains of the coming generations, and a new species, of a sort, was coming slowly into being. Locke knew that well. In his own time he, too, had been a child genius.

Other parents might meet the problem in other ways, he thought stubbornly. Not himself. He *knew* what was best for Absalom. Other parents might send their genius children to one of the creches where they could develop among their own kind. Not Locke.

"Absalom's place is here," he said aloud. "With me, where I can——" He caught the housekeeper's eye and shrugged again, irritably, going back to the conversation that had broken off. "Of course he's bright. But not bright enough yet to go to Baja California and study entropic logic. Entropic logic! It's too advanced for the boy. Even you ought to realize that. It isn't like a lollypop you can hand the kid—first making sure there's castor oil in the bathroom closet. Absalom's immature. It would actually be dangerous to send him to the Baja California University now to study with men three times his age. It would involve mental strain he isn't fit for yet. I don't want him turned into a psychopath."

Abigail's prim mouth pursed up sourly.

"You let him take calculus."

"Oh, leave me alone." Locke glanced down again at the small boy on the play court. "I think," he said slowly, "that it's time for another rapport with Absalom."

The housekeeper looked at him sharply, opened her thin lips to speak, and then closed them with an almost audible snap of disapproval. She didn't understand entirely, of course, how a rapport worked or what it accomplished. She only knew that there were ways in which it was possible to enforce hypnosis, to pry open a mind willy-nilly and search it for contraband thoughts. She shook her head, lips pressed tight.

"Don't try to interfere in things you don't understand," Locke said. "I tell you, I know what's best for Absalom. He's in the same place I was thirty-odd years ago. Who could know better? Call him in, will you? I'll be in my study."

Abigail watched his retreating back, a pucker between her brows. It was hard to know what was best. The mores of the day demanded rigid good conduct, but sometimes a person had trouble deciding in her own mind what was the right thing to do. In the old days, now, after the atomic wars, when license ran riot and anybody could do anything he pleased, life must have been easier. Nowadays, in the violent backswing to a Puritan culture, you were expected to think twice and search your soul before you did a doubtful thing.

Well, Abigail had no choice this time. She clicked on the wall microphone and spoke into it.

"Absalom?"

"Yes, Sister Schuler?"

"Come in. Your father wants you."

In his study Locke stood quiet for a moment, considering. Then he reached for the house microphone.

"Sister Schuler, I'm using the televisor. Ask Absalom to wait."

He sat down before his private visor. His hands moved deftly.

"Get me Dr. Ryan, the Wyoming Quizkid Creche. Joel Locke calling."

Idly as he waited he reached out to take an old-fashioned cloth-bound book from a shelf of antique curiosa. He read:

But Absalom sent spies throughout all the tribes of Israel, saying, As soon as ye hear the sound of the trumpet, then ye shall say, Absalom reigneth in Hebron.

"Brother Locke?" the televisor asked.

The face of a white-haired, pleasant-featured man showed on the screen. Locke replaced the book and raised his hand in greeting.

"Dr. Ryan. I'm sorry to keep bothering you."

"That's all right," Ryan said. "I've plenty of time. I'm supposed to be supervisor at the creche, but the kids are running it to suit themselves." He chuckled. "How's Absalom?"

"There's a limit," Locke said sourly. "I've given the kid his head, outlined a broad curriculum, and now he wants to study entropic logic. There are only two universities that handle the subject, and the nearest's in Baja California."

"He could commute by 'copter, couldn't he?" Ryan asked, but Locke grunted disapproval.

"Take too long. Besides, one of the requirements is inboarding, under a strict regime. The discipline, mental and physical, is supposed to be necessary in order to master entropic logic. Which is spinach. I got the rudiments at home, though I had to use the tri-disney to visualize it."

Ryan laughed.

"The kids here are taking it up. Uh—are you sure you understood it?"

"Enough, yeah. Enough to realize it's nothing for a kid to study until his horizons have expanded."

"We're having no trouble with it," the doctor said. "Don't forget that Absalom's a genius, not an ordinary youngster."

"I know. I know my responsibility too. A normal home environment has to be maintained to give Absalom some sense of security—which is one reason I don't want the boy to live in Baja California just now. I want to be able to protect him."

"We've disagreed on that point before. All the quizkids are pretty self-sufficient, Locke."

"Absalom's a genius, and a child. Therefore he's lacking in a sense of proportion. There are more dangers for him to

avoid. I think it s a grave mistake to give the quizkids their
heads and let them do what they like. I refused to send
Absalom to a creche for an excellent reason. Putting all the
boy geniuses in a batch and letting them fight it out—
completely artificial environment."

"I'm not arguing," Ryan said. "It's your business.
Apparently you'll never admit that there's a sine curve of
geniuses these days. A steady increase. In another generation——"

"I was a child genius myself, but I got over it," Locke
said irritably. "I had enough trouble with my father. He was
a tyrant, and if I hadn't been lucky, he'd have managed to
warp me psychologically way out of line. I adjusted, but I
had trouble. I don't want Absalom to have that trouble.
That's why I'm using psychonamics."

"Narcosynthesis? Enforced hypnotism?"

"It's not enforced," Locke snapped. "It's a valuable
mental catharsis. Under hypnosis, he tells me everything
that's on his mind, and I can help him."

"I didn't know you were doing that," Ryan said slowly.
"I'm not at all sure it's a good idea."

"I don't tell you how to run your creche."

"No. But the kids do. A lot of them are smarter than I
am."

"Immature intelligence is dangerous. A kid will skate on
thin ice without making a test first. Don't think I'm holding
Absalom back. I'm just running tests for him first. I make
sure the ice will hold him. Entropic logic I can understand,
but he can't—yet. So he'll have to wait on that."

"Well?"

Locke hesitated. "Uh—do you know if your boys have
been communicating with Absalom?"

"I don't know," Ryan said. "I don't interfere with their
lives."

"All right, I don't want them interfering with mine, or
with Absalom's. I wish you'd find out if they're getting in
touch with him."

There was a long pause. Then Ryan said slowly:

"I'll try. But if I were you, Brother Locke, I'd let
Absalom go to Baja California if he wants to."

"I know what I'm doing," Locke said, and broke the
beam. His gaze went toward the Bible again.

Entropic logic!

Once the boy reached maturity, his somatic and physiological symptoms would settle toward the norm, but meanwhile the pendulum still swung wildly. Absalom needed strict control, for his own good.

And, for some reason, the boy had been trying to evade the hypnotic rapports lately. There was something going on.

Thoughts moved chaotically through Locke's mind. He forgot that Absalom was waiting for him, and remembered only when Abigail's voice, on the wall transmitter, announced the evening meal.

At dinner Abigail Schuler sat like Atropos between father and son, ready to clip the conversation whenever it did not suit her. Locke felt the beginnings of a long-standing irritation at Abigail's attitude that she had to protect Absalom against his father. Perhaps conscious of that, Locke himself finally brought up the subject of Baja California.

"You've apparently been studying the entropic logic thesis." Absalom did not seem startled. "Are you convinced yet that it's too advanced for you?"

"No, Dad," Absalom said, "I'm not convinced of that."

"The rudiments of calculus might seem easy to a youngster. But when he got far enough into it—— I went over that entropic logic, Son, through the entire book, and it was difficult enough for me. And I've a mature mind."

"I know you have. And I know I haven't—yet. But I still don't think it would be beyond me."

"Here's the thing," Locke said. "You might develop psychotic symptoms if you studied that thing, and you might not be able to recognize them in time. If we could have a rapport every night, or every other night, while you were studying——"

"But it's in Baja California!"

"That's the trouble. If you want to wait for my sabbatical, I can go there with you. Or one of the nearer universities may start the course. I don't want to be unreasonable. Logic should show you my motive."

"It does," Absalom said. "That part's all right. The only difficulty's an intangible, isn't it? I mean, you think my mind couldn't assimilate entropic logic safely, and I'm convinced that it could."

"Exactly," Locke said. "You've the advantage of know-

ing yourself better than I could know you. You're handi-
capped by immaturity, lack of a sense of proportion. And
I've had the advantage of more experience."

"Your own, though, Dad. How much would such values
apply to me?"

"You must let me be the judge of that, Son."

"Maybe," Absalom said. "I wish I'd gone to a quizkid
creche, though."

"Aren't you happy here?" Abigail asked, hurt, and the
boy gave her a quick, warm look of affection.

"Sure I am, Abbie. You know that."

"You'd be a lot less happy with dementia praecox,"
Locke said sardonically. "Entropic logic, for instance,
presupposes a grasp of temporal variations being assumed
for problems involving relativity."

"Oh, that gives me a headache," Abigail said. "And if
you're so worried about Absalom's overtraining his mind,
you shouldn't talk to him like that." She pressed buttons
and slid the cloisonné metal dishes into the compartment.
"Coffee, Brother Locke . . . milk, Absalom . . . and I'll take
tea."

Locke winked at his son, who merely looked solemn.
Abigail rose with her teacup and headed toward the
fireplace. Seizing the little hearth broom, she whisked away
a few ashes, relaxed amid cushions, and warmed her skinny
ankles by the wood fire. Locke patted back a yawn.

"Until we settle this argument, Son, matters must stand.
Don't tackle that book on entropic logic again. Or anything
else on the subject. Right?"

There was no answer.

"Right?" Locke insisted.

"I'm not sure," Absalom said after a pause. "As a matter
of fact, the book's already given me a few ideas."

Looking across the table, Locke was struck by the
incongruity of that incredibly developed mind in the
childish body.

"You're still young," he said. "A few days won't matter.
Don't forget that legally I exercise control over you, though
I'll never do that without your agreement that I'm acting
justly."

"Justice for you may not be justice for me," Absalom
said, drawing designs on the tablecloth with his fingernail.

"We'll discuss it again until we've thrashed it out right. Now I've some papers to correct."

He went out.

"He's acting for the best, Absalom," Abigail said.

"Of course he is, Abbie," the boy agreed. But he remained thoughtful.

The next day Locke went through his classes in an absentminded fashion, and at noon he televised Dr. Ryan at the Wyoming Quizkid Creche. Ryan seemed entirely too casual and noncommittal. He said he had asked the quizkids if they had been communicating with Absalom, and they had said no.

"But they'll lie at the drop of a hat, of course, if they think it advisable," Ryan added, with inexplicable amusement.

"What's so funny?" Locke inquired.

"I don't know," Ryan said. "The way the kids tolerate me. I'm useful to them at times, but originally I was supposed to be supervisor here. Now the boys supervise me."

"Are you serious?"

Ryan sobered.

"I've a tremendous respect for the quizkids. And I think you're making a very grave mistake in the way you're handling your son. I was in your house once, a year ago. It's *your* house. Only one room belongs to Absalom. He can't leave any of his possessions around anywhere else. You're dominating him tremendously."

"I'm trying to help him."

"Are you sure you know the right way?"

"Certain," Locke snapped. "Even if I'm wrong, does that mean I'm committing fl—filio——"

"That's an interesting point," Ryan said casually. "You could have thought of the right words for matricide, parricide, or fratricide easily enough. But it's seldom one kills his son. The word doesn't come to the tongue quite as instantly."

Locke glared at the screen. "What the devil do you mean?"

"Just be careful." Ryan said. "I believe in the mutant theory, after running this creche for fifteen years."

"I was a child genius myself," Locke repeated.

"Uh-huh," Ryan said, his eyes intent. "I wonder if you know that the mutation's supposed to be cumulative? Three generations ago two per cent of the population were child geniuses. Two generations ago, five per cent. One generation—a sine curve, Brother Locke. And the I.Q. mounts proportionally. Wasn't your father a genius too?"

"He was," Locke admitted. "But a maladjusted one."

"I thought so. Mutations take time. The theory is that the transition is taking place right now, from homo sapiens to homo superior."

"I know. It's logical enough. Each generation of mutations—this dominant mutation at least—taking another step forward till homo superior is reached. What that will be——"

"I don't think we'll ever know," Ryan said quietly. "I don't think we'd understand. How long will it take, I wonder? The next generation? I don't think so. Five more generations, or ten or twenty? And each one taking another step, realizing another buried potentiality of homo, until the summit is reached. Superman, Joel."

"Absalom isn't a superman," Locke said practically. "Or a superchild, for that matter."

"Are you sure?"

"Good lord! Don't you suppose I know my own son?"

"I won't answer that," Ryan said. "I'm certain that I don't know all there is to know about the quizkids in my creche. Beltram, the Denver Creche supervisor, tells me the same thing. These quizkids are the next step in the mutation. You and I are members of a dying species, Brother Locke."

Locke's face changed. Without a word he clicked off the televisor.

The bell was ringing for his next class. But Locke stayed motionless, his cheeks and forehead slightly damp.

Presently, his mouth twisted in a curiously unpleasant smile; he nodded and turned from the televisor . . .

He got home at five. He came in quietly, by the side entrance, and took the elevator upstairs. Absalom's door was closed, but voices were coming through it faintly. Locke listened for a time. Then he rapped sharply on the panel.

"Absalom. Come downstairs. I want to talk to you."

In the living room he told Abigail to stay out for a while. With his back to the fireplace, he waited until Absalom came.

The enemies of my lord the king, and all that rise against thee to do thee hurt, be as that young man is.

The boy entered without obvious embarrassment. He came forward and he faced his father, the boy face calm and untroubled. He had poise, Locke saw, no doubt of that.

"I overheard some of your conversation, Absalom," Locke said.

"It's just as well," Absalom said coolly. "I'd have told you tonight anyway. I've got to go on with that entropic logic course."

Locke ignored that. "Who were you vising?"

"A boy I know. Malcolm Roberts, in the Denver Quizkid Creche."

"Discussing entropic logic with him, eh? After what I told you?"

"You'll remember that I didn't agree."

Locke put his hands behind him and interlaced his fingers.

"Then you'll also remember that I mentioned that I had legal control over you."

"Legal," Absalom said, "yes. Moral, no."

"This has nothing to do with morals."

"It has, though. And with ethics. Many of the youngsters—younger than I—at the quizkid creches are studying entropic logic. It hasn't harmed them. I must go to a creche, or to Baja California. I must."

Locke bent his head thoughtfully.

"Wait a minute," he said. "Sorry, Son. I got emotionally tangled for a moment. Let's go back on the plane of pure logic."

"All right," Absalom said, with a quiet, imperceptible withdrawal.

"I'm convinced that that particular study might be dangerous for you. I don't want you to be hurt. I want you to have every possible opportunity, especially the ones I never had."

"No," Absalom said, a curious note of maturity in his high voice. "It wasn't lack of opportunity. It was incapability."

"What?" Locke said.

"You could never allow yourself to be convinced I could safely study entropic logic. I've learned that. I've talked to other quizkids."

"Of private matters?"

"They're of my race," Absalom said. "You're not. And please don't talk about filial love. You broke that law yourself long ago."

"Keep talking," Locke said quietly, his mouth tight. "But make sure it's logical."

"It is. I didn't think I'd ever have to do this for a long time, but I've got to now. You're holding me back from what I've got to do."

"The step mutation. Cumulative. I see."

The fire was too hot. Locke took a step away from the hearth. Absalom made a slight movement of withdrawal. Locke looked at him intently.

"It *is* a mutation," the boy said. "Not the complete one, but Grandfather was one of the first steps. You are farther along than he was. And I'm farther than you. My children will be closer toward the ultimate mutation. The only psychonamic experts worth anything are the child geniuses of your generation."

"Thanks."

"You're afraid of me," Absalom said. "You're afraid of me and jealous of me."

Locke started to laugh. "What about logic now?"

The boy swallowed. "It *is* logic. Once you were convinced that the mutation was cumulative, you couldn't bear to think I'd displace you. It's a basic psychological warp in you. You had the same thing with Grandfather, in a different way. That's why you turned to psychonamics, where you were a small god, dragging out the secret minds of your students, molding their brains as Adam was molded. You're afraid that I'll outstrip you. And I will."

"That's why I let you study anything you wanted, I suppose?" Locke asked. "With this exception."

"Yes, it is. A lot of child geniuses work so hard they burn themselves out and lose their mental capacities entirely.

You wouldn't have talked so much about the danger if—under these circumstances—it hadn't been the one thing paramount in your mind. Sure you gave me my head. And, subconsciously, you were hoping I *would* burn myself out, so I wouldn't be a possible rival any more."

"I see."

"You let me study math, plane geometry, calculus, non-Euclidean, but you kept pace with me. If you didn't know the subject already, you were careful to bone up on it, to assure yourself that it was something you *could* grasp. You made sure I couldn't outstrip you, that I wouldn't get any knowledge you couldn't get. And that's why you wouldn't let me take entropic logic."

There was no expression on Locke's face.

"Why?" he asked coldly.

"You couldn't understand it yourself," Absalom said. "You tried it, and it was beyond you. You're not flexible. Your logic isn't flexible. It's founded on the fact that a second hand registers sixty seconds. You've lost the sense of wonder. You've translated too much from abstract to concrete. I *can* understand entropic logic. I can understand it!"

"You've picked this up in the last week," Locke said.

"No. You mean the rapports. A long time ago I learned to keep part of my mind blanked off under your probing."

"That's impossible!" Locke said, startled.

"It is for you. I'm a further step in the mutation. I have a lot of talents you don't know anything about. And I know this—I'm not far enough advanced for my age. The boys in the creches are ahead of me. Their parents followed natural laws—it's the role of homo sapiens to protect homo superior, as it's the role of any parent to protect its young. Only the immature parents are out of step—like you."

Locke was still quite impassive.

"I'm immature? And I hate you? I'm jealous of you? You're quite settled on that?"

"Is it true or not?"

Locke didn't answer. "You're still inferior to me mentally," he said, "and you will be for some years to come. Let's say, if you want it that way, that your superiority lies in your—flexibility and your homo superior talents. Whatever they are. Against that, balance the fact that I'm a

physically mature adult and you weigh less than half of what
I do. I'm legally your guardian. And I'm stronger than you
are."

Absalom swallowed again, but said nothing. Locke rose a
little higher, looking down at the boy. His hand went to his
middle, but found only a lightweight zipper.

He walked to the door. He turned.

"I'm going to prove to you that you're my inferior," he
said coldly and quietly. "You're going to admit it to me."

Absalom said nothing.

Locke went upstairs. He touched the switch on his
bureau, reached into the drawer, and withdrew an elastic
lucite belt. He drew its cool, smooth length through his
fingers once. Then he turned to the dropper again.

His lips were white and bloodless by now.

At the door of the living room he stopped, holding the
belt. Absalom had not moved, but Abigail Schuler was
standing beside the boy.

"Get out, Sister Schuler," Locke said.

"You're not going to whip him," Abigail said, her head
held high, her lips purse-string tight.

"Get out."

"I won't. I heard every word. And it's true, all of it."

"Get out, I tell you!" Locke screamed.

He ran forward, the belt uncoiled in his hand. Absalom's
nerve broke at last. He gasped with panic and dashed away,
blindly seeking escape where there was none.

Locke plunged after him.

Abigail snatched up the little hearth broom and thrust it
at Locke's legs. The man yelled something inarticulate as he
lost his balance. He came down heavily, trying to brace
himself against the fall with stiff arms.

His head struck the edge of a chair seat. He lay
motionless.

Over his still body, Abigail and Absalom looked at each
other. Suddenly the woman dropped to her knees and began
sobbing.

"I've killed him," she forced out painfully. "I've killed
him—but I couldn't let him whip you, Absalom—I
couldn't!"

The boy caught his lower lip between his teeth. He came
forward slowly to examine his father.

"He's not dead."

Abigail's breath came out in a long, shuddering sigh.

"Go on upstairs, Abbie," Absalom said, frowning a little. "I'll give him first aid. I know how."

"I can't let you——"

"Please, Abbie," he coaxed. "You'll faint or something. Lie down for a bit. It's all right, really."

At last she took the dropper upstairs. Absalom, with a thoughtful glance at his father, went to the televisor.

He called the Denver Creche. Briefly he outlined the situation.

"What had I better do, Malcolm?"

"Wait a minute." There was a pause. Another young face showed on the screen. "Do this," an assured, high-pitched voice said, and there followed certain intricate instructions. "Got that straight, Absalom?"

"I have it. It won't hurt him?"

"He'll live. He's psychotically warped already. This will just give it a different twist, one that's safe for you. It's projection. He'll externalize all his wishes, feelings, and so forth. On you. He'll get his pleasure only out of what *you* do, but he won't be able to control you. You know the psychonamic key to his brain. Work with the frontal lobe chiefly. Be careful of Broca's area. We don't want aphasia. He must be made harmless to you, that's all. Any killing would be awkward to handle. Besides, I suppose you wouldn't want that."

"No," Absalom said. "H-he's my father."

"All right," the young voice said. "Leave the screen on. I'll watch and help."

Absalom turned toward the unconscious figure on the floor.

For a long time the world had been shadowy now. Locke was used to it. He could still fulfill his ordinary functions, so he was not insane, in any sense of the word.

Nor could he tell the truth to anyone. They had created a psychic bloc. Day after day he went to the university and taught psychonamics and came home and ate and waited in hopes that Absalom would call him on the televisor.

And when Absalom called, he might condescend to tell something of what he was doing in Baja California. What he had accomplished. What he had achieved. For those things mattered now. They were the only things that mattered. The projection was complete.

Absalom was seldom forgetful. He was a good son. He called daily, though sometimes, when work was pressing, he had to make the call short. But Joel Locke could always work at his immense scrapbooks, filled with clippings and photographs about Absalom. He was writing Absalom's biography too.

He walked otherwise through a shadow world, existing in flesh and blood, in realized happiness, only when Absalom's face appeared on the televisor screen. But he had not forgotten anything. He hated Absalom, and hated the horrible, unbreakable bond that would forever chain him to his own flesh—the flesh that was not quite his own, but one step farther up the ladder of the new mutation.

Sitting there in the twilight of unreality, his scrapbooks spread before him, the televisor set never used except when Absalom called but standing ready before his chair, Joel Locke nursed his hatred and a quiet, secret satisfaction that had come to him.

Someday Absalom would have a son. Someday. Someday.

THE MONSTER

by Lester Del Rey

His feet were moving with an automatic monotony along the sound-deadening material of the flooring. He looked at them, seeing them in motion, and listened for the little taps they made. Then his eyes moved up along the rough tweed of his trousers to the shorter motion of his thighs. There was something good about the movement, almost a purpose.

He tried making his arms move, and found that they ac-

Copyright, 1951, by Popular Publications, Inc., reprinted by permission of Argosy Magazine, the author, and his agent, Scott Meredith.

cepted the rhythm, the right arm moving forward with the left leg, giving a feeling of balance. It was nice to feel the movement, and nice to know that he could walk so smoothly.

His eyes tired of the motion quickly, however, and he glanced along the hall where he was moving. There were innumerable doors along it; it was a long hall, with a bend at the end. He reached the bend, and began to wonder how he could make the turn. But his feet seemed to know better than he, since one of them shortened its stride automatically, and his body swung right before picking up the smooth motion again.

The new hallway was like the old one, painted white, with the long row of doors. He began to wonder idly what might lie behind all the doors. A universe of hallways and doors that branched off into more hallways? It seemed purposeless to him. He slowed his steps, just as a series of sounds reached him from one of the doors. It was speech—and that meant there was someone else in this universe in which he had found himself. He stopped outside the door, turning his head to listen. The sounds were muffled, but he could make out most of the words.

Politics, his mind told him. The word had some meaning to him, but not much. Someone inside was talking to someone else about the best way to avoid the battle on the moon, now that both powers had bases there. There was a queer tone of fear to the comments on the new iron-chain reaction bombs and what they could do from the moon.

It meant nothing to him, except that he was not alone, and that it stirred up knowledge in his head of a world like a ball in space with a moon that circled it. He tried to catch more conversation, but it had stopped, and the other doors seemed silent. Then he found a door behind which a speaker was cursing at the idea of introducing robots into a world already a mess, calling another by name.

That hit the listener, sending shocks of awareness through his consciousness. He had no name! Who was he? Where was he? And what had come before he found himself here?

He found no answers, savagely though he groped through his reluctant mind. A single word emerged—amnesia, loss of memory. Did that mean he had once had memories? Then he tried to reason out whether an amnesiac would have a feeling of personality, but could not guess. He could not even be sure he had none.

He stared at the knob of the door, wondering if the men inside would know the answers. His hand moved to the knob slowly. Then, before he could act, there was the sudden, violent sound of running footsteps down the hall.

He swung about to see two men come plunging around the corner toward him. It hadn't occurred to him that legs could move so quickly. One man was thicker than he was, dressed in a dirty smock of some kind, and the other was neat and trim, in figure and dress, in a khaki outfit he wore like a badge. The one in khaki opened his mouth.

"There he is! Stop him! You—Expeto! Halt! George ——"

Expeto—George Expeto! So he did have a name—unless the first name belonged to the other man. No matter, it was a name. George accepted it and gratitude ran through him sharply. Then he realized that senselessness of the order. How could he halt when he was already standing still? Besides, there were those rapid motions . . .

The two men let out a yell as George charged into motion, finding that his legs could easily hold the speed. He stared doubtfully at another corner, but somehow his responses were equal to it. He started to slow to a halt—just as something whined by his head and spattered against a white wall. His mind catalogued it as a bullet from a silent zep gun, and bullets were used in animosity. The two men were his enemies.

He considered it, and found he had no desire to kill them; besides, he had no gun. He doubled his speed, shot down another hall, ran into stairs and took them at a single leap. It was a mistake. They led to a narrower hallway, obviously recently blocked off, with a single door. And the man with the zep gun was charging after him as he hesitated.

He hit the door with his shoulder and was inside, in a strange room of machinery and tables and benches. Most of it was strange to his eyes, though he could recognize a small, portable boron-reactor and generator unit. It was obviously one of the new hundred-kilowatt jobs.

The place was a blind alley! Behind him the man in khaki leaped through the ruined door, his zep gun ready. But the panting, older figure of the man in the smock was behind him, catching his arm.

"No! Man, you'd get a hundred years of Lunar Prison for shooting Expeto. He's worth his weight in general's stars! If he——"

"Yeah, if! George, we can't risk it. Security comes first. And if he isn't, we can't have another paranoiac running around. Remember the other?"

Expeto dropped his shoulders, staring at them and the queer fear that was in them. "I'm not George?" he asked slowly. "But I've got to be George. I've got to have a name."

The older man nodded. "Sure, George, you're George—George Expeto. Take it easy, Colonel Kallik! Sure you're George. And I'm George—George Enders Obanion. Take it easy, George, and you'll be all right. We're not going to hurt you. We want to help you."

It was a ruse, and Expeto knew it. They didn't want to help—he was somehow important, and they wanted him for something. His name wasn't George—just Expeto. The man was lying. But there was nothing else to do; he had no weapons.

He shrugged. "Then tell me something about myself."

Obanion nodded, catching at the other man's hand. "Sure, George. See that chart on the wall, there behind you—— *Now!*"

Expeto had barely time to turn and notice there was no chart on the wall before he felt a violent motion at his back and a tiny catching reaction as the other's hand hit him. Then he blanked out.

He came back to consciousness abruptly, surprised to find that there was no pain in his head. A blow sufficient to knock him out should have left afterpains. He was alone with his thoughts.

They weren't good thoughts. His mind was seizing on the words the others had used, and trying to dig sense out of them. Amnesia was a rare thing—too rare. But paranoia was more common. A man might first feel others were persecuting him, then be sure of it, and finally lose all reality in his fantasies of persecution and his own importance. Then he was a paranoiac, making up fantastic lies to himself but cunning enough and seemingly rational at times.

But they *had* been persecuting him! There'd been the man with the gun—and they'd said he was important! Or had he only imagined it? If someone important had paranoia, would they deliberately induce amnesia as a curative step?

And who was he and where? On the first, he didn't care—George Expeto would do. The second took more thought, but he had begun to decide it was a hospital—or asylum. The room here was whitewashed, and the bed was the only furniture. He stared down at his body. They'd strapped him down, and his arms were encased in thin metal chains!

He tried to recall all he could of hospitals, but nothing came. If he had ever been sick, there was no memory of it. Nor could he remember pain, or what it was like, though he knew the word.

The door opened then, cautiously, and a figure in white came in. Expeto stared at the figure, and a slow churning began in his head. The words were reluctant this time, but they came, mere surface whispers that he had to fight to retain. But the differences in the figure made them necessary. The longer hair, the softer face, the swelling at the breast, and something about the hips stirred his memories just enough.

"You're—woman!" He got the word out, not sure it would come.

She jumped at his voice, reaching for the door which she had closed slowly. Fear washed over her face, but she nodded, gulping. "I—of course. But I'm just a technician, and they'll be here, and—— They've fastened you down!"

That seemed to bring her back to normal, and she came over, her eyes sweeping over him curiously, while one eyebrow lifted, and she whistled. "Um, not bad. Hi, Romeo. Too bad you're a monster! You don't look mean."

"So you came to satisfy your curiosity," he guessed, and his mind puzzled over it, trying to identify the urge that drove men to stare at beasts in cages. He was just a beast to them, a monster—but somehow important. And in the greater puzzle of it all, he couldn't even resent her remark. Instead, something that had been bothering him since he'd found the word came to the surface. "Why are there men and women—and who am I?"

She glanced at her watch, her ear to the door. Then she glided over to him. "I guess you're the most important man in the world—if you're a man, and not pure monster. Here."

She found his hand had limited freedom in the chains and moved it over her body, while he stared at her. Her eyes were intent on him. "Well. Now do you know why there are men and women?" Her stare intensified as he shook his head, and her lips firmed. "My God, it's true—you couldn't act that well! That's all I wanted to know! And now they'll take over the whole moon! Look, don't tell them I was here—they'll kill you if you do. Or do you know what death is? Yeah, that's it, *kaput!* Don't talk, then. Not a word!"

She was at the door, listening. Finally she opened it, and moved out. . . .

There was no sound from the zep gun, but the *splaatt* of the bullet reached Expeto's ears. He shuddered, writhing within himself as her exploding body jerked back out of sight. She'd been pleasant to look at. Maybe that was what women were for.

Obanion was over him then, while a crowd collected in the hall, all wearing khaki. "We're not going to kill you, Expeto. We knew she'd come—or hoped she would. Now, if I unfasten your chains, will you behave? We've only got four hours left. O.K., Colonel Kallik?"

The colonel nodded. Behind him, the others were gathering something up and leaving.

"She's the spy, all right. That must make the last of them. Clever. I'd have sworn she was O.K. But they tipped their hand in letting Expeto's door stay unbolted before. Well, the trap worked. Sorry about cutting down your time."

Obanion nodded, and now it was a group of men in white uniforms who came in, while the khaki-clad men left. They were wheeling in assorted machines, something that might have been an encephalograph, a unitary cerebrotrope, along with other instruments.

Expeto watched them, his mind freezing at the implications. But he wasn't insane. His thoughts were lucid. He opened his mouth to protest, just as Obanion swung around.

"Any feeling we're persecuting you, Expeto? Maybe you'd like to get in a few licks, to break my skull and run away where you'd be understood. You might get away with it; you're stronger than I am. Your reaction time is better too. See, I'm giving you the idea. And you've only got four hours in which to do it."

Expeto shook his head. That way lay madness. Let his mind feel he was persecuted and he'd surely be the paranoiac he'd heard mentioned. There had to be another answer. This was a hospital—and men were healed in hospitals. Even of madness. It could only be a test.

"No," he denied slowly, and was surprised to find it was

true. "No, I don't want to kill you, Doctor. If I've been
insane, it's gone. But I can't remember—I can't remember!"

He pulled his voice down from its shriek, shook his head
again and tried to restrain himself. "I'll co-operate. Only tell
me who I am. What have I done that makes people call me a
monster? My God, give me an anchor to hold me steady,
and then do what you want."

"You're better off not knowing, since you seem to be able
to guess when I'm lying." Obanion motioned the other men
up, and they waited while Expeto took the chair they
pointed out. Then they began clamping devices on his head.
"You're what the girl said—the spy. You're the most
important man in the world right now—if you can stay
sane. You're the one man who carries the secret of how we
can live on the moon, protect Earth from aggressive powers,
even get to the stars someday."

"But I can't remember—anything!"

"It doesn't matter. The secret's in you and we know how
to use it. All right, now I'm going to give you some tests, and
I want you to tell me exactly what comes into your mind.
The instruments will check on it, so lying won't do any
good. Ready?"

It went on and on, while new shifts came in. The clock on
the wall indicated only an hour, but it might have been a
century, when Obanion sighed and turned his work over to
another.

Expeto's thoughts were reeling. He grabbed the breather
gratefully, let his head thump back. There must be a way.

"What day is this?" he asked. At their silence he frowned.
"Co-operate means both working together. I've been doing
my part. Or is it too much to answer a simple question?"

The new man nodded slowly. "You're right. You deserve
some answers, if I can give them without breaking security.
It's June eighth, nineteen sixty-one—11 P.M."

It checked with figures that had appeared in the back of
his mind, ruining the one theory he'd had. "The President is
William Olsen?"

The doctor nodded, killing the last chance at a theory.
For a time he'd thought that perhaps the aggressive
countries had won, and that this was their dictatorship. If
he'd been injured in a war——— But it was nonsense, since

no change had occurred in his time sense or in the Administration.

"How'd I get here?"

The doctor opened his mouth, then closed it firmly. "Forget that, Expeto. You're here. Get this nonsense of a past off your mind—you never had one, understand? And no more questions. We'll never finish in less than three hours, as it is."

Expeto stood up slowly, shaking himself. "You're quite right. You won't finish. I'm sick of this. Whatever I did, you've executed your justice in killing the me that was only a set of memories. And whatever I am, I'll find myself. To hell with the lot of you!"

He expected zep guns to appear, and he was right. The walls suddenly opened in panels, and six armed men were facing him, wearing the oppressive khaki. But something in him seemed to take over. He had the doctor in one arm and a zep gun from the hand of a major before anyone else could move. He faced them, waiting for the bullets that would come, but they drew back, awaiting orders. Expeto's foot found the door, kicked at it; the lock snapped.

Obanion's voice cut through it all. "Don't! No shooting! Expeto, I'm the one you want. Let Smith go, and I'll accompany you, until you're ready to let me go. Fair enough?"

Smith was protesting, but Obanion cut him short. "My fault, since I'm responsible. And the Government be damned. I'm not going to have a bunch of good men killed. His reaction's too fast. We can learn things this way, maybe better. All right, Expeto—or do you want to kill them?"

Expeto dropped the gun a trifle and nodded, while the emotions in his head threatened to make him blank out. He knew now that he could never kill even one of them. But they apparently weren't so sure. "Take me outside, and you can go back," he told Obanion.

The doctor wiped sweat from his forehead; managed a pasty smile and nodded. Surprisingly, he stepped through a different door, and down a short hall, where men with rifles stood irresolutely. Then they were outside.

Obanion turned to go back, and then hesitated. Surprisingly, he dropped an arm onto Expeto's shoulder. "Come on back inside. We can understand you. Or—— All right, I guess you're going. Thanks for taking my offer."

The door closed, and Expeto was alone. Above him most
of the building was dark, but he saw a few lighted windows,
and some with men and women working over benches and
with equipment. There was no sign of beds. All right, so it
was some government laboratory.

The most important monster in the world, the useful
paranoiac they'd saved by amnesia . . . The monster they
intended to persecute back to paranoia, in hopes he'd
recover his memory and the secret they wanted. Let them
have the secret—but let him have peace and quiet, where
his brain could recover by itself. Then he'd gladly give it to
them. Or would he? Would he really be a monster again? Or
might he learn the strange reason for there being men and
women, the puzzle which seemed so simple that the woman
had felt mere contact would solve it?

Funny that there were so many sciences, but no science of
life—or was there? Maybe he'd been such a scientist—
psychology, zoology, biology, whatever they'd call it from
the Greek. Maybe the secret lay there, and it had completely
burned out that part of his mind.

Then he heard the sound of a motor and knew they
weren't going to let him go. He wasn't to have a moment of
freedom if they could prevent it. He swung about sharply,
studying the horizon. There were lights and a town. There'd
be people, and he could hide among them.

He whipped his legs into action, driving on at a full run.
The light of the moon was barely enough for him to see the
ground clearly, but he managed a good deal more speed
than the hallways had permitted. He heard the car behind
on the road he found, and doubled his speed, while the
sound of the motor slowly weakened as the distance
increased.

He breathed easier when he hit the outskirts of the town,
and slowed to a casual walk, imitating the steps of a few
people he saw about. This was better. In the myriad of
streets and among countless others, he would be lost. The
only trouble was that he was on a main street, and the lights
would give him away to anyone who knew him.

He picked up a paper from a waste receptacle and moved
off to the left, seeking a less brilliantly lighted street. Now
and again he glanced at the print, looking for some trace
But aside from the news that his mind recognized as normal
for the times, there was nothing on any mysterious, all-

important person, nor on anyone who was either a monster or a savior.

Ahead of him a lone girl was tapping along the sidewalk. He quickened his step, and she looked back, making the identity complete as her tiny bolero drifted back in the breeze to expose all but the tip of her breasts. She hesitated as he caught up with her, looking up uncertainly. "Yes?"

She couldn't know the answers. Obviously she had never seen him. How could she tell him what he wanted to know?

"Sorry. I thought you were someone else? No, wait. You can tell me something. Where can I find a place to stay?"

"Oh. Well, the Alhambra, I guess." She smiled a little. "Back there—see where the sign is?"

She brushed against his arm as she turned, and a faint gasp sounded. Her hand suddenly contracted on his bare skin, then jerked back sharply. She began stepping slowly away.

"No!" It was a small wail as he caught her shoulder. Then she slumped against him, wilting as he pulled her toward his face. He released her, to see her fall down in a sagging heap.

For a moment the sickness in him rose in great waves, undulating and horrible as he dropped beside her. But when he felt the pulse in her hand still beating, it left. He hadn't killed her, only frightened her into unconsciousness.

He stood there, tasting that. *Only* frightened her that much!

And finally he turned about and headed for the Alhambra. There was nothing he could do for her; she'd recover, in time, and it would be better if she didn't see him there. Then maybe she'd decide it was all a fantasy.

Bitterly he watched a streak mount the horizon, remembering that the men had been discussing the two bases on the moon in the room where he'd first heard voices. They could face war and only fear it vaguely. But he could drive someone senseless by touching them!

He found the night clerk busy watching a television set with the screen badly adjusted to an overbalance of red, and signed the register with the full name he'd hoped once was his. George Expeto, from—make it from New York. It wouldn't matter.

"Five dollars," the clerk told him.

Dollars? He shook his head slowly, trying to think. Something about dollars and cents. But it made no sense.

The clerk's eyes were hard. "No dough, eh? O.K., try to fool someone else. No baggage, no dough, no room. Scram."

Expeto stood irresolutely, trying to make sense out of it still. Dollars—something . . . The clerk had swung back to watching the set, and he reached out for the scrawny shoulder, drawing the man around.

"But look——" Then it was no use. The shoulder had crumpled in his hand like a rotten stick, and the man had lapsed into a faint with a single shriek.

Expeto stood outside, swaying while the sickness washed away slowly; he told himself the doctors would fix the man up—that was what they were for. They'd fix him, and no real harm had been done. He hadn't meant to hurt the man. He'd only meant to ask him what dollars were and how to get them.

Then he moved on into a little park and dropped onto a seat. But the sickness was still there, a sickness he hadn't noticed, but which had been growing on him even before he'd hurt the clerk. It was as if something were slowly eroding his mind. Even the curious memory of ideas and words were going!

He was sitting there, his head in his hands, trying to catch himself, when the car drove up. Obanion and Kallik got out, but Obanion came over alone.

"Come on, Expeto. It won't work. You might as well come back. And there's only an hour left!"

Expeto got up slowly, nodding wearily. The doctor was right—there was no place in the world for such a monster as he.

"Left before what?" he asked dully, as he climbed into the rear of the car and watched Obanion lock the door and the glass slide between him and the front seat.

For a second Obanion hesitated, then he shrugged. "All right. Maybe you should know. In another hour you'll be dead! And nothing can prevent it."

Expeto took it slowly, letting the thought sink into the muddying depths of his mind. But he was important—they'd told him so. Or had they? They'd chased him about, bound him down, refused to tell him what he needed, refused him even civil decency and told him he was the hope of the world. Or had he only imagined it?

"I never wanted anything but myself. Only myself. And

they wouldn't let me have that—not even for a few hours. They had to hound me——." He realized he was muttering aloud and stopped it.

But from the front seat the voices came back, muffled by the glass, Kallik speaking first. "See, paranoia all right. Thinks he's being persecuted."

"He is." Obanion nodded slowly. "With the time limit the Government insisted on, the ruin of our plans by the spies that got through, and the need to get the facts, what else could we do? If they'd let us animate him for a week—but six hours' limit on the vital crystals! We've had to be brutal."

"You talk as if he were a human being. Remember the other—XP One? Crazy, killing people, or trying to. I tell you, the robots can't be made trustworthy yet, no matter what you cybernetics boys have found in the last ten years. This one only had six hours instead of ten for the other, and he's already threatened us and hurt two people."

"Maybe. We don't know all the story yet." Obanion wiped his forehead. "And damn it, he is human. That's what makes it tough, knowing we've got to treat him like a machine. Maybe we grew his brain out of silicones and trick metal crystals, and built his body in a laboratory, but the mechanical education he got made him a lot more human than some people, or should have made him so. If I can prove he isn't crazy——"

E x p e t o—Experiment Two—stared at the hand he held before his face. He bent the fingers, looking at the veins and muscles. Then, slowly, with his other hand, he twisted at them, stretching them out and out, until there could be no doubt that they were rubbery plastic.

A monster! A thing grown in a laboratory, made out of mechanical parts, and fed bits of human education from tapes in cybernetics machines! A thing that would walk on the moon without air and take over enemy bases, do men's work, but who could never be taken as a man by human beings, who grew from something or other but were never built. A thing to be animated for a few hours and deliberately set to die at the end of that time, as a precaution—because it had no real life, and it wasn't murder to kill a built thing!

A thing that somehow couldn't kill men, it seemed, judging by the sickness he'd felt when he'd hurt or threatened them. But a thing of which they couldn't be sure—until they'd tested him and found he was complete and sane.

He rocked back and forth on the seat, moaning a little. He didn't want to die; but already the eroded places in his brain were growing larger. It didn't matter; he had never been anyone; he never could be anyone. But he didn't want to die!

"Half an hour left," the cyberneticist, Obanion, said slowly. "And less than that unless we make sure he doesn't exert himself. He's about over."

Then the car was coming into the garage, and Obanion got out with Kallik. Expeto went with them quietly, knowing that Obanion was right. Already he was finding it hard to use his legs or control what passed for muscles. They went back to the room with the instruments and the waiting technicians.

For a moment he looked at the humans there. Obanion's eyes were veiled, but the others were open to his gaze. And there was no pity there. Men don't pity a car that is too old and must go to the scrap heap. He was only a machine, no matter how valuable. And after him other machines would see the faces of men turned away from them, generation after generation.

Slowly he kicked at the chair, tipping it over without splintering it, and his voice came out as high and shrill as his faltering control could force it. "No! No more! You've persecuted me enough. You've tried to kill me—me, the hope of your puny race! You've laughed at me and tortured me. But I'm smarter than you—greater than you! I can kill you—all of you—the whole world, with my bare hands."

He saw shock on Obanion's face, and sadness, and for that he was almost sorry. But the smug satisfaction of Kallik as the zep gun came up and the horror on the faces of the others counteracted it. He yelled once, and charged at them.

For a moment he was afraid that he would not be stopped before he had to injure at least one of them. But then the zep gun in Kallik's hand spoke silently, and the bullet smashed against the mockery of Expeto's body.

He lay there, watching them slowly recover from their fright. It didn't matter when one of them came over and began kicking him senselessly. It didn't even matter when Obanion put a stop to it.

His senses were fading now, and he knew that the excitement had shortened his brief time, and that the crystals were about to break apart and put an end to his short existence. But in a curious way, while he still hated and feared death, he was resigned to it.

They'd be better off. Maybe the first experimental robot had known that. Expeto let the thought linger, finding it good. He couldn't believe the other had grown insane; it, too, must have found the bitter truth, and tried to do the only possible thing, even when that involved genuine injury to a few of the humans.

Now they'd have two such failures, and it would be perhaps years before they'd risk another when their checks failed to show the reason for the nonexistent flaws. They'd have to solve their own problems of war or peace without mechanical monsters to make them almost gods in power while teaching them the disregard of devils for life other than their own.

And there'd be no more of his kind to be used and despised and persecuted. Persecuted? The word stirred up thoughts—something about paranoia and insanity.

But it faded. Everything faded. And he sank through vague content into growing blackness. His thoughts were almost happy as death claimed him.

JAY SCORE

by Eric Frank Russell

There are very good reasons for everything they do. To the uninitiated some of their little tricks and some of their regulations seem mighty peculiar—but rocketing through the cosmos isn't quite like paddling a bathtub across a farm pond, no sir!

This stunt of using mixed crews, for instance, is pretty sensible when you look into it. On the outward runs toward Mars, the asteroids and beyond, they have white Terrestrials to run the engines and do the navigating, because they're the ones who perfected rocket ships, know most about them, and can handle them like nobody else. All ship's surgeons are black Terrestrials because, for some reason nobody's ever been able to explain, no Negro gets gravity bends or space nausea. Every outside repair gang is composed of Martians, because they use very little air, are tiptop metal workers, and fairly immune to cosmic-ray burn.

As for the inward trips to Venus, they mix them pretty much the same—except that the emergency pilot is always a big clunker like Jay Score. There's a reason for that—he was the reason! I'm not likely to forget him; he sort of sticks in the mind. What a guy!

Fortune put me at the top of the gangway the first time he appeared. Our ship was the *Upskadaska City,* a brand-new freighter with limited passenger accommodation, registered in the Venusian port from which she took her name. Needless to say, she was known among spacefarers as the *Upsydaisy.*

We were in the Colorado Rocket Basin, just north of Denver, with a fair load aboard, mostly watchmaking machinery, scientific instruments, agricultural equipment, aeronautical jigs and tools for Upskadaska, as well as a case of radium needles for the Venusian Cancer Research Institute. There were eight passengers, all agriculturists. We'd kangarooed the vessel and were waiting for the blow-brothers-blow siren due in forty minutes, when Jay Score arrived.

He was six feet nine, about three hundred pounds, and he toted his bulk with the easy grace of a ballet dancer. A big guy like that, moving like that, was something worth watching. He came up the duralumin gangway with the nonchalance of a tripper boarding the bus for Jackson's Creek, and he was dangling from his hamlike right fist a rawhide case not quite big enough to hold his bed and maybe a wardrobe or two.

At the top he took in the crossed swords on my cap, said, "Morning, Sarge. I'm the new E.P. I've got to report to Captain McNulty."

I knew a fresh emergency pilot was due. Jeff Durkin had been promoted to the snooty Martian scentbox *Prometheus.* So this was his successor! He was a Terrestrial, all right, but

neither white nor black. His expressionless but capable face
looked as if covered with old, well-seasoned leather. His
eyes held fires, almost like phosphorescence. There was an
air about him that marked him out as an exceptional
individual.

"Welcome, Tiny," I said. I didn't offer my hand, because
I wanted to use it later on. "Open your satchel and leave it
in the sterilizing chamber. You'll find the skipper in the
bow."

"Thanks!" he responded, without the glimmer of a smile.
He stepped into the air lock, swinging the rawhide bungalow
at his side.

"We blast in forty minutes," I warned him.

Didn't see anything more of Jay Score until we were two
hundred thousand out, with Earth a greenish moon at the
end of our vapor wake. Then I heard him in the passage
asking where he could find the sergeant at arms. He was
directed through my door.

"Sarge," he said, handing over his official requisition,
"I've come to collect the trimmings." When he leaned on
the barrier, the whole framework creaked, and the top tube
sagged in the middle.

"Hey!" I shouted.

"Sorry!" He unleaned. The barrier stood much better
while he had his weight on his dogs.

I stamped his requisition, went into the armory, got him
his needle ray pistol and an issue of capsules for same. The
biggest Venusian mud skis I could find were about seven
sizes too small and a yard too short for him, but they had to
do. He got a can of thin, multipurpose oil, a jar of graphite,
a Lepanto powerpack for his microwave radiophone and,
finally, a bunch of nutweed pellicules marked: "Compli-
ments of the Bridal Planet Aromatic Herbal Corporation."

Shoving back the spicy junk lumps, he said, "You have
'em—they give me the staggers." The rest of the stuff he
gathered without so much as twitching an eyebrow. I've
never seen anyone so poker-faced.

All the same, the way he eyed the spacesuits seemed
somewhat wistful. There were thirty bifurcated ones for the
Terrestrials, all hanging on the wall like sloughed skins.
There were also six head-and-shoulder helmets for the

Martians, since they needed no more than three pounds of air. There wasn't a suit for him. I couldn't have fitted him with one if my life had depended on it—it'd have been like trying to can an elephant.

Well, he lumbered out lightly, if you get what I mean. The casual way he transported his tonnage made me think that I'd sure like to be someplace else if ever he got on a rampage. Not that I thought him likely to run amuck—he was amiable enough, though sphinxlike. But I was fascinated by his air of calm certainty, and by his motion, which was fast and eerie and silent. The latter, I guess, was because he favored an inch of sponge rubber under his dogs.

I kept my eyes on Jay Score while the *Upsydaisy* made good time on her crawl through the void. Yes, I was curious about him because his type was a new one on me—and I've seen plenty in my time. He remained uncommunicative but always polite, while his work was smooth, efficient, and in every way satisfactory. McNulty took a great fancy to him—and he never had been one to greet a newcomer with love and kisses.

Three days out, Jay made a great hit with the Martians. As everyone knows, those goggle-eyed, ten-tentacled, half-breathing kibitzers have stuck harder than glue to the Solar System Chess Championship for more than two centuries. Nobody outside of Mars will ever pry them loose. They're nuts about it, and many's the time I've seen a bunch of them go through all the colors of the spectrum in sheer excitement when somebody had shifted a pawn after thirty minutes of profound consideration.

One rest time, Jay spent his whole eight hours under three pounds of pressure in the starboard air lock. Over the lock phones came long silences punctuated by wild and shrill twitterings, as if he and the octopuses were turning the place into a madhouse. At the end of the time we found our outside gang exhausted. Seems Jay had consented to play Kli Yang and had forced him to a stalemate. Kli had been sixth runner-up in the last solar melee, had been beaten only ten times—each time by a brother Martian, of course.

The red-planet gang had the finger on him after that. Every rest time they waylaid him and dragged him into the air lock. When we were eleven days out, he played the six of them simultaneously, lost two games, stalemated three, won one. They thought he was a whiz—for a Terrestrial. Knowing them, I thought so too. So did McNulty. He stuck the sporting data in the log.

You'll remember the stunt that the audiopress of 2270 boosted as "McNulty's Miracle Move"? Sure, it's practically a legend of the spaceways. Afterward, when we'd got safely back, McNulty disclaimed all the credit and put it where it rightfully belonged. The audiopress had a good excuse, as usual. They said he was the captain, wasn't he? And his name made the phrase alliterative, didn't it? Seems like there must be a sect of audio journalists who've got to be alliterative to gain salvation.

What precipitated that crazy stunt and whitened my hair was a chunk of flotsam. Said junk was a gob of meteoric nickel iron which was ambling along at the usual cosmic speed of *pssst!* Its orbit was on the planetary plane, and it approached at right angles to our sunward course.

It gave us the business. I'd never have believed anything so small could have made such a slam. To the present day I can hear the whistle of air as it made a break for freedom through that jagged hole.

We lost a lot of political juice before the autodoors sealed the section. Pressure had dropped to nine pounds when the compensators held it and slowly began to build it up again. The drop didn't worry the Martians—nine pounds was still like inhaling pigwash to them.

There was one engineer in that sealed section. A second beat the doors by the toe of his left boot and got clear. But the first, we thought, had drawn his number and eventually would be floated out like so many spacemen who've come to the end of their duty.

The guy who got clear was leaning against a bulwark, skin white with the narrowness of his squeak, when Jay came pounding in. His jaw was working, and his eyes were like lamps, but his voice was cool and easy.

He said, "Get out and seal this room. I'll make a snatch. Open up and let me through fast when I knock."

With that, he shoved out the other. We sealed the room by closing another autodoor. We couldn't see what the big hunk was doing, but the telltale showed he'd released and opened the door to the damaged section. Ten seconds later the light went out, showing the door was closed again. Came a hard, urgent knock. We opened. Jay plunged through like

a bat out of hell, the engineer's limp body cuddled in his
thick arms. He bore it like it was no more than a kitten, and
the way he took it down the passage threatened to carry him
clear through the nose of the ship.

Meanwhile, we found we were in a No. 1 mess. The
rockets weren't functioning any more. The Venturi tubes
were O.K., and the combustion chambers undamaged.
The injectors worked without a hitch—providing you
pumped them by hand. We'd lost none of our precious fuel,
and the shell was intact save for that one jagged hole. What
made us useless was the wrecking of our co-ordinated
feeding and firing controls. They'd been located in that
damaged section and now they were as much scrap.

This was more than serious. General opinion called it
certain death. I'm pretty certain that McNulty shared the
morbid notion even if his official report did describe it as
"an embarrassing predicament." But that's just like McNulty. It's a wonder he didn't define our feelings by recording that we were nonplused.

Anyway, the Martian squad poured out, some honest
work being required of them for the first time in six trips.
Pressure had crawled back to fourteen, and they had to
come into it to put on their head-and-shoulder contraptions.

Kli Yang sniffed, waved a disgusted tentacle, and chir-
ruped, "I could swim." He eased up when we got his dingbat
fixed and exhausted it to his customary three pounds. That's
the Martian idea of sarcasm—whenever it's thicker than
they like they make sinuous backstrokes and say, "I could
swim."

To give them their due, they were good. They can cling to
polished ice and work for twelve hours on a ration of oxygen that wouldn't satisfy a Terrestrial for more than ninety
minutes. I saw them beat it through the air lock, their goggle
eyes peering through their inverted goldfish bowls, their
tentacles clutching power lines, sealing plates, and quasi-arc
welders. Blue lights made little auroras outside the ports as
they began to cut, shape, and seal that ragged hole.

All the time, we continued to bullet onward toward the
Sun. But for this cursed misfortune we'd have swung a curve
into the orbit of Venus in four hours' time. Then we'd have
let her catch us up, and we'd have carefully decelerated to a
safe landing. But when that peewee planetoid picked on us
we were still headed straight for the biggest and brightest

furnace hereabouts. That was the way we were still going, our original velocity being steadily increased by the pull of our fiery destination. I wanted to be cremated—but not yet!

Up in the bow navigation, Jay Score was in constant conference with Captain McNulty and the two astrocomputator operators. Outside, the Martians continued to crawl around, fizzing and spitting with flashes of ghastly blue light. The engineers, of course, weren't waiting for them to finish their job—four in spacesuits entered the damaged section and started the task of creating order out of chaos.

I envied all those busy guys and so did many of the others. There's a lot of consolation in being able to do something even in a hopeless situation. There's a lot of misery in being compelled to play with one's fingers while others are active.

Two Martians came in through the lock, grabbed some more plates and crawled out again. One picked up a pocket chess set, but I took it off him. Then I went along to see Sam Hignett, our Negro surgeon.

Sam had dragged back the engineer from the very rim of the grave. He'd done it with oxygen and heart massage. Only his long, dextrous fingers could have done it. It was a feat that had been brought off before—but not often.

It seemed that Sam didn't know just what had happened and didn't care. He was like that when he had a patient on his hands. Deftly, he closed the chest incision with silver clips, painted the pinched flesh with iodized plastic, cooled the stuff to hardness with a spray of ether.

"Sam," I told him, "you're a marvel!"

"Jay gave me a chance," he said. "He got him here in time."

"Why put the blame on him?" I joked.

"Sergeant," he answered, quite seriously, "I'm the ship's doctor. I do the best I can. I couldn't have saved this man if Jay hadn't got him to me in time."

"All right, all right," I agreed. "Have it your own way." A good fellow, Sam. But he was like all doctors—you know, ethical. I left him with his breathing patient.

McNulty came toddling along the catwalk as I went back. He checked up on the fuel tanks. He did it personally, and that meant something. He looked worried, and that meant a devil of a lot. It meant that I needn't bother writing my last will and testament, because it'd never be read.

I watched his portly form dive back into bow navigation, and heard him say, "Jay, I guess you——" before the closing door cut off his voice.

Seemed to have a lot of faith in Jay Score. Well, Jay looked capable enough. The skipper and the laconic E.P. were still acting like cronies even while heading for the final frizzle.

One of the emigrating agriculturists came out of his cabin and caught me before I regained the armory. Looking at me wide-eyed, he said, "Sergeant, there's a half moon showing through my port."

He continued to pop them at me while I popped mine at him. Venus showing half her pan meant that we were crossing her orbit. He knew it, too—I could tell by the way he bugged them.

"Well," he persisted, "how long is this mishap likely to delay us?"

"No knowing," I replied, quite truthfully. I scratched my head, trying to look confident and stupid at one and the same time. "Captain McNulty will do the best he can. Put your trust in him. Poppa knows best!"

"You don't think that we are—er—in any danger?"

"Oh, not at all!"

"You're a liar," he said.

"I know it," said I.

That unhorsed him. He went into his cabin, dissatisfied, apprehensive. Pretty soon he'd see Venus in a three-quarter phase and he'd tell the others. Then the fat would be in the fire—our fat in the solar fire.

The last vestiges of hope had drained away just about the time that a terrific roar and a violent tremble told that the long-dead rockets were back in action. The noise didn't last more than a few seconds; they were shut off quickly, the brief burst serving to show that repairs were effective and satisfactory.

The noise brought out the agriculturist at full gallop. He knew the worst by now, and so did the others. It had been impossible to conceal the truth for the three days since he'd seen Venus as a half moon. She was far behind now, and we were cutting the orbit of Mercury. But still the passengers clung desperately to the chance of somebody performing a miracle.

Charging into the armory, he said, "The rockets are working again! Does that mean——"

"Nothing," I told him, seeing no use in building false hopes.

"But can't we turn around and go back?" He mopped the perspiration trickling down his jowls. It wasn't so much that he was scared as the unpleasant fact that interior conditions were now anything but arctic.

"Sir," I said, "we're moving so all-fired fast that there's nothing to do but hold a lily."

"My ranch," he growled bitterly. "I was allotted five thousand acres of the best Venusian tobacco-growing country, not to mention a range of uplands for beef."

"Sorry, brother, but the days of the West are through."

Crrrump! went the rockets again. The burst bent me backward and made him bow forward like he had a bad bellyache. Somebody up in bow navigation—McNulty or Jay Score—was blowing them when he felt the whim. I couldn't see any sense in it.

"What's that for?" demanded the complainant, regaining the perpendicular.

"Boys will be boys," I said.

Snorting his disgust, he went back to his cabin. A typical Terrestrial emigrant, big and healthy and tough, he was more peeved than worried.

Half an hour later the general call sounded on the buzzers all over the ship. It was a ground signal, never used in space, and it meant that the entire crew and all other occupants of the vessel were summoned to the central cabin. Imagine guys being called from their posts in full flight! Something unique in the history of space navigation must have been behind that call, probably a compose-yourselves-for-the-end speech by McNulty.

Expecting the skipper to preside over the last rites, I wasn't surprised to find him standing on the tiny dais as we assembled. A faint scowl lay over the plump features, but it faded into a ghost of a smile when the Martians mooched in and one of them did some imitation shark-dodging.

Erect beside McNulty, expressionless as usual, Jay Score looked at that Martian as if he were a pane of glass. Then his strangely lit orbs roamed idly away as if they'd seen nothing more boring. The swim joke was getting stale, anyway.

"Men and vedras," began McNulty—the latter being Martian for "adults," and more Martian sarcasm too— "I've no need to enlarge upon the awkwardness of our position." That man sure could pick his words—awkward! "Already we are nearer the sun than any space vessel has ever been in the whole history of cosmic navigation."

"Comic navigation," murmured Kli Yang, with tactless wit.

"We'll need your humor to entertain us later," observed Jay Score in a voice so flat that Kli Yang subsided.

"We're moving toward the luminary," went on McNulty, his scowl reappearing, "faster than any space vessel ever moved before. Bluntly, there's not more than one chance in ten thousand of us getting out of this alive." He favored Kli Yang with a challenging glare, but that tentacled individual was now subdued. "However, there is that one chance— and we're going to take it!"

We gaped at him, wondering what the devil he meant. Every one of us knew that it was absolutely impossible to make a U-bend without touching the Sun, neither would we be able to fight our way back in the reverse direction with all that mighty drag upon us. There was nothing to do but go onward, onward—until the last searing blast scattered our disrupted molecules all over the block.

"What we propose to do is to try a cometary," continued McNulty. "Jay and myself and the astrocomputator operators reckon it's barely possible that we can do it and pull through."

That was plain enough. The stunt was a theoretical one frequently debated by mathematicians and astronavigators, and often used by writers in stories. But this time it was to be the real thing. The idea is to build up all the velocity that can be got, and at the same time to angle into the path of an elongated elliptical orbit like that of a comet. In theory, the vessel then *might* skim the Sun so fast that it would swing like a pendulum far out to the opposite side of the orbit whence it had come. A sweet little trick—but could we make it?

"Calculations show our present condition fair enough to permit a small chance of success," said McNulty. "We've power enough and fuel enough to build up the necessary velocity, to strike the requisite angle, and to maintain both for the proper time. The only point about which I have grave doubt is that of whether we can survive at our nearest to the Sun." He wiped perspiration as if unconsciously to emphasize the shape of things to come. "I won't mince words, men—it's going to be a sample of hell!"

"We're ready, Skipper," said somebody, and a low murmur of support ran around the cabin.

Kli Yang got up, simultaneously waggled four arms for attention, and twittered, "It is an idea. It is excellent. I, Kli Yang, endorse it on behalf of my fellow vedras. We shall all cram into the refrigerator and breathe the Terrestrial stink while the Sun goes past?"

McNulty let pass the crack about human odor, nodded, and said, "Everyone will be packed into the cold room and endure it as best they can."

"Exactly," said Kli. "Quite," he added with bland disregard of superfluity. Wiggling a tentacle tip at McNulty, he carried on, "But we can't control the ship while we're squatting in the icebox like three and a half dozen strawberry sundaes. There'll have to be control from bow navigation. One individual could hold her on her course—until he gets fried. So somebody's got to be the fryee."

He gave the tip another sinuous wiggle, being under the delusion that it was fascinating his listeners into complete attention. "And since it cannot be denied that we Martians are far less susceptible to extremes of heat, I suggest that ——"

"Nuts!" said McNulty. His gruffness deceived nobody. The Martians were nuisances—but grand guys.

"All right." Kli's chirrup rose to a shrill, protesting yelp. "Who else is going to be a crisp?"

"Me, maybe—or not," said Jay Score. It was queer the way he said it—just as if he were a candidate so obvious that only the stone-blind couldn't see him.

He was right, at that! Jay was the very one for the job. If anyone could take what was going to come through the fore observation ports, it was Jay Score. He was big and tough, built for just such a task as this. He had a lot of stuff that none of us had, and, after all, was a fully qualified E.P.

But it was funny the way I felt about him. I could imagine him up in front, all alone, nobody there, but our lives depending on how much he could take—while the flaming Sun extended its searing fingers . . .

"You!" ejaculated Kli, breaking my thought. His goggle eyes bulged angrily at the big, laconic figures on the dais. "You would! I'm ready to mate in four moves, and you get yourself locked away."

"Six," contradicted Jay disinterestedly. "You can't do it in less than six."

"Four," Kli fairly howled. "And right at this point you ———"

It was too much for McNulty. He looked as if on the verge of a stroke. His purple face turned on the semaphoring Kli.

"To hell with your blasted chess!" he roared. "Return to your stations, all of you. Make ready for the boost. I'll sound the general call immediately it is necessary to take cover, and then you're all to go to the cold room." He looked around, the purple gradually fading as his blood pressure went down. "That is, all except Jay."

Seemed like old times with the rockets going full belt. They roared away steadily, like we were running with a tail of thunder. Inside the vessel, the atmosphere got hotter and hotter until moisture glistened on the metal walls and plenty more of same trickled steadily down our backs. What it was like up in bow navigation I didn't know and didn't care to discover. The Martians weren't inconvenienced yet—and it was one time their wacky composition was to be envied.

I didn't keep check of the time, but I'd had two spells of duty with an intervening sleep period and rest time before the buzzers sounded the general call. By then things were pretty bad. I was no longer perspiring—I was slowly melting into my boots.

Sam, of course, endured it most easily of all the Terrestrials, and had persisted enough to drag his patient completely out of danger. That engineer was one lucky guy! We'd put him in the cool room right away, with Sam in frequent attendance.

The rest of us dribbled in when the buzzer went. Our sanctuary was more than a mere refrigerator; it was the strongest and coolest section of the vessel, an armored, triply shielded compartment holding the instrument lockers, two sick bays and a large lounge for the benefit of nauseated passengers. It held us all comfortably.

All but the Martians. It held them, but not comfortably. They're never comfortable at fourteen pounds, which they regard as not only thick but also smelly—something like breathing treacle impregnated with old goat.

Under our very eyes Kli Yang produced a bottle of hooloo scent, handed it to his half parent Kli Morg. The latter took it, stared distastefully at us, then sniffed at it in an ostentatious manner that was positively insulting. But nobody said anything.

All were present except McNulty and Jay Score. The skipper appeared two hours later. It must have been raw up in front, because he looked terrible. His haggard face was beaded and glossy, his formerly plump cheeks sunken and blistered. His usually spruce, well-fitting uniform hung upon him sloppily. It needed only one glance to tell that he'd had a darned good roasting—as much as he could stand.

Walking unsteadily, he crossed the floor, went into the first-aid cubby, stripped himself with slow, painful movements. Sam rubbed him all over with tannic jelly—we could hear the tormented skipper grunting hoarsely as Sam put plenty of pep into the job.

The heat was now on us with a vengeance. It pervaded the walls, the floor, the air, and it created a multitude of stinging sensations in every muscle of my body. Several of the engineers took off their boots and jerkins. After a while the passengers followed suit, discarding much of their outer clothing. My agriculturist sat a miserable figure in tropical silks, moody over what might have been.

Coming out of the cubby, McNulty flopped onto a bunk, and said, "If we're all O.K. in four hours' time, we're out of the woods!"

At that moment the rockets faltered. We knew at once what was wrong. A fuel tank had emptied and the relay had failed to cut in. An engineer should have been ready to switch the conduits. In the heat and excitement, someone had blundered.

The fact barely had time to sink in before Kli Yang was out through the door. He'd been sitting nearest to it, and was gone before anyone realized the fact. Twenty seconds later the rockets renewed their steady thrum.

A speaking-tube whistle shrilled right by my ear. Solar

radiation had made the radiophones useless these last two days. Pulling out the whistle, I croaked a throaty, "Well?" into the tube, and heard Jay's voice coming back from bow.

"Who did it?"

"Kli Yang," I told him. "He's still outside."

"Probably gone for the domes," guessed Jay. "Tell him I said thanks!"

"What's it like around where you live?" I asked.

"Fierce," he replied. "It isn't so good . . . for vision." Silence for a moment, then, "Guess I can . . . stick it . . . somehow. Strap in ready for next time I blow the . . . whistle."

"Why?" I half yelled, half rasped.

"Going to rotate her—distribute the heat."

A faint squeak told that he'd plugged his end of the tube. Shoving the whistle back, I told the others to strap down in readiness for Jay's signal. The Martians didn't have to bother, since they had enough first-class suckers to weld them to a sun-fishing meteor.

Kli came back and showed Jay's guess to be correct. He was dragging the squads' head-and-shoulder pieces. The load was about as much as he could pull now that the temperature was up to the point where even he was beginning to wilt.

The Martian moochers donned their gadgets gladly, carefully sealing the seams, then evacuating them down to three pounds. It made them a lot happier. Remembering that we Terrestrials use spacesuits to keep air in, it seemed queer seeing those guys wearing theirs to keep air out.

They'd just finished and had laid out a chessboard when the whistle squeaked. We braced ourselves; the Martians clamped down their suckers. Slowly and steadily the *Upsydaisy* began to turn upon her longitudinal axis. The chessboard and pieces tried to stay put, failed, crawled along the floor, up the wall, and across the ceiling. Solar pull was making them stick to the sunward side, of course. I saw Kli Morg's strained, heat-ridden face glooming at a black bishop while it skittered around—and I guess that inside his goldfish boll were resounding some potent samples of Martian invective.

"Three hours and a half," gasped McNulty.

That four-hour estimate could only mean two hours of

approach to the deadline, and two hours of retreat from it. So the moment when we had two hours to go would be the moment when we were at our nearest to the solar furnace, the moment of our greatest peril.

I wasn't aware of that potent instant, since I passed out twenty minutes before it arrived, and recovered consciousness an hour and a half after it. My dazed mind took what seemed an endless time to realize that we now had only half an hour to go, thirty minutes to safety!

What had happened in the interval could only be left to my imagination—and I didn't care to think much about that time. The Sun blazing with ferocity infinitely greater than a tiger's eye—and a thousand times hungrier. The corona licking out toward this tiny shipload of footlings, half-dead entities. And up in front of the vessel, behind its totally inadequate quartz windows, Jay sitting alone and facing the mounting inferno, staring, staring, staring . . .

Getting to my feet, I teetered uncertainly, fell over like a bundle of rags. The ship wasn't rotating any longer and we seemed to be bulleting along in perfectly normal fashion. What brought me down was sheer weakness. I felt lousy.

The Martians had already recovered. I knew they'd be the first. One of them logged me up and held me steady while I got back a percentage of my former control. I noticed that another had sprawled himself right across the unconscious McNulty and three of the passengers. Yes, he'd shielded them from some of the heat. His action was successful too, for they were the next to come to life.

Struggling to the tube, I extracted the whistle, blew down the funnel. It was a weak, ineffectual blow that brought me no response. Just a waste of good breath on which I was darned short. I hung there dazedly for a full three minutes, then summoned my returning strength, extended my aching chest, blew as hard as I could and heard the shrill cheep of the whistle at the other end. But Jay didn't answer.

Several more attempts didn't bring me the slightest response. The effort cost me a dizzy spell, and down I flopped again. The heat was still terrific; I felt as dehydrated as a mummy dug out of sand a million years old.

Kli Yang opened the door, crept out with dragging, pain-stricken motion. He was still wearing his head-and-shoulder piece. Five minutes later he came back, spoke through his helmet's diaphragm:

"Couldn't get near bow navigation. At the midway catwalk it's hotter than an oven, and all the atmosphere's sealed off." He answered the question in my eyes. "Yes, the autodoors are closed—there can't be any air in bow navigation."

No air meant the navigation windows had gone *phut*. Nothing else could have emptied the cabin. Well, we'd spares for that job, and could make good the damage once we were in the clear. Meanwhile, here we were roaring along, maybe on our correct course and maybe not, with an empty, airless navigation room, and with a speaking tube that gave us nothing but ghastly silence.

Sitting around, we picked up strength. The last one to come out of his coma was the sick engineer. Sam brought him round all right. It was just then that McNulty got excited.

"Four hours!" he shouted. "We've done it!"

We raised a hollow cheer. By Jupiter, the superheated atmosphere seemed to grow ten degrees cooler with the news! Funny how relief can breed strength. In one minute we conquered all weakness and were rarin' to go. But it was another four hours before a quartet of engineers in spacesuits bore their burden from the airless navigation room.

They carried him into Sam's little place—a long, heavy, silent figure.

I said, "Jay, Jay, how're you making out?"

He must have heard me, for he moved the fingers of his right hand and emitted a chesty grinding noise before they carried him inside. Two of the engineers went to his cabin, brought back his huge rawhide case. They shut the door, staying in with Sam, leaving me and the Martians hanging around outside. Kli Yang wandered up and down the passage as if he didn't know what to do with his tentacles.

Sam came out after an hour, and we jumped him on the spot.

"How's Jay?"

"Blind as a statue," he said, shaking his head. "And his voice isn't there any more. He's taken an awful beating."

"So that's why he didn't answer on the tube." I looked him straight in the eyes. "Can you—can you do anything for him, Sam?"

"I only wish I could!" His black face showed his feelings. "You know how much I'd like to put him right, Sergeant—but I can't." He made a gesture of futility. "He's completely beyond my modest skill. Maybe when we get back to Earth—" His voice petered out, and he went back inside.

Kli Yang said miserably, "I am saddened."

A scene I'll never forget as long as I live was that evening we spent as guests of the Astro Club in New York. That club was then—as it is still—the most exclusive group of human beings ever gathered together. To qualify for membership, you had to perform a feat of astronavigation tantamount to a miracle. There were only nine members in those days, and there are only twelve now.

Mace Waldron, the famous pilot who saved that Martian liner in 2263, was the chairman. Classy in his soup-and-fish, he stood at the top of the table with Jay Score sitting at his side. At the other end of the table sat McNulty, a broad smirk of satisfaction on his jovial pan. Beside the skipper was old, white-haired Knud Johannsen, the genius who designed the J-series, and a figure known to every spaceman.

Along the sides, and somewhat self-conscious, sat the entire crew of the *Upsydaisy,* including the Martians, plus three of our passengers who'd postponed their trips for this occasion. There were also a couple of audio journalists with their scanners and mikes.

"Gentlemen and vedras," said Mace, "this is an event without precedent in the history of humanity or this club. Perhaps because of that, I feel it to be doubly an honor and a privilege to propose that Emergency Pilot Jay Score be accepted as a fully qualified and worthy member of the Astro Club."

"Seconded!" shouted three members simultaneously.

"Thank you, gentlemen." He cocked an inquiring eyebrow. Eight hands went up in unison. "Carried," he said. "Unanimously!" Glancing down at the still taciturn Jay Score, he launched into a eulogy. It went on and on, while Jay sat there with a listless air.

Down at the other end, I saw McNulty's gratified smirk wax stronger and stronger. At his side, old Knud was gazing down the table with a fatherly fondness that was almost

fatuous. The crew gave plenty of attention to the subject of
the eulogy, and the scanners were fixed upon him too.

I returned my attention to where all the others were
directing their attention, and the victim sat there, his
restored eyes bright and glittering, but his face immobile
despite the talk, the publicity, the beam of paternal pride
from Johannsen.

But after ten minutes of this, I saw J.20 begin to fidget.
Don't let anybody kid you that a robot can't have feelings!

BETELGEUSE BRIDGE

by William Tenn

You tell them, Alvarez, old boy; you know how to
talk to them. This isn't my kind of public relations. All I
care about is that they get the pitch exactly right, with all the
implications and complications and everything just the way
they really were.

If it hurts, well, let them yell. Just use your words and get
it right. Get it all.

You can start with the day the alien spaceship landed
outside Baltimore. Makes you sick to think how we never
tumbled, doesn't it, Alvarez? No more than a hop, skip, and
a jet from the Capitol dome, and we thought it was just a
lucky accident.

Explain why we thought it was so lucky. Explain about
the secrecy it made possible, the farmer who tele-
phoned the news was placed in special and luxurious
custody, how a hand-picked cordon of M.P.s paced five
square miles off into an emergency military reservation a
few hours later, how Congress was called into secret session
and the way it was all kept out of the newspapers.

How and why Trowson, my old sociology prof, was
consulted once the problem became clear. How he blinked
at the brass hats and striped pants and came up with the
answer.

Me. I was the answer.

How my entire staff and I were plucked out of our New York offices, where we were quietly earning a million bucks, by a flying squad of the F.B.I. and air-mailed to Baltimore. Honestly, Alvarez, even after Trowson explained the situation to me, I was still irritated. Government hush-hush always makes me uncomfortable. Though I don't have to tell you how grateful I was for it later.

The spaceship itself was such a big surprise that I didn't even wet my lips when the first of the aliens *slooshed* out. After all those years of streamlined cigar shapes the Sunday supplement artists had dreamed up, that colorful and rococo spheroid rearing out of a barley field in Maryland looked less like an interplanetary vessel than an oversized ornament for a what-not table. Nothing that seemed like a rocket jet anywhere.

"And there's your job." The prof pointed. "Those two visitors."

They were standing on a flat metal plate surrounded by the highest the republic had elected or appointed. Nine feet of slimy green trunk tapering up from a rather wide base to a pointed top, and dressed in a tiny pink-and-white shell. Two stalks with eyes on them that swung this way and that, and seemed muscular enough to throttle a man. And a huge wet slash of a mouth that showed whenever an edge of the squirming base lifted from the metal plate.

"Snails," I said. *"Snails!"*

"Or slugs," Trowson amended. "Gastropodal mollusks in any case." He gestured at the roiling white bush of hair that sprouted from his head. "But, Dick, that vestigial bit of coiled shell is even less an evolutionary memento than this. They're an older—and smarter—race."

"Smarter?"

He nodded. "When our engineers got curious, they were very courteously invited inside to inspect the ship. They came out with their mouths hanging."

I began to get uncomfortable. I ripped a small piece off my manicure. "Well, naturally, prof; if they're so alien, so different—"

"Not only that. Superior. Get that, Dick, because it'll be very important in what you have to do. The best engineering minds that this country can assemble in a hurry are like a crowd of South Sea Islanders trying to analyze the rifle and

compass from what they know of spears and wind storms.
These creatures belong to a galaxy-wide civilization composed of races *at least* as advanced as they; we're a
bunch of backward hicks in an unfrequented hinterland of
space that's about to be opened to exploration. Exploi-
tation, perhaps, if we can't measure up. We have to give a
very good impression and we have to learn fast."

A dignified official with a brief case detached himself
from the nodding, smiling group around the aliens and
started for us.

"*Whew!*" I commented brilliantly. "Fourteen ninety-
two, repeat performance." I thought for a moment, not too
clearly. "But why send the Army and Navy after *me?* I'm
not going to be able to read blueprints from—from———"

"Betelgeuse. Ninth planet of the star Betelgeuse. No,
Dick, we've already had Dr. Warbury out here. They
learned English from him in two hours, although he hasn't
identified a word of theirs in three days! And people like
Lopez, like Mainzer, are going quietly psychotic trying to
locate their power source. We have the best minds we can
get to do the learning. Your job is different. We want you as
a top-notch advertising man, a public-relations executive.
You're the good impression part of the program."

The official plucked at my sleeve and I shrugged him
away. "Isn't that the function of government glad-hand-
ers?" I asked Trowson.

"No. Don't you remember what you said when you first
saw them? *Snails!* How do you think this country is going to
take to the idea of snails—giant snails—who sneer con-
descendingly at our skyscraper cities, our atomic bombs, our
most advanced mathematics? We're a conceited kind of
monkey. Also, we're afraid of the dark."

There was a gentle official tap on my shoulder. I said
"Please!" impatiently. I watched the warm little breeze
ruffle Professor Trowson's slept-in clothes and noticed the
tiny red streaks in his weary eyes.

" 'Mighty Monsters from Outer Space.' Headlines like
that, Prof?"

"Slugs with superiority complexes. *Dirty* slugs, more
likely. We're lucky they landed in this country, and so close
to the Capitol too. In a few days we'll have to call in the
heads of other nations. Then, sometime soon after, the news
will be out. We don't want our visitors attacked by mobs

drunk on superstition, planetary isolation, or any other form of tabloid hysteria. We don't want them carrying stories back to their civilization of being shot at by a suspendered fanatic who screamed, 'Go back where you come from, you furrin seafood!' We want to give them the impression that we are a fairly amiable, fairly intelligent race, that we can be dealt with reasonably well."

I nodded. "Yeah. So they'll set up trading posts on this planet instead of garrisons. But what do I do in all this?"

He punched my chest gently. "You, Dick—you do a job of public relations. You sell these aliens to the American people!"

The official had maneuvered around in front of me. I recognized him. He was the Undersecretary of State.

"Would you step this way, please?" he said. "I'd like to introduce you to our distinguished guests."

So he stepped, and I stepped, and we scrunched across the field and clanked across the steel plate and stood next to our gastropodic guests.

"Ahem," said the Undersecretary politely.

The nearer snail bent an eye toward us. The other eye drew a bead on the companion snail, and then the great slimy head arched and came down to our level. The creature raised, as it were, one cheek of its foot and said, with all the mellowness of air being pumped through a torn inner tube, "Can it be that you wish to communicate with my unworthy self, respected sir?"

I was introduced. The thing brought two eyes to bear on me. The place where its chin should have been dropped to my feet and snaked around there for a second. Then it said, "You, honored sir, are our touchstone, the link with all that is great in your noble race. Your condescension is truly a tribute."

All this tumbled out while I was muttering "How," and extending a diffident hand. The snail put one eyeball in my palm and the other on the back of my wrist. It didn't shake; it just put the things there and took them away again. I had the wit not to wipe my hands on my pants, which was my immediate impulse. The eyeball wasn't exactly dry, either.

I said, "I'll do my best. Tell me, are you—uh—ambassadors, sort of? Or maybe just explorers?"

"Our small worth justifies no titles," said the creature,

"yet we are both; for all communication is ambassadorship of a kind, and any seeker after knowledge is an explorer."

I was suddenly reminded of an old story with the punchline, "Ask a foolish question and you get a foolish answer." I also wondered suddenly what snails eat.

The second alien glided over and eyed me. "You may depend upon our utmost obedience," it said humbly. "We understand your awesome function and we wish to be liked to whatever extent it is possible for your admirable race to like such miserable creatures as ourselves."

"Stick to that attitude and we'll get along," I said.

By and large, they were a pleasure to work with. I mean there was no temperament, no up-staging, no insistence on this camera angle or that mention of a previously published book or the other wishful biographical apocrypha about being raised in a convent, like with most of my other clients.

On the other hand, they weren't easy to talk to. They'd take orders, sure. But ask them a question. Any question:

"How long did the trip take you?"

"'How long' in your eloquent tongue indicates a frame of reference dealing with duration. I hesitate to discuss so complex a problem with one as learned as yourself. The velocities involved make it necessary to answer in relative terms. Our lowly and undesirable planet recedes from this beauteous system during part of its orbital period, advances toward it during part. Also, we must take into consideration the direction and velocity of our star in reference to the cosmic expansion of this portion of the continuum. Had we come from Cygnus, say, or Bootes, the question could be answered somewhat more directly; for those bodies travel in a contiguous arc skewed from the ecliptic plane in such a way that——"

Or a question like, "Is your government a democracy?"

"A democracy is a rule of the people, according to your rich etymology. We could not, in our lowly tongue, have expressed it so succinctly and movingly. One must govern oneself, of course. The degree of governmental control on the individual must vary from individual to individual and in the individual from time to time. This is so evident to as comprehensive a mind as yours that I trust you forgive me my inanities. The same control applies, naturally, to individuals considered in the mass. When faced with a universal necessity, the tendency exists among civilized species to unite to fill the need. Therefore, when no such necessity exists, there is less reason for concerted effort. Since this applies to all species, it applies even to such as us. On the other hand——"

See what I mean? A little of that got old quickly with me. I was happy to keep my nose to my own grindstone.

The Government gave me a month for the preparatory propaganda. Originally, the story was to break in two weeks, but I got down on my hands and knees and bawled that a publicity deadline required at least five times that. So they gave me a month.

Explain that carefully, Alvarez. I want them to understand exactly what a job I faced. All those years of lurid magazine covers showing extremely nubile females being menaced in three distinct colors by assorted monstrosities; those horror movies, those invasion-from-outer-space novels, those Sunday supplement fright splashes—all those sturdy psychological ruts I had to retrack. Not to mention the shudders elicited by mention of "worms," the regulation distrust of even human "furriners," the superstitious dread of creatures who had no visible place to park a soul.

Trowson helped me round up the men to write the scientific articles, and I dug up the boys who could pseudo them satisfactorily. Magazine mats were ripped apart to make way for yarns speculating gently on how far extraterrestrial races might have evolved beyond us, how much more ethical they might have become, how imaginary seven-headed creatures could still apply the Sermon on the Mount. Syndicated features popped up describing "Humble Creatures Who Create Our Gardens," "Snail Racing, the Spectacular New Spectator Sport," and so much stuff on "The Basic Unity of All Living Things" that I began to get uncomfortable at even a vegetarian dinner. I remember hearing there was a perceptible boom in mineral waters and vitamin pills. . . .

And all this, mind you, without a word of the real story breaking. A columnist did run a cute and cryptic item about someone having finally found meat on the flying saucers, but half an hour of earnest discussion in an abandoned fingerprint file room prejudiced him against further comment along this line.

The video show was the biggest problem. I don't think I could have done it on time with anything less than the resources and influence of the United States Government behind me. But a week before the official announcement, I had both the video show and the comic strip in production.

I think fourteen—though maybe it was more—of the country's best comedy writers collaborated on the project, not to mention the horde of illustrators and university psychologists who combined to sweat out the delightful little drawings. We used the drawings as the basis for the puppets on the TV show and I don't think anything was ever so gimmicked up with Popular Appeal—and I do mean *Popular*—as "Andy and Dandy."

Those two fictional snails crept into the heart of America like a virus infection: overnight, everybody was talking about their anthropomorphic antics, repeating their quotable running gags and adjuring each other not to miss the next show. ("You *can't* miss it, Steve; it's on every channel anyway. Right after supper.") I had the tie-ins, too: Andy and Dandy dolls for the girls, snail scooters for the boys, everything from pictures on cocktail glasses to kitchen decalcomanias. Of course, a lot of the tie-ins didn't come off the production line till after the Big Announcement.

When we gave the handouts to the newspapers, we "suggested" what headlines to use. They had a choice of ten. Even the New York *Times* was forced to shriek "REAL ANDY AND DANDY BLOW IN FROM BETELGEUSE," and under that a four-column cut of blond Baby Ann Joyce with the snails.

Baby Ann had been flown out from Hollywood for the photograph. The cut showed her standing between the two aliens and clutching an eye stalk of each in her trusting, chubby hands.

The nicknames stuck. Those two slimy intellectuals from another star became even more important than the youthful evangelist who was currently being sued for bigamy.

Andy and Dandy had a ticker-tape reception in New York. They obligingly laid a cornerstone for the University of Chicago's new library. They posed for the newsreels everywhere, surrounded by Florida oranges, Idaho potatoes, Milwaukee beer. They were magnificently coopera-tive.

From time to time I wondered what they thought of us. They had no facial expressions, which was scarcely odd, since they had no faces. Their long eye stalks swung this way and that as they rode down shrieking Broadway in the back seat of the mayor's car; their gelatinous body-foot would heave periodically and the mouth under it make a smacking noise, but when the photographers suggested that they curl around the barely clad beauties, the time video rigged up a Malibu Beach show, Andy and Dandy wriggled over and complied without a word. Which is more than I can say for the barely clad beauties.

And when the winning pitcher presented them with an autographed baseball at that year's World Series, they bowed gravely, their pink shell tops glistening in the sunlight, and said throatily into the battery of microphones: "We're the happiest fans in the universe!"

The country went wild over them.

"But we can't keep them here," Trowson predicted. "Did you read about the debate in the U.N. General Assembly yesterday? We are accused of making secret alliances with non-human aggressors against the best interests of our own species."

I shrugged. "Well, let them go overseas. I don't think anyone else will be more successful extracting information from them than we were."

Professor Trowson wriggled his short body up on a corner of his desk. He lifted a folderful of typewritten notes and grimaced as if his tongue were wrapped in wool.

"Four months of careful questioning," he grumbled. "Four months of painstaking interrogation by trained sociologists using every free moment the aliens had, which admittedly wasn't much. Four months of organized investigation, of careful data sifting." He dropped the folder disgustedly to the desk and some of the pages splashed out. "And we know more about the social structure of Atlantis than Betelgeuse IX."

We were in the wing of the Pentagon assigned to what the brass hats, in their own cute way, had christened Project Encyclopedia. I strolled across the large, sunny office and glanced at the very latest organizational wall chart. I pointed to a small rectangle labeled "Power Source Sub-Section" depending via a straight line from a larger

rectangle marked "Alien Physical Science Inquiry Section."
In the small rectangle, very finely printed, were the names of
an army major, a WAC corporal, and Drs. Lopez, Vinthe,
and Mainzer.

"How're they doing?" I asked.

"Not much better, I'm afraid." Trowson turned away
with a sigh from peering over my shoulder. "At least I de-
duce that from the unhappy way Mainzer bubbles into his
soup spoon at lunch. Conversation between sub-sections
originating in different offices on the departmental level is
officially discouraged, you know. But I remember Mainzer
from the university cafeteria. He bubbled into his soup the
very same way when he was stuck on his solar refraction
engine."

"Think Andy and Dandy are afraid we're too young to
play with matches? Or maybe apelike creatures are too
unpleasant-looking to be allowed to circulate in their
refined and esthetic civilization?"

"I don't *know*, Dick." The prof ambled back to his desk
and leafed irritably through his sociological notes. "If
anything like that is true, why would they give us free run of
their ship? Why would they reply so gravely and courteously
to every question? If only their answers weren't so vague in
our terms! But they are such complex and artistically
minded creatures, so chockful of poetic sentiment and good
manners that it's impossible to make mathematical or even
verbal sense out of their vast and circumlocutory explanations. Sometimes, when I think of their highly polished
manners and their seeming lack of interest in the structure of their society, when I put that together with their
spaceship, which looks like one of those tiny jade carvings
that took a lifetime to accomplish———"

He trailed off and began riffling the pages like a
Mississippi steamboat gambler going over somebody else's
deck of cards.

"Isn't it possible we just don't have enough stuff as yet to
understand them?"

"Yes. In fact, that's what we always come back to.
Warbury points to the tremendous development in our
language since the advent of technical vocabularies. He says
that this process, just beginning with us, already affects our
conceptual approach as well as our words. And, naturally,
in a race so much further along——— But if we could only

find a science of theirs which bears a faint resemblance to one of ours!"

I felt sorry for him, standing there blinking futilely out of gentle, academic eyes.

"Cheer up, Prof. Maybe by the time old Suckfoot and his pal come back from the Grand Tour, you'll have unsnarled a sophistry and we'll be off this 'Me, friend; you come from across sea in great bird with many wings' basis that we seem to have wandered into."

And there you are, Alvarez: a cheap advertising small-brain like me, and I was that close. I should have said something then. Bet you wouldn't have nodded at me heavily and said, "I hope so, Dick. I desperately hope so." But, come to think of it, not only Trowson was trotting up that path. So was Warbury. So were Lopez, Vinthe, and Mainzer. So was I, among others.

I had a chance to relax when Andy and Dandy went abroad. My job wasn't exactly over, but the public relations end was meshing right along, with me needed only once in a while to give a supervisory spin. Chiefly, I maintained close contact with my opposite number in various other sovereign states, giving out with experienced advice on how to sell the Boys from Betelgeuse. They had to adjust it to their own mass phobias and popular myths; but they were a little happier about it than I had been without any clear idea of what public behavior to expect of our visitors.

Remember, when *I'd* started, I hadn't even been sure those snails were housebroken.

I followed them in the newspapers. I pasted the pictures of the Mikado receiving them next to their nice comments on the Taj Mahal. They weren't nearly so nice to the Akhund of Swat, but then when you think of what the Akhund said about them . . .

They tended to do that everywhere, giving just a little better than they got. For example, when they were presented with those newly created decorations in Red Square (Dandy got the Order of Extraterrestrial Friends of Soviet Labor, while, for some abstruse reason, the Order of Heroic Interstellar Champion of the Soviet People was conferred upon Andy), they came out with a long, ringing speech about the scientific validity of communist government. It made for cheering, flower-tossing crowds in the Ukraine and Poland but a certain amount of restiveness in these United States.

But before I had to run my staff into overtime hours, whipping up press releases which recapitulated the aliens' statement before the joint houses of Congress and their lovely, sentimental comments at Valley Forge, the aliens were in Berne, telling the Swiss that only free enterprise could have produced the yodel, the Incabloc escapement in watches, and such a superb example of liberty; hadn't they had democracy long enough to have had it first, and wasn't it wonderful?

By the time they reached Paris I had the national affection pretty much under control again, although here and there a tabloid still muttered peevishly in its late city final. But, as always, Andy and Dandy put the clincher on. Even then I wondered whether they really liked DeRoges's latest abstraction for itself alone.

But they bought the twisted sculpture, paying for it, since they had no cash of their own, with a thumb-sized gadget which actually melted marble to any degree of pattern delicacy the artist desired, merely by being touched to the appropriate surface. DeRoges threw away his chisels blissfully, but six of the finest minds in France retired to intensive nervous breakdowns after a week of trying to solve the tool's working principles.

It went over big here:

ANDY AND DANDY
PASS AS THEY GO

Betelgeuse Businessmen
Show Appreciation
for Value Received.

This newspaper notes with pleasure the sound shopper's ethics behind the latest transaction of our distinguished guests from the elemental void. Understanding the inexorable law of supply and demand, these representatives of an advanced economic system refuse to succumb to the "gimmies." If certain other members of the human race were to examine carefully the true implications of . . .

So when they returned to the United States after being presented at the British court, they got juicy spreads in all the newspapers, a tug-whistle reception in New York harbor and the mayor's very chiefest deputy there on City Hall steps to receive them.

And even though people were more or less accustomed to them now, they were somehow never shoved off page one. There was the time a certain furniture polish got a testimonial out of them in which the aliens announced that they'd had particularly happy and glossy results on their tiny shell toppers with the goo; and they used the large financial rewards of the testimonial to buy ten extremely rare orchids and have them sunk in plastic. And there was the time . . .

I missed the television show on which it broke. I had gone to a side-street movie theater that night to see a revival of one of my favorite Chaplin pictures; and I'd never enjoyed the ostentatious greet-the-great hysterics of *Celebrity Salon* anyway. I hadn't any idea of how long the M.C., Bill Bancroft, had waited to get Andy and Dandy on his program, and how much he was determined to make it count when the big night arrived.

Reconstructed and stripped of meaningless effusion, it went something like this:

Bancroft asked them if they weren't anxious to get home to the wife and kiddies. Andy explained patiently, for perhaps the thirty-fourth time, that, since they were hermaphrodites, they had no family in any humanly acceptable sense. Bancroft cut into the explanation to ask them what ties they *did* have. Chiefly the revitalizer, says Andy politely.

Revitalizer? What's a revitalizer? Oh, a machine they have to expose themselves to every decade or so, says Dandy. There's at least one revitalizer in every large city on their home planet.

Bancroft makes a bad pun, waits for the uproarious audience to regain control, then asks: And this revitalizer—just what does it do? Andy goes into a long-winded explanation, the gist of which is that the revitalizers stir up cytoplasm in animal cells and refresh them.

I see, cracks Bancroft; the pause every decade that refreshes. And then, after being refreshed, you have what as a result? "Oh," muses Dandy, "you might say we have no fear of cancer or any degenerative disease. Besides that, by exposing ourselves to revitalizers at regular intervals throughout our lifetime and refreshing our body cells, we quintuple our life expectancy. We live five times longer than we should. That's about what the revitalizer does, you might say," says Dandy. Andy, after thinking a bit, agrees. "That's about it."

Pandemonium, and not mild. Newspaper extras in all languages, including the Scandinavian. Lights burning late at night in the U. N. Headquarters with guards twenty deep around the site.

When President of the Assembly Sadhu asked them why they'd never mentioned revitalizers before, they did the snail equivalent of shrugging and said the Betelgeuse IX equivalent of nobody ever asked them.

President Sadhu cleared his throat, waved all complications aside with his long brown fingers and announced, "That is not important. Not now. We must have revitalizers."

It seemed to take the aliens awhile to understand that. When they finally became convinced that we, as a species, were utterly entranced with the prospect of two to four centuries of life instead of fifty or sixty years, they went into a huddle.

But their race didn't make these machines for export, they explained regretfully. Just enough to service their population. And while they *could* see as how we might like and must obviously deserve to have these gadgets, there was none to ferry back from Betelgeuse.

Sadhu didn't even look around for advice. "What would your people want?" he asked. "What would they like in exchange for manufacturing these machines for us? We will pay almost any price within the power of this entire planet." A rumbling, eager "yes" in several languages rolled across the floor of the Assembly.

Andy and Dandy couldn't think of a thing. Sadhu begged them to try. He personally escorted them to their spaceship, which was now parked in a restricted area in Central Park. "Good night, gentlemen," said President of the Assembly Sadhu. "Try—please try hard to think of an exchange."

They stayed inside their ship for almost six days while the world almost went insane with impatience. When I think of all the fingernails bitten that week by two billion people . . .

"Imagine!" Trowson whispered to me. He was pacing the floor as if he fully intended to walk all the way to Betelgeuse. "We'd just be children on a quintupled life scale, Dick. All my achievement and education, all yours, would be just the beginning! A man could learn five professions in such a life—and think what he could accomplish in one!"

I nodded, a little numb. I was thinking of the books I could read, the books I might write, if the bulk of my life stretched ahead of me and the advertising profession as just a passing phase at the beginning of it. Then again, somehow I'd never married, never had had a family. Not enough free time, I had felt. And now, at forty, I was too set in my ways. But a man can unset a lot in a century . . .

In six days the aliens came out. With a statement of price.

They believed they could persuade their people to manufacture a supply of revitalizers for us if—— An IF writ very large indeed.

Their planet was woefully short of radioactive minerals, they explained apologetically. Barren worlds containing radium, uranium, and thorium had been discovered and claimed by other races, but the folk of Betelgeuse IX were forbidden by their ethics to wage aggressive war for territorial purposes. We had plenty of radioactive ore, which we used chiefly for war and biological research. The former was patently undesirable and the latter would be rendered largely unnecessary by the revitalizers.

So, in exchange, they wanted our radioactive elements. All of them, they stated humbly.

All right, we were a little surprised, even stunned. But the protests never *started* to materialize. There was an overwhelming chorus of "sold!" from every quadrant of the globe. A couple of generals here, a few militaristic statesmen there managed to raise direly pointing forefingers before they were whisked out of position. A nuclear physicist or two howled about the future of subatomic research, but the peoples of the earth howled louder.

"Research? How much research can you do in a lifetime of three hundred years?"

Overnight, the United Nations became the central office of a planet-wide mining concession. National boundaries were superseded by pitchblende deposits and swords were beaten into pickaxes. Practically anyone with a good, unable arm enlisted in the shovel brigades for two or more months out of the year. Comaraderie flew on the winds of the world.

Andy and Dandy politely offered to help. They marked out on detail contour maps the spots to be mined, and that included areas never suspected of radioactivity. They supplied us with fantastic but clear line drawings of devices for extracting the stuff from the ores in which it assayed poorly, and taught us the exact use of these devices, if not their basic principle.

They hadn't been joking. They wanted it all.

Then, when everything was running smoothly, they buzzed off for Betelgeuse to handle their part of the bargain.

Those two years were the most exhilarating of my life. And I'd say everyone feels the same, don't they, Alvarez? The knowledge that the world was working together, cheerfully, happily, for life itself. I put *my* year in at the Great Slave Lake, and I don't think anyone of my age and weight lifted more pitchblende.

Andy and Dandy came back in two huge ships, manned by weird snail-like robots. The robots did everything, while Andy and Dandy went on being lionized. From the two ships, almost covering the sky, the robots ferried back and forth in strange, spiral aircraft, bringing revitalizers down, carrying refined radioactive elements aloft. No one paid the slightest attention to their methods of instantaneous extraction from large quantities of ore: we were interested in just one throbbing thought—the revitalizers.

They worked. And that, so far as most of us were concerned, was that.

The revitalizers *worked*. Cancer disappeared; heart disease and kidney disease became immediately arrested. Insects which were introduced into the square one-story lab structures lived for a year instead of a few months. And humans—doctors shook their heads in wonder over people who had gone through.

All over the planet, near every major city, the long, patient, slowly moving lines stood outside the revitalizers, which were rapidly becoming something else.

"Temples!" shouted Mainzer. "They look on them as temples. A scientist investigating their operation is treated by the attendants like a dangerous lunatic in a nursery. Not that a man can find a clue in those ridiculously small motors. I no longer ask what their power source can be. Instead, I ask if they have a power source at *all!*"

"The revitalizers are very precious now, in the beginning," Trowson soothed him. "After a while the novelty will wear off and you'll be able to investigate at your leisure. Could it be solar power?"

"No!" Mainzer shook his huge head positively. "Not solar power. Solar power I am sure I could recognize. As I am sure that the power supply of their ships and whatever runs these—these revitalizers are two entirely separate things. On the ships I have given up. But the revitalizers I believe I could solve. If only they would let me examine them. Fools! So terribly afraid I might damage one, and they would have to travel to another city for their elixir!"

We patted his shoulder, but we weren't really interested. Andy and Dandy left that week, after wishing us well in their own courteous and complex fashion. Whole population groups blew kisses at their mineral-laden ships.

Six months after they left, the revitalizers stopped.

"Am I certain?" Trowson snorted at my dismayed face. "One set of statistics proves it: look at your death rate. It's back to pre-Betelgeuse normal. Or ask any doctor. Any doctor who can forget his U.N. security oath, that is. There'll be really wild riots when the news breaks, Dick."

"But *why?*" I asked him. "Did we do something wrong?"

He started a laugh that ended with his teeth clicking frightenedly together. He rose and walked to the window, staring out into the star-diseased sky. "We did something wrong, all right. We trusted. We made the same mistake all natives have made when they met a superior civilization. Mainzer and Lopez have taken one of the revitalizer engine units apart. There was just a trace of it left, but this time they found the power source. Dick, my boy, the revitalizers were run on the fuel of completely pure radioactive elements!"

I needed a few moments to file that properly. Then I sat down in the easy chair very, very carefully. I made some hoarse, improbable sounds before croaking: "Prof, do you mean they wanted that stuff for themselves, for their *own* revitalizers? That everything they did on this planet was carefully planned so that they could con us with a maxi-

mum of friendliness all around? It doesn't seem—it just
can't—— Why, with their superior science, they could have
conquered us if they'd cared to. They could have——"

"No, they couldn't have," Trowson whipped out. He
turned to face me and flung his arms across each other.
"They're a decadent, dying race; they wouldn't have attempted to conquer us. Not because of their ethics—this
huge, horrible swindle serves to illustrate *that* aspect of
them—but because they haven't the energy, the concentration, the interest. Andy and Dandy are probably representative of the few remaining who have barely enough
git-up-and-go to *trick* backward peoples out of the all-
important, life-sustaining revitalizer fuel."

The implications were just beginning to soak into my
cortex. Me, the guy who did the most complete and colossal
public-relations job of all time—I could just see what my
relations with the public would be like if I was ever connected with this shambles.

"And without atomic power, Prof, we won't have space
travel!"

He gestured bitterly. "Oh, we've been taken, Dick; the
whole human race has been had. I know what you're going
through, but think of me! I'm the failure, the man
responsible. I'm supposed to be a sociologist! How could I
have missed? *How?* It was all there: the lack of interest in
their own culture, the overintellectualization of esthetics,
the involved methods of thought and expression, the
exaggerated etiquette, even the very first thing of theirs we
saw—their ship—was too heavily stylized and intricately
designed for a young, trusting civilization.

"They *had* to be decadent; every sign pointed to that
conclusion. And of course the fact that they resort to the
methods of fueling their revitalizers that we've experienced
—when if we had their science, what might we not do, what
substitutes might we not develop! No wonder they couldn't
explain their science to us; I doubt if they understand it fully
themselves. They are the profligate, inadequate and sneak-
thief heirs of what was once a soaring race!"

I was following my own unhappy images. "And we're still
hicks. Hicks who've been sold the equivalent of the
Brooklyn Bridge by some dressed-up sharpies from
Betelgeuse."

Trowson nodded. "Or a bunch of poor natives who have

sold their island home to a group of European explorers for a handful of brightly colored glass beads."

But of course we were both wrong, Alvarez. Neither Trowson nor I had figured on Mainzer or Lopez or the others. Like Mainzer said, a few years earlier and we would have been licked. But man had entered the atomic age some time before 1945 and people like Mainzer and Vinthe had done nuclear research back in the days when radioactive elements abounded on Earth. We had that and we had such tools as the cyclotron, the betatron. And, if our present company will pardon the expression, Alvarez, we are a young and vigorous race.

All we had to do was the necessary research.

The research was done. With a truly effective world government, with a population not only interested in the problem but recently experienced in working together—and with the grim incentive we had, Alvarez, the problem, as you know, was solved.

We developed artificial radioactives and refueled the revitalizers. We developed atomic fuels out of the artificial radioactives and we got space travel. We did it comparatively fast, and we weren't interested in a ship that just went to the Moon or Mars. We wanted a star ship. And we wanted it so bad, so fast, that we have it now too.

Here we are. Explain the situation to them, Alvarez, just the way I told it to you, but with all the knee-bending and gobbledegook that a transplanted Brazilian with twelve years oriental trading experience can put into it. You're the man to do it—I can't talk like that. It's the only language those decadent slugs understand, so it's the only way we can talk to them. So talk to them, these slimy snails, these oysters on the quarter shell, those smart-alecky slugs. Don't forget to mention to them that the supply of radioactives they got from us won't last forever. Get that down in fine detail.

Then stress the fact that we've got artificial radioactives, and that they've got some things we know we want and lots of other things we mean to find out about.

Tell them, Alvarez, that we've come to collect tolls on that Brooklyn Bridge they sold us.

SURVIVAL SHIP

by Judith Merril

Half a million people actually made the round trip to Space Station One that day to watch the take-off in person. And back on Earth a hundred million video screens flashed the picture of Captain Melnick's gloved hand waving a dramatic farewell at the port, while the other hand slowly pressed down the lever that would fire the ship out beyond the orbit of the artificial satellite, past the Moon and the planets, into unknown space.

From Station One, Earth, and Moon, a hundred million winged wishes added their power to the surge of the jets, as a rising spiral of fire inside the greatest rocket tower ever built marked the departure of the thrice-blessed ship, *Survival*. In the great churches, from pole to pole, services were held all day, speeding the giant vessel on its way, calling on the aid of the Lord for the Twenty and Four who manned the ship.

At mountain-top telescopes a dozen cameras faithfully transmitted the messages of great unblinking glass eyes. Small home sets and massive pulpit screens alike looked to the sky to follow the flare dimming in the distance, to watch the man-made star falling away.

Inside the great ship Melnick's hand left the firing lever, then began adjusting the chin rest and the earphones of the acceleration couch. The indicator dashboard, designed for prone eye level, leaped into focus. Securing the couch straps with the swift competence of habit, the captain intently watched the sweep of the big second hand around the take-off timer, aware at the same time that green lights were beginning to glow at the other end of the board. The indicator reached the first red mark.

"The show's over, everybody. We're in business!" The mike built into the chin rest carried the captain's taut voice all over the ship. "Report, all stations!"

"Number one, all secure!" Melnick mentally ticked off the first green light, glowing to prove the astrogator's couch was in use.

"Number two, all secure!"

"Number three . . ." "Four . . ." "Five." The rhythmic sing-song of pinpoint timing in take-off was second nature by now to the whole crew. One after another, the green lights glowed for safety, punctuating the litany, and the gong from the timer put a period neatly in place after the final "All secure!"

"Eight seconds to black out," the captain's voice warned. "Seven . . . six . . . stand by." The first wave of acceleration shock reeled into twenty-four helmet-sheathed heads on twenty-four individually designed head rests. "Five——" *It's got to work,* Melnick was thinking, fighting off unconsciousness with fierce intensity. "Four——" *It's got to . . . got to . . .* "Three——" *got to . . . got to . . .* "Two——" *got to . . .*

At the space station, a half-million watchers were slowly cleared from the giant take-off platform. They filed in long orderly lines down the ramps to the interior, and waited there for the smaller Earth rockets that would take them home. Waiting, they were at once elated and disappointed. They had seen no more than could be seen at the same place on any other day. The entire rocket area had been fenced off, with a double cordon of guards to make sure that too-curious visitors stayed out of range. Official explanations mentioned the new engine, the new fuel, the danger of escaping gases—but nobody believed it. Every one of the half-million visitors knew what the mystery was: the crew, and nothing else. Giant video screens all over the platform gave the crowd details and closeups, the same they would have seen had they stayed comfortably at home. They saw the captain's gloved hand, at the last, but not the captain's face.

There was muttering and complaining, but there was something else too. Each man, woman, and child who went to the station that day would be able to say, years later, "I was there when the *Survival* took off. You never saw anything so big in your life."

Because it wasn't just another planet hop. It wasn't just

like the hundreds of other take-offs. It was the *Survival*, the greatest spaceship ever engineered. People didn't think of the *Survival* in terms of miles-per-second; they said, "Sirius in fifteen years!"

From Sunday supplements to dignified periodicals, nearly every medium of communication on Earth had carried the story. Brightly colored graphs made visibly simple the natural balance of life forces in which plants and animals could maintain a permanently fresh atmosphere as well as a self-perpetuating food supply. Lecture demonstrations and videocasts showed how centrifugal force would replace gravity.

For months before take-off, the press and video followed the preparations with daily intimate accounts. The world over, people knew the nicknames of pigs, calves, chickens, and crew members—and even the proper botanical name of the latest minor masterpiece of the biochemists, a hybrid plant whose root, stems, leaves, buds, blossoms, and fruit were all edible, nourishing, and delicious, and which had the added advantage of being the thirstiest CO_2 drinker ever found.

The public knew the nicknames of the crew, and the proper name of the plant. But they never found out, not even the half million who went to the field to see for themselves, the real identity of the Twenty and Four who comprised the crew. They knew that thousands had applied; that it was necessary to be single, under twenty-five, and a graduate engineer in order to get as far as the physical exam; that the crew was mixed in sex, with the object of filling the specially equipped nursery and raising a second generation for the return trip, if, as was hoped, a lengthy stay on Sirius's planet proved possible. They knew, for that matter, all the small characteristics and personal idiosyncrasies of the crew members—what they ate, how they dressed, their favorite games, theaters, music, books, cigarettes, preachers, and political parties. There were only two things the public didn't know, and couldn't find out: the real names of the mysterious Twenty and Four, and the reason why those names were kept secret.

There were as many rumors as there were newsmen or radio reporters, of course. Hundreds of explanations were offered at one time or another. But still nobody knew—nobody except the half hundred Very Important Persons who had planned the project, and the Twenty and Four themselves.

And now, as the pinpoint of light faded out of the screens of televisors all over Earth, the linear and rotary acceleration of the great ship began to adjust to the needs of the human body. "Gravity" in the living quarters gradually approached Earth-normal. Tortured bodies relaxed in the acceleration couches, where the straps had held them securely positioned through the initial stage, so as to keep the blood and guts where they belonged, and to prevent the stomach from following its natural tendency to emerge through the backbone. Finally, stunned brain cells awoke to the recognition that danger signals were no longer coming through from shocked, excited tissues.

Captain Melnick was the first to awake. The row of lights on the board still glowed green. Fumbling a little with the straps, Melnick watched tensely to see if the indicator lights were functioning properly, sighing with relief as the one at the head of the board went dead, operated automatically by the removal of body weight from the couch.

It was right—it was essential—for the captain to wake up first. If any of the men had showed superior recuperative powers, it could be bad. Melnick thought wearily of the years and years ahead during which this artificial dominance had to be maintained in defiance of all Earth conditioning. But of course it would not be that bad, really. The crew had been picked for ability to conform to the unusual circumstances; they were all without strong family ties or prejudices. Habit would establish the new castes soon enough, but the beginning was crucial. Survival was more than a matter of plant-animal balance and automatic gravity.

While the captain watched, another light went out, and then another. Officers, both of them. Good. Three more lights died out together. Then men were beginning to awaken, and it was reassuring to know that their own couch panels would show them that the officers had revived first. In any case, there was no more time for worrying. There were things to be done.

A detail was sent off immediately to attend to the animals, release them from the confinement of the specially prepared acceleration pens, and check them for any possible damage incurred in spite of precautions. The proportions of human, animal, and plant life had been worked out carefully beforehand for maximum efficiency and for comfort. Now that the trip had started, the miniature world had to maintain its status quo or perish.

As soon as enough of the crew were awake, Lieutenant Johnson, the third officer, took a group of eight out to make an inspection of the hydroponic tanks that lined the hull. Nobody expected much trouble here. Being at the outermost part of the ship, the plants were exposed to high "gravity." The outward pull exerted on them by rotation should have held their roots in place, even through the tearing backward thrust of the acceleration. But there was certain to be a large amount of minor damage, to stems and leaves and buds, and whatever there was would need immediate repair. In the ship's economy the plants had the most vital function of all—absorbing carbon dioxide from dead air already used by humans and animals, and deriving from it the nourishment that enabled their chlorophyll systems to release fresh oxygen for re-use in breathing.

There was a vast area to inspect. Row upon row of tanks marched solidly from stem to stern of the giant ship, all around the inner circumference of the hull. Johnson split the group of eight into four teams, each with a biochemist in charge to locate and make notes of the extent of the damage, and an unclassified man as helper, to do the actual dirty work, crawling out along the catwalks to mend each broken stalk.

Other squads were assigned to check the engines and control mechanisms, and the last two women to awake got stuck with the booby prize—first shift in the galley. Melnick squashed their immediate protests with a stern reminder that they had hardly earned the right to complain; but privately the captain was pleased at the way it had worked out. This first meal on board was going to have to be something of an occasion. A bit of ceremony always helped; and above all, social procedures would have to be established immediately. A speech was indicated—a speech Melnick did not want to have to make in the presence of all twenty-four crew members. As it worked out, the Four would almost certainly be kept busy longer than the others. If these women had not happened to wake up last . . .

The buzzing of the intercom broke into the captain's speculations. "Lieutenant Johnson reporting, sir." Behind the proper, crisp manner, the young lieutenant's voice was frightened. Johnson was third in command, supervising the inspection of the tanks.

"Having trouble down there?" Melnick was deliberately informal, knowing the men could hear over the intercom, and anxious to set up an immediate feeling of unity among the officers.

"One of the men complaining, sir." The young lieutenant sounded more confident already. "There seems to be some objection to the division of work."

Melnick thought it over quickly and decided against any more public discussion on the intercom. "Stand by. I'll be right down."

All over the ship airducts and companionways led from the inner-level living quarters "down" to the outer level of tanks; Melnick took the steps three at a time and reached the trouble zone within seconds after the conversation ended.

"Who's the troublemaker here?"

"Kennedy—on assignment with Petty Officer Giorgio for plant maintenance."

"You have a complaint?" Melnick asked the swarthy, dungareed man whose face bore a look of sullen dissatisfaction.

"Yeah." The man's voice was deliberately insolent. The others had never heard him speak that way before, and he seemed to gain confidence from the shocked surprise they displayed. "I thought I was supposed to be a pampered darling this trip. How come I do all the dirty work here, and Georgie gets to keep so clean?"

His humor was too heavy to be effective. "Captain's orders, that's why," Melnick snapped. "Everybody has to work double time till things are squared away. If you don't like the job here, I can fix you up fine in the brig. Don't worry about your soft quarters. You'll get 'em later and plenty of 'em. It's going to be a long trip, and don't forget it." The captain pointed significantly to the chronometer built into the overhead. "But it's not much longer to dinner. You'd better get back to work if you want to hit the chow while it's hot. Mess call in thirty minutes."

Melnick took a chance and turned abruptly away, terminating the interview. It worked. Sullen but defeated, Kennedy hoisted himself back up on the catwalk, and then began crawling out to the spot Giorgio pointed out. Not daring to express their relief, lieutenant and captain exchanged one swift look of triumph before Melnick walked wordlessly off.

In the big control room that would be mess hall, social hall, and general meeting place for all of them for fifteen years to come—or twice that time if Sirius's planet turned out to be uninhabitable—the captain waited for the crew members to finish their checkup assignments. Slowly they gathered in the lounge, ignoring the upholstered benches around the sides and the waiting table in the center, standing instead in small awkward groups. An undercurrent of excitement ran through them all, evoking deadly silences and erupting in bursts of too-noisy conversation, destroying the joint attempt at an illusion of nonchalance. They all knew—or hoped they knew—what the subject of the captain's first speech would be, and behind the façade of bronzed faces and trimly muscled bodies they were all curious, even a little afraid.

Finally there were twenty of them in the room, and the captain rose and rapped for order.

"I suppose," Melnick began, "you will all want to know our present position and the results of the checkup." Nineteen heads turned as one, startled and disappointed at the opening. "However," the captain continued, smiling at the change of expressions the single word brought, "I imagine you're all as hungry and—er—impatient as I am, so I shall put off the more routine portions of my report until our other comrades have joined us. There is only one matter which should properly be discussed immediately."

Everyone in the room was acutely conscious of the Four. They had all known, of course, how it would be. But on Earth there had always been other, ordinary men around to make them less aware of it. Now the general effort to maintain an air of artificial ease and disinterest was entirely abandoned as the captain plunged into the subject most on everyone's mind.

"Our ship is called the *Survival*. You all know why. Back on Earth, people think they know why too; they think it's because of our planets and artificial gravity, and the hundreds of other engineering miracles that keep us going. Of course, they also know that our crew is mixed, and that our population is therefore"—the captain paused, letting an anticipatory titter circle the room—"is therefore by no means fixed. What they don't know, naturally, is the division of sexes in the crew.

"You're all aware of the reason for the secrecy. You know that our organization is in direct opposition to the ethical principles on which the peace was established after World War IV. And you know how the planners of this trip had to struggle with the authorities to get this project approved. When consent was granted, finally, it was only because the highest prelates clearly understood that the conditions of our small universe were in every way different from those on Earth—and that the division proposed was *necessary for survival.*"

The captain paused, waiting for the last words to sink in, and studying the attitudes of the group. Even now, after a year's conditioning to counteract earthly mores, there were some present who listened to this public discussion of dangerous and intimate matters with flushed faces and embarrassed smiles.

"You all realize, of course, that this consent was based, finally, on the basic principle itself." Automatically, out of long habit unbroken by that year's intensive training, the captain made the sign of the olive branch. *"Survival of the race is the first duty of every ethical man and woman."* The command was intoned meaningfully, almost pontifically, and brought its reward as confusion cleared from some of the flushed faces. "What we are doing, our way of life now, has the full approval of the authorities. We must never forget that.

"On Earth, survival of the race is best served by the increasing strength of family ties. It was not thought wise to endanger those ties by letting the general public become aware of our—unorthodox—system here on board. A general understanding, on Earth, of the true meaning of the phrase, 'the Twenty and the Four,' could only have aroused a furor of discussion and argument that would, in the end, have impeded survival both there and here.

"The knowledge that there are twenty of one sex on board, and only four of the other—that children will be born outside of normal family groups, and raised jointly—I need not tell you how disastrous that would have been." Melnick paused, raising a hand to dispel the muttering in the room.

"I wanted to let you know, before the Four arrive, that I have made some plans which I hope will carry us through the initial period in which difficulties might well arise. Later, when the groups of six—five of us, and one of them in each—have been assigned their permanent quarters, I think it will be possible, in fact necessary, to allow a greater amount of autonomy within those groups. But for the time being, I have arranged a—shall we call it a dating schedule?" Again the captain paused, waiting for tension to relieve itself in laughter. "I have arranged dates for all of you with each of them during convenient free periods over the next month. Perhaps at the end of that time we will be able to choose groups; perhaps it will take longer. Maternity schedules, of course, will not be started until I am certain that the grouping is satisfactory to all. For the time being, remember this:

"We are not only more numerous than they, but we are stronger and, in our social placement here, more fortunate. We must become accustomed to the fact that they are our responsibility. It is because we are hardier, longer-lived, less susceptible to pain and illness, better able to withstand, mentally, the difficulties of a life of monotony, that we are placed as we are—and not alone because we are the bearers of children."

Over the sober silence of the crew, the captain's voice rang out. "Lieutenant Johnson," Melnick called to the golden-haired, sun-tanned woman near the door, "will you call the men in from the tank rooms now? They can finish their work after dinner."

KEYHOLE

by Murray Leinster

There's a story about a psychologist who was studying the intelligence of a chimpanzee. He led the chimp into a room full of toys, went out, closed the door and put his eye to the keyhole to see what the chimp was doing. He found himself gazing into a glittering interested brown eye only inches from his own. The chimp was looking through the keyhole to see what the psychologist was doing.

When they brought Butch into the station in Tycho Crater he seemed to shrivel as the gravity coils in the air lock went on. He was impossible to begin with. He was all big eyes and skinny arms and legs, and he was very young and he didn't need air to breathe. Worden saw him as a limp bundle of bristly fur and terrified eyes as his captors handed him over.

"Are you crazy?" demanded Worden angrily. "Bringing him in like this? Would you take a human baby into eight gravities? Get out of the way!"

He rushed for the nursery that had been made ready for somebody like Butch. There was a rebuilt dwelling-cave on one side. The other side was a human schoolroom. And under the nursery the gravity coils had been turned off so that in that room things had only the weight that was proper to them on the Moon.

The rest of the station had coils to bring everything up to normal weight for Earth. Otherwise the staff of the station would be seasick most of the time. Butch was in the Earth-gravity part of the station when he was delivered, and he couldn't lift a furry spindly paw.

In the nursery, though, it was different. Worden put him on the floor. Worden was the uncomfortable one there—his weight only twenty pounds instead of a normal hundred and sixty. He swayed and reeled as a man does on the Moon without gravity coils to steady him.

But that was the normal thing to Butch. He uncurled himself and suddenly flashed across the nursery to the reconstructed dwelling-cave. It was a pretty good job, that cave. There were the five-foot chipped rocks shaped like dunce caps, found in all residences of Butch's race. There was the rocking stone on its base of other flattened rocks. But the spear stones were fastened down with wire in case Butch got ideas.

Butch streaked it to these familiar objects. He swarmed up one of the dunce-cap stones and locked his arms and legs about its top, clinging close. Then he was still. Worden regarded him. Butch was motionless for minutes, seeming to take in as much as possible of his surroundings without moving even his eyes.

Suddenly his head moved. He took in more of his environment. Then he stirred a third time and seemed to look at Worden with an extraordinary intensity—whether of fear or pleading Worden could not tell.

"Hmm," said Worden, "so that's what those stones are for! Perches or beds or roosts, eh? I'm your nurse, fella. We're playing a dirty trick on you but we can't help it."

He knew Butch couldn't understand, but he talked to him as a man does talk to a dog or a baby. It isn't sensible, but it's necessary.

"We're going to raise you up to be a traitor to your kinfolk," he said with some grimness. "I don't like it, but it has to be done. So I'm going to be very kind to you as part of the conspiracy. Real kindness would suggest that I kill you instead—but I can't do that."

Butch stared at him, unblinking and motionless. He looked something like an Earth monkey but not too much so. He was completely impossible but he looked pathetic.

Worden said bitterly, "You're in your nursery, Butch. Make yourself at home!"

He went out and closed the door behind him. Outside he glanced at the video screens that showed the interior of the nursery from four different angles. Butch remained still for a long time. Then he slipped down to the floor. This time he ignored the dwelling-cave of the nursery.

He went interestedly to the human-culture part. He examined everything there with his oversized soft eyes. He touched everything with his incredibly handlike tiny paws. But his touches were tentative. Nothing was actually disturbed when he finished his examination.

He went swiftly back to the dunce-cap rock, swarmed up it, locked his arms and legs about it again, blinked rapidly and seemed to go to sleep. He remained motionless with closed eyes until Worden grew tired of watching him and moved away.

The whole affair was preposterous and infuriating. The first men to land on the Moon knew that it was a dead world. The astronomers had been saying so for a hundred years, and the first and second expeditions to reach Luna from Earth found nothing to contradict the theory.

But a man from the third expedition saw something moving among the upflung rocks of the Moon's landscape and he shot it and the existence of Butch's kind was discovered. It was inconceivable of course that there should be living creatures where there was neither air nor water. But Butch's folk did live under exactly those conditions.

The dead body of the first living creature killed on the Moon was carried back to Earth and biologists grew indignant. Even with a specimen to dissect and study they were inclined to insist that there simply wasn't any such creature. So the fourth and fifth and sixth lunar expeditions hunted Butch's relatives very earnestly for further specimens for the advancement of science.

The sixth expedition lost two men whose spacesuits were punctured by what seemed to be weapons while they were hunting. The seventh expedition was wiped out to the last man. Butch's relatives evidently didn't like being shot as biological specimens.

It wasn't until the tenth expedition of four ships established a base in Tycho Crater that men had any assurance of being able to land on the Moon and get away again. Even then the staff of the station felt as if it were under permanent siege.

Worden made his report to Earth. A baby lunar creature had been captured by a tractor party and brought into Tycho Station. A nursery was ready and the infant was there now, alive. He seemed to be uninjured. He seemed not to mind an environment of breathable air for which he had no use. He was active and apparently curious and his intelligence was marked.

There was so far no clue to what he ate—if he ate at all—though he had a mouth like the other collected specimens and the toothlike concretions which might serve as teeth. Worden would of course continue to report in detail. At the moment he was allowing Butch to accustom himself to his new surroundings.

He settled down in the recreation room to scowl at his companion scientists and try to think, despite the program beamed on radar frequency from Earth. He definitely didn't like his job, but he knew that it had to be done. Butch had to be domesticated. He had to be persuaded that he was a human being, so human beings could find out how to exterminate his kind.

It had been observed before, on Earth, that a kitten raised with a litter of puppies came to consider itself a dog and that even pet ducks came to prefer human society to that of their own species. Some talking birds of high intelligence appeared to be convinced that they were people and acted that way. If Butch reacted similarly he would become a traitor to his kind for the benefit of man. And it was necessary!

Men had to have the Moon, and that was all there was to it. Gravity on the Moon was one eighth that of gravity on Earth. A rocket ship could make the Moon voyage and carry a cargo, but no ship yet built could carry fuel for a trip to Mars or Venus if it started out from Earth.

With a fueling stop on the Moon, though, the matter was simple. Eight drums of rocket fuel on the Moon weighed no more than one on Earth. A ship itself weighed only one eighth as much on Luna. So a rocket that took off from Earth with ten drums of fuel could stop at a fuel base on the Moon and soar away again with two hundred, and sometimes more.

With the Moon as a fueling base men could conquer the solar system. Without the Moon, mankind was earthbound. Men had to have the Moon!

But Butch's relatives prevented it. By normal experience there could not be life on an airless desert with such monstrous extremes of heat and cold as the Moon's surface experienced. But there was life there. Butch's kinfolk did not breathe oxygen. Apparently they ate it in some mineral combination and it interacted with other minerals in their bodies to yield heat and energy.

Men thought squids peculiar because their blood stream used copper in place of iron, but Butch and his kindred seemed to have complex carbon compounds in place of both. They were intelligent in some fashion, it was clear. They used tools, they chipped stone, and they had long, needlelike stone crystals which they threw as weapons.

No metals, of course, for lack of fire to smelt them. There couldn't be fire without air. But Worden reflected that in ancient days some experimenters had melted metals and set wood ablaze with mirrors concentrating the heat of the sun. With the naked sunlight of the Moon's surface, not tempered by air and clouds, Butch's folk could have metals if they only contrived mirrors and curved them properly like the mirrors of telescopes on Earth.

Worden had an odd sensation just then. He looked around sharply as if somebody had made a sudden movement. But the video screen merely displayed a comedian back on Earth, wearing a funny hat. Everybody looked at the screen.

As Worden watched, the comedian was smothered in a mass of soapsuds and the studio audience two hundred and thirty thousand miles away squealed and applauded the exquisite humor of the scene. In the Moon station in Tycho Crater somehow it was less than comical.

Worden got up and shook himself. He went to look again at the screens that showed the interior of the nursery. Butch was motionless on the absurd cone-shaped stone. His eyes were closed. He was simply a furry, pathetic little bundle, stolen from the airless wastes outside to be bred into a traitor to his race.

Worden went to his cabin and turned in. Before he slept, though, he reflected that there was still some hope for Butch. Nobody understood his metabolism. Nobody could guess at what he ate. Butch might starve to death. If he did he would be lucky. But it was Worden's job to prevent it.

Butch's relatives were at war with men. The tractors that crawled away from the station—they went amazingly fast on the Moon—were watched by big-eyed furry creatures from rock crevices and from behind the boulders that dotted the lunar landscape.

Needle-sharp throwing stones flicked through emptiness. They splintered on the tractor bodies and on the tractor ports, but sometimes they jammed or broke a tread and then the tractor had to stop. Somebody had to go out and clear things or make repairs. And then a storm of throwing stones poured upon him.

A needle-pointed stone, traveling a hundred feet a second, hit just as hard on Luna as it did on Earth—and it traveled farther. Spacesuits were punctured. Men died. Now tractor treads were being armored and special repair-suits were under construction, made of hardened steel plates.

Men who reached the Moon in rocket ships were having to wear armor like medieval knights and men-at-arms!

There was a war on. A traitor was needed. And Butch was elected to be that traitor.

When Worden went into the nursery again—the days and nights on the Moon are two weeks long apiece, so men ignored such matters inside the station—Butch leaped for the dunce-cap stone and clung to its top. He had been fumbling around the rocking stone. It still swayed back and forth on its plate. Now he seemed to try to squeeze himself to unity with the stone spire, his eyes staring enigmatically at Worden.

"I don't know whether we'll get anywhere or not," said Worden conversationally. "Maybe you'll put up a fight if I touch you. But we'll see."

He reached out his hand. The small furry body—neither hot nor cold but the temperature of the air in the station—resisted desperately. But Butch was very young. Worden peeled him loose and carried him across the room to the human schoolroom equipment. Butch curled up, staring fearfully.

"I'm playing dirty," said Worden, "by being nice to you, Butch. Here's a toy."

Butch stirred in his grasp. His eyes blinked rapidly. Worden put him down and wound up a tiny mechanical toy. It moved. Butch watched intently. When it stopped he looked back at Worden. Worden wound it up again. Again Butch watched. When it ran down a second time the tiny handlike paw reached out.

With an odd tentativeness, Butch tried to turn the winding key. He was not strong enough. After an instant he went loping across to the dwelling-cave. The winding key was a metal ring. Butch fitted that over a throw-stone point, and twisted the toy about. He wound it up. He put the toy on the floor and watched it work. Worden's jaw dropped.

"Brains!" he said wryly. "Too bad, Butch! You know the principle of the lever. At a guess you've an eight-year-old human brain! I'm sorry for you, fella!"

At the regular communication hour he made his report to Earth. Butch was teachable. He only had to see a thing done once—or at most twice—to be able to repeat the motions involved.

"And," said Worden, carefully detached, "he isn't afraid of me now. He understands that I intend to be friendly.

While I was carrying him I talked to him. He felt the vibration of my chest from my voice.

"Just before I left him I picked him up and talked to him again. He looked at my mouth as it moved and put his paw on my chest to feel the vibrations. I put his paw at my throat. The vibrations are clearer there. He seemed fascinated. I don't know how you'd rate his intelligence but it's above that of a human baby."

Then he said with even greater detachment, "I am disturbed. If you must know, I don't like the idea of exterminating his kind. They have tools, they have intelligence. I think we should try to communicate with them in some way—try to make friends—stop killing them for dissection."

The communicator was silent for the second and a half it took his voice to travel to Earth and the second and a half it took to come back. Then the recording clerk's voice said briskly, "Very good, Mr. Worden! Your voice was very clear!"

Worden shrugged his shoulders. The lunar station in Tycho was a highly official enterprise. The staff on the Moon had to be competent—and besides, political appointees did not want to risk their precious lives—but the Earth end of the business of the Space Exploration Bureau was run by the sort of people who do get on official payrolls. Worden felt sorry for Butch—and for Butch's relatives.

In a later lesson session Worden took an empty coffee tin into the nursery. He showed Butch that its bottom vibrated when he spoke into it, just as his throat did. Butch experimented busily. He discovered for himself that it had to be pointed at Worden to catch the vibrations.

Worden was unhappy. He would have preferred Butch to be a little less rational. But for the next lesson he presented Butch with a really thin metal diaphragm stretched across a hoop. Butch caught the idea at once.

When Worden made his next report to Earth he felt angry.

"Butch has no experience of sound as we have, of course," he said curtly. "There's no air on the Moon. But sound travels through rocks. He's sensitive to vibrations in solid objects just as a deaf person can feel the vibrations of a dance floor if the music is loud enough.

"Maybe Butch's kind has a language or a code of sounds sent through the rock underfoot. They do communicate somehow! And if they've brains and a means of communication they aren't animals and shouldn't be exterminated for our convenience!"

He stopped. The chief biologist of the Space Exploration Bureau was at the other end of the communication beam then. After the necessary pause for distance his voice came blandly.

"Splendid, Worden! Splendid reasoning! But we have to take the longer view. Exploration of Mars and Venus is a very popular idea with the public. If we are to have funds—and the appropriations come up for a vote shortly—we have to make progress toward the nearer planets. The public demands it. Unless we can begin work on a refueling base on the Moon, public interest will cease!"

Worden said urgently, "Suppose I send some pictures of Butch? He's very human, sir! He's extraordinarily appealing! He has personality! A reel or two of Butch at his lessons ought to be popular!"

Again that irritating wait while his voice traveled a quarter-million miles at the speec of light and the wait for the reply.

"The—ah—lunar creatures, Worden," said the chief biologist regretfully, "have killed a number of men who have been publicized as martyrs to science. We cannot give favorable publicity to creatures that have killed men!" Then he added blandly, "But you are progressing splendidly, Worden—*splendidly!* Carry on!"

His image faded from the video screen. Worden said naughty words as he turned away. He'd come to like Butch. Butch trusted him. Butch now slid down from that crazy perch of his and came rushing to his arms every time he entered the nursery.

Butch was ridiculously small—no more than eighteen inches high. He was preposterously light and fragile in his nursery, where only Moon gravity obtained. And Butch was such an earnest little creature, so soberly absorbed in everything that Worden showed him!

He was still fascinated by the phenomena of sound. Humming or singing—even Worden's humming and singing—entranced him. When Worden's lips moved now Butch struck an attitude and held up the hoop diaphragm with a tiny finger pressed to it to catch the vibrations Worden's voice made.

Now too when he grasped an idea Worden tried to convey he tended to swagger. He became more human in his actions with every session of human contact. Once, indeed, Worden looked at the video screens which spied on Butch and saw him—all alone—solemnly going through every gesture and every movement Worden had made. He was pretending to give a lesson to an imaginary still-tinier companion. He was pretending to be Worden, apparently for his own satisfaction!

Worden felt a lump in his throat. He was enormously fond of the little mite. It was painful that he had just left Butch to help in the construction of a vibrator-microphone device which would transfer his voice to rock vibrations and simultaneously pick up any other vibrations that might be made in return.

If the members of Butch's race did communicate by tapping on rocks or the like, men could eavesdrop on them—could locate them, could detect ambushes in preparation, and apply mankind's deadly military countermeasures.

Worden hoped the gadget wouldn't work. But it did. When he put it on the floor of the nursery and spoke into the microphone, Butch did feel the vibrations underfoot. He recognized their identity with the vibrations he'd learned to detect in air.

He made a skipping exultant hop and jump. It was plainly the uttermost expression of satisfaction. And then his tiny foot pattered and scratched furiously on the floor. It made a peculiar scratchy tapping noise which the microphone picked up. Butch watched Worden's face, making the sounds which were like highly elaborated footfalls.

"No dice, Butch," said Worden unhappily. "I can't understand it. But it looks as if you've started your treason already. This'll help wipe out some of your folks."

He reported it reluctantly to the head of the station. Microphones were immediately set into the rocky crater floor outside the station and others were made ready for exploring parties to use for the detection of Moon creatures near them. Oddly enough, the microphones by the station yielded results right away.

It was near sunset. Butch had been captured near the middle of the three-hundred-and-thirty-four-hour lunar day. In all the hours between—a week by Earth time—he had had no nourishment of any sort. Worden had conscientiously offered him every edible and inedible substance in the station. Then at least one sample of every mineral in the station collection.

Butch regarded them all with interest but without appetite. Worden—liking Butch—expected him to die of starvation and thought it a good idea. Better than encompassing the death of all his race, anyhow. And it did seem to him that Butch was beginning to show a certain sluggishness, a certain lack of bounce and energy. He thought it was weakness from hunger.

Sunset progressed. Yard by yard, fathom by fathom, half mile by half mile, the shadows of the miles-high western walls of Tycho crept across the crater floor. There came a time when only the central hump had sunlight. Then the shadow began to creep up the eastern walls. Presently the last thin jagged line of light would vanish and the colossal cup of the crater would be filled to overflowing with the night.

Worden watched the incandescent sunlight growing even narrower on the cliffs. He would see no other sunlight for two weeks' Earth time. Then abruptly an alarm bell rang. It clanged stridently, furiously. Doors hissed shut, dividing the station into airtight sections.

Loudspeakers snapped, *"Noises in the rock outside! Sounds like Moon creatures talking nearby! They may plan an attack! Everybody into spacesuits and get guns ready!"*

At just that instant the last thin sliver of sunshine disappeared. Worden thought instantly of Butch. There was no spacesuit to fit him. Then he grimaced a little. Butch didn't need a spacesuit.

Worden got into the clumsy outfit. The lights dimmed. The harsh airless space outside the station was suddenly bathed in light. The multimillion-lumen beam, made to guide rocket ships to a landing even at night, was turned on to expose any creatures with designs on its owners. It was startling to see how little space was really lighted by the beam and how much of stark blackness spread on beyond.

The loud-speaker snapped again. *"Two Moon creatures! Running away! They're zigzagging! Anybody who wants to take a shot*——" The voice paused. It didn't matter. Nobody is a crack shot in a spacesuit. *"They left something behind!"* said the voice in the loudspeaker. It was sharp and uneasy.

"I'll take a look at that," said Worden. His own voice startled him but he was depressed. "I've got a hunch what it is."

Minutes later he went out through the air lock. He moved lightly despite the cumbrous suit he wore. There were two other staff members with him. All three were armed and the searchlight beam stabbed here and there erratically to expose any relative of Butch who might try to approach them in the darkness.

With the light at his back Worden could see that trillions of stars looked down upon Luna. The zenith was filled with infinitesimal specks of light of every conceivable color. The familiar constellations burned ten times as brightly as on Earth. And Earth itself hung nearly overhead. It was three-quarters full—a monstrous bluish giant in the sky, four times the Moon's diameter, its ice caps and continents mistily to be seen.

Worden went forebodingly to the object left behind by Butch's kin. He wasn't much surprised when he saw what it was. It was a rocking stone on its plate with a fine impalpable dust on the plate, as if something had been crushed under the egg-shaped upper stone acting as a mill.

Worden said sourly into his helmet microphone, "It's a present for Butch. His kinfolk know he was captured alive. They suspect he's hungry. They've left some grub for him of the kind he wants or needs most."

That was plainly what it was. It did not make Worden feel proud. A baby—Butch—had been kidnaped by the enemies of its race. That baby was a prisoner and its captors would have nothing with which to feed it. So someone, greatly daring—Worden wondered somberly if it was Butch's father and mother—had risked their lives to leave food for him with a rocking stone to tag it for recognition as food.

"It's a dirty shame," said Worden bitterly. "All right! Let's carry it back. Careful not to spill the powdered stuff!"

His lack of pride was emphasized when Butch fell upon the unidentified powder with marked enthusiasm. Tiny pinch by tiny pinch Butch consumed it with an air of vast satisfaction. Worden felt ashamed.

"You're getting treated pretty rough, Butch," said Worden. "What I've already learned from you will cost a good many hundred of your folks' lives. And they're taking chances to feed you! I'm making you a traitor and myself a scoundrel."

Butch thoughtfully held up the hoop diaphragm to catch the voice vibrations in the air. He was small and furry and absorbed. He decided that he could pick up sounds better from the rock underfoot. He pressed the communicator microphone on Worden. He waited.

"*No!*" said Worden roughly. "Your people are too human. Don't let me find out any more, Butch. Be smart and play dumb!"

But Butch didn't. It wasn't very long before Worden was teaching him to read. Oddly, though, the rock microphones that had given the alarm at the station didn't help the tractor parties at all. Butch's kinfolk seemed to vanish from the neighborhood of the station altogether. Of course if that kept up the construction of a fuel base could be begun and the actual extermination of the species carried out later. But the reports on Butch were suggesting other possibilities.

"If your folks stay vanished," Worden told Butch, "it'll be all right for a while—and only for a while. I'm being urged to try to get you used to Earth gravity. If I succeed, they'll want you on Earth in a zoo. And if that works—why, they'll be sending other expeditions to get more of your kinfolk to put in other zoos."

Butch watched Worden, motionless.

"And also"—Worden's tone was very grim—"there's some miniature mining machinery coming up by the next rocket. I'm supposed to see if you can learn to run it."

Butch made scratching sounds on the floor. It was unintelligible of course, but it was an expression of interest at least. Butch seemed to enjoy the vibrations of Worden's voice, just as a dog likes to have his master talk to him. Worden grunted.

"We humans class you as an animal, Butch. We tell ourselves that all the animal world should be subject to us. Animals should work for us. If you act too smart we'll hunt down all your relatives and set them to work digging minerals for us. You'll be with them. But I don't want you to work your heart out in a mine, Butch! It's wrong!"

Butch remained quite still. Worden thought sickishly of small furry creatures like Butch driven to labor in airless mines in the Moon's frigid depths. With guards in spacesuits watching lest any try to escape to the freedom they'd known before the coming of men. With guns mounted against revolt. With punishments for rebellion or weariness.

It wouldn't be unprecedented. The Indians in Cuba when the Spanish came . . . Negro slavery in both Americas . . . concentration camps . . .

Butch moved. He put a small furry paw on Worden's knee. Worden scowled at him.

"Bad business," he said harshly. "I'd rather not get fond of you. You're a likable little cuss but your race is doomed. The trouble is that you didn't bother to develop a civilization. And if you had, I suspect we'd have smashed it. We humans aren't what you'd call admirable."

Butch went over to the blackboard. He took a piece of pastel chalk—ordinary chalk was too hard for his Moon-gravity muscles to use—and soberly began to make marks on the slate. The marks formed letters. The letters made words. The words made sense.

YOU, wrote Butch quite incredibly in neat pica lettering, GOOD FRIEND.

He turned his head to stare at Worden. Worden went white. "I haven't taught you those words, Butch!" he said very quietly. "What's up?"

He'd forgotten that his words, to Butch, were merely vibrations in the air or in the floor. He'd forgotten they had no meaning. But Butch seemed to have forgotten it too. He marked soberly:

MY FRIEND GET SPACESUIT. He looked at Worden and marked once more. TAKE ME OUT. I COME BACK WITH YOU.

He looked at Worden with large incongruously soft and appealing eyes. And Worden's brain seemed to spin inside his skull. After a long time Butch printed again—YES.

Then Worden sat very still indeed. There was only Moon gravity in the nursery and he weighed only one eighth as much as on Earth. But he felt very weak. Then he felt grim.

"Not much else to do, I suppose," he said slowly. "But I'll have to carry you through Earth gravity to the air lock."

He got to his feet. Butch made a little leap up into his

arms. He curled up there, staring at Worden's face. Just before Worden stepped through the door Butch reached up a skinny paw and caressed Worden's cheek tentatively.

"Here we go!" said Worden. "The idea was for you to be a traitor. I wonder——"

But with Butch a furry ball, suffering in the multiplied weight Earth gravity imposed upon him, Worden made his way to the air lock. He donned a spacesuit. He went out.

It was near sunrise then. A long time had passed and Earth was now in its last quarter and the very highest peak of all that made up the crater wall glowed incandescent in the sunshine. But the stars were still quite visible and very bright. Worden walked away from the station, guided by the Earth-shine on the ground underfoot.

Three hours later he came back. Butch skipped and hopped beside his spacesuited figure. Behind them came two other figures. They were smaller than Worden but much larger than Butch. They were skinny and furry and they carried a burden. A mile from the station he switched on his suit radio. He called. A startled voice answered in his earphones.

"It's Worden," he said dryly. "I've been out for a walk with Butch. We visited his family and I've a couple of his cousins with me. They want to pay a visit and present some gifts. Will you let us in without shooting?"

There were exclamations. There was confusion. But Worden went on steadily toward the station while another high peak glowed in sunrise light and a third seemed to burst into incandescence. Dawn was definitely on the way.

The air-lock door opened. The party from the airless Moon went in. When the air lock filled, though, and the gravity coils went on, Butch and his relatives became helpless. They had to be carried to the nursery. There they uncurled themselves and blinked enigmatically at the men who crowded into the room where gravity was normal for the Moon and at the other men who stared in the door.

"I've got a sort of message," said Worden. "Butch and his relatives want to make a deal with us. You'll notice that they've put themselves at our mercy. We can kill all three of them. But they want to make a deal."

The head of the station said uncomfortably, "You've managed two-way communication, Worden?"

"*I* haven't," Worden told him. "*They* have. They've

proved to me that they've brains equal to ours. They've been treated as animals and shot as specimens. They've fought back—naturally! But they want to make friends. They say that we can never use the Moon except in spacesuits and in stations like this, and they could never take Earth's gravity. So there's no need for us to be enemies. We can help each other."

The head of the station said dryly, "Plausible enough, but we have to act under orders, Worden. Did you explain that?"

"They know," said Worden. "So they've got set to defend themselves if necessary. They've set up smelters to handle metals. They get the heat by sun mirrors, concentrating sunlight. They've even begun to work with gases held in containers. They're not far along with electronics yet, but they've got the theoretic knowledge and they don't need vacuum tubes. They live in a vacuum. They can defend themselves from now on."

The head said mildly, "I've watched Butch, you know, Worden. And you don't look crazy. But if this sort of thing is sprung on the armed forces on Earth there'll be trouble. They've been arguing for armed rocket ships. If your friends start a real war for defense—if they can—maybe rocket warships will be the answer."

Worden nodded.

"Right. But our rockets aren't so good that they can fight this far from a fuel store, and there couldn't be one on the Moon with all of Butch's kinfolk civilized—as they nearly are now and as they certainly will be within the next few weeks. Smart people, these cousins and such of Butch!"

"I'm afraid they'll have to prove it," said the head. "Where'd they get this sudden surge in culture?"

"From us," said Worden. "Smelting from me, I think. Metallurgy and mechanical engineering from the tractor mechanics. Geology—call it lunology here—mostly from you."

"How's that?" demanded the head.

"Think of something you'd like Butch to do," said Worden grimly, "and then watch him."

The head stared and then looked at Butch. Butch—small and furry and swaggering—stood up and bowed profoundly from the waist. One paw was placed where his heart could be. The other made a grandiose sweeping gesture. He straightened up and strutted, then climbed swiftly into Worden's lap and put a skinny furry arm about his neck.

"That bow," said the head, very pale, "is what I had in mind. You mean——"

"Just so," said Worden. "Butch's ancestors had no air to make noises in for speech. So they developed telepathy. In time, to be sure, they worked out something like music—sounds carried through rock. But like our music it doesn't carry meaning. They communicate directly from mind to mind. Only we can't pick up communications from them and they can from us."

"They read our minds!" said the head. He licked his lips. "And when we first shot them for specimens they were trying to communicate. Now they fight."

"Naturally," said Worden. "Wouldn't we? They've been picking our brains. They can put up a terrific battle now. They could wipe out this station without trouble. They let us stay so they could learn from us. Now they want to trade."

"We have to report to Earth," said the head slowly, "but——"

"They brought along some samples," said Worden. "They'll swap diamonds, weight for weight, for records. They like our music. They'll trade emeralds for textbooks—they can read now! And they'll set up an atomic pile and swap plutonium for other things they'll think of later. Trading on that basis should be cheaper than a war!"

"Yes," said the head. "It should. That's the sort of argument men will listen to. But how——"

"Butch," said Worden ironically. "Just Butch! We didn't capture him—they planted him on us! He stayed in the station and picked our brains and relayed the stuff to his relatives. We wanted to learn about them, remember? It's like the story of the psychologist. . . ."

There's a story about a psychologist who was studying the intelligence of a chimpanzee. He led the chimp into a room full of toys, went out, closed the door and put his eye to the keyhole to see what the chimp was doing. He found himself gazing into a glittering interested brown eye only inches from his own. The chimp was looking through the keyhole to see what the psychologist was doing.

MISBEGOTTEN MISSIONARY

by Isaac Asimov

He had slipped aboard the ship! There had been dozens waiting outside the energy barrier when it had seemed that waiting would do no good. Then the barrier had faltered for a matter of two minutes (which showed the superiority of unified organisms over life fragments) and he was across.

None of the others had been able to move quickly enough to take advantage of the break, but that didn't matter. All alone, he was enough. No others were necessary.

And the thought faded out of satisfaction and into loneliness. It was a terribly unhappy and unnatural thing to be parted from all the rest of the unified organism, to be a life fragment oneself. How could these aliens stand being fragments?

It increased his sympathy for the aliens. Now that he experienced fragmentation himself, he could feel, as though from a distance, the terrible isolation that made them so afraid. It was fear born of that isolation that dictated their actions. What but the insane fear of their condition could have caused them to blast an area, one mile in diameter, into dull-red heat before landing their ship? Even the organized life ten feet deep in the soil had been destroyed in the blast.

He engaged reception, listening eagerly, letting the alien thought saturate him. He enjoyed the touch of life upon his consciousness. He would have to ration that enjoyment. He must not forget himself.

But it could do no harm to listen to thoughts. Some of the fragments of life on the ship thought quite clearly, considering that they were such primitive, incomplete creatures. Their thoughts were like tiny bells.

Roger Oldenn said, "I feel contaminated. You know what I mean? I keep washing my hands and it doesn't help."

Jerry Thorn hated dramatics and didn't look up. They were still maneuvering in the stratosphere of Saybrook's Planet and he preferred to watch the panel dials. He said, "No reason to feel contaminated. Nothing happened."

"I hope not," said Oldenn. "At least they had all the field men discard their spacesuits in the air lock for complete disinfection. They had a radiation bath for all men entering from outside. I *suppose* nothing happened."

"Why be nervous, then?"

"I don't know. I wish the barrier hadn't broken down."

"Who doesn't? It was an accident."

"I wonder." Oldenn was vehement. "I was here when it happened. My shift, you know. There was no reason to overload the power line. There was equipment plugged into it that had no damn business near it. None whatsoever."

"All right. People are stupid."

"Not that stupid. I hung around when the Old Man was checking into the matter. None of them had reasonable excuses. The armor-baking circuits, which were draining off two thousand watts, had been put into the barrier line. They'd been using the second subsidiaries for a week. Why not this time? They couldn't give any reason."

"Can you?"

Oldenn flushed. "No, I was just wondering if the men had been"—he searched for a word—"hypnotized into it. By those things outside."

Thorn's eyes lifted and met those of the other levelly. "I wouldn't repeat that to anyone else. The barrier was down only two minutes. If anything had happened, if even a spear of grass had drifted across it would have shown up in our bacteria cultures within half an hour, in the fruit-fly colonies in a matter of days. Before we got back it would show up in the hamsters, the rabbits, maybe the goats. Just get it through your head, Oldenn, that nothing happened. Nothing."

Oldenn turned on his heel and left. In leaving, his foot came within two feet of the object in the corner of the room. He did not see it.

He disengaged his reception centers and let the thoughts flow past him unperceived. These life fragments were not important, in any case, since they were not fitted for the continuation of life. Even as fragments, they were incomplete.

The other types of fragments now—they were different. He had to be careful of them. The temptation would be great, and he must give no indication, none at all, of his existence on board ship till they landed on their home planet.

He focused on the other parts of the ship, marveling at the diversity of life. Each item, no matter how small, was sufficient to itself. He forced himself to contemplate this, until the unpleasantness of the thought grated on him and he longed for the normality of home.

Most of the thoughts he received from the smaller fragments were vague and fleeting, as you would expect. There wasn't much to be had from them, but that meant their need for completeness was all the greater. It was that which touched him so keenly.

There was the life fragment which squatted on its haunches and fingered the wire netting that enclosed it. Its thoughts were clear, but limited. Chiefly, they concerned the yellow fruit a companion fragment was eating. It wanted the fruit very deeply. Only the wire netting that separated the fragments prevented its seizing the fruit by force.

He disengaged reception in a moment of complete revulsion. *These fragments competed for food!*

He tried to reach far outward for the peace and harmony of home, but it was already an immense distance away. He could reach only into the nothingness that separated him from sanity.

He longed at the moment even for the feel of the dead soil between the barrier and the ship. He had crawled over it last night. There had been no life upon it, but it had been the soil of home, and on the other side of the barrier there had still been the comforting feel of the rest of organized life.

He could remember the moment he had located himself on the surface of the ship, maintaining a desperate suction grip until the air lock opened. He had entered, moving cautiously between the outgoing feet. There had been an inner lock and that had been passed later. Now he lay here, a life fragment himself, inert and unnoticed.

Cautiously, he engaged reception again at the previous focus. The squatting fragment of life was tugging furiously at the wire netting. It still wanted the other's food, though it was the less hungry of the two.

Larsen said, "Don't feed the damn thing. She isn't hungry; she's just sore because Tillie had the nerve to eat before she herself was crammed full. The greedy ape! I wish we were back home and I never had to look another animal in the face again."

He scowled at the older female chimpanzee frowningly and the chimp mouthed and chattered back to him in full reciprocation.

Rizzo said, "Okay, okay. Why hang around here, then? Feeding time is over. Let's get out."

They went past the goat pens, the rabbit hutches, the hamster cages.

Larsen said bitterly, "You volunteer for an exploration voyage. You're a hero. They send you off with speeches—and make a zoo keeper out of you."

"They give you double pay."

"All right, so what? I didn't sign up just for the money. They said at the original briefing that it was even odds we wouldn't come back, that we'd end up like Saybrook. I signed up because I wanted to do something important."

"Just a bloomin' bloody hero," said Rizzo.

"I'm not an animal nurse."

Rizzo paused to lift a hamster out of the cage and stroke it. "Hey," he said, "did you ever think that maybe one of these hamsters has some cute little baby hamsters inside, just getting started?"

"Wise guy! They're tested every day."

"Sure, sure." He muzzled the little creature, which vibrated its nose at him. "But just suppose you came down one morning and found them there. New little hamsters looking up at you with soft, green patches of fur where the eyes ought to be."

"Shut up, for the love of Mike," yelled Larsen.

"Little soft, green patches of shining fur," said Rizzo, and put the hamster down with a sudden loathing sensation.

He engaged reception again and varied the focus. There wasn't a specialized life fragment at home that didn't have a rough counterpart on shipboard.

There were the moving runners in various shapes, the

moving swimmers, and the moving fliers. Some of the fliers were quite large, with perceptible thoughts; others were small, gauzy-winged creatures. These last transmitted only patterns of sense perception, imperfect patterns at that, and added nothing intelligent of their own.

There were the non-movers, which, like the non-movers at home, were green and lived on the air, water, and soil. These were a mental blank. They knew only the dim, dim consciousness of light, moisture, and gravity.

And each fragment, moving and non-moving, had its mockery of life.

Not yet. Not yet. . . .

He clamped down hard upon his feelings. Once before, these life fragments had come, and the rest at home had tried to help them—too quickly. It had not worked. This time they must wait.

If only these fragments did not discover him.

They had not, so far. They had not noticed him lying in the corner of the pilot room. No one had bent down to pick up and discard him. Earlier, it had meant he could not move. Someone might have turned and stared at the stiff wormlike thing, not quite six inches long. First stare, then shout, and then it would all be over.

But now, perhaps, he had waited long enough. The take-off was long past. The controls were locked; the pilot room was empty.

It did not take him long to find the chink in the armor leading to the recess where some of the wiring was. They were dead wires.

The front end of his body was a rasp that cut in two a wire of just the right diameter. Then, six inches away, he cut it in two again. He pushed the snipped-off section of the wire ahead of him packing it away neatly and invisibly into a corner of recess. Its outer covering was a brown elastic material and its core was gleaming, ruddy metal. He himself could not reproduce the core, of course, but that was not necessary. It was enough that the pellicle that covered him had been carefully bred to resemble a wire's surface.

He returned and grasped the cut sections of the wire before and behind. He tightened against them as his little suction disks came into play. Not even a seam showed.

They could not find him now. They could look right at him and see only a continuous stretch of wire.

Unless they looked very closely indeed and noted that, in a certain spot on this wire, there were two tiny patches of soft and shining green fur.

"It is remarkable," said Dr. Weiss, "that little green hairs can do so much."

Captain Loring poured the brandy carefully. In a sense, this was a celebration. They would be ready for the jump through hyper-space in two hours, and after that, two days would see them back on Earth.

"You are convinced, then, the green fur is the sense organ?" he asked.

"It is," said Weiss. Brandy made him come out in splotches, but he was aware of the need of celebration—quite aware. "The experiments were conducted under difficulties, but they were quite significant."

The captain smiled stiffly. " 'Under difficulties' is one way of phrasing it. I would never have taken the chances you did to run them."

"Nonsense. We're all heroes aboard this ship, all volunteers, all great men with trumpet, fife, and fanfarade. You took the chance of coming here."

"You were the first to go outside the barrier."

"No particular risk was involved," Weiss said. "I burned the ground before me as I went, to say nothing of the portable barrier that surrounded me. Nonsense, Captain. Let's all take our medals when we come back; let's take them without attempt at gradation. Besides, I'm a male."

"But you're filled with bacteria to here." The captain's hand made a quick, cutting gesture three inches above his head. "Which makes you as vulnerable as a female would be."

They paused for drinking purposes.

"Refill?" asked the captain.

"No, thanks. I've exceeded my quota already."

"Then one last for the spaceroad." He lifted his glass in the general direction of Saybrook's Planet, no longer visible, its sun only a bright star in the visiplate. "To the little green hairs that gave Saybrook his first lead."

Weiss nodded. "A lucky thing. We'll quarantine the planet, of course."

The captain said, "That doesn't seem drastic enough.

Someone might always land by accident someday and not have Saybrook's insight, or his guts. Suppose he did not blow up his ship, as Saybrook did. Suppose he got back to some inhabited place."

The captain was somber. "Do you suppose they might ever develop interstellar travel on their own?"

"I doubt it. No proof, of course. It's just that they have such a completely different orientation. Their entire organization of life has made tools unnecessary. As far as we know, even a stone ax doesn't exist on the planet."

"I hope you're right. Oh, and, Weiss, would you spend some time with Drake?"

"The Galactic Press fellow?"

"Yes. Once we get back, the story of Saybrook's Planet will be released for the public and I don't think it would be wise to oversensationalize it. I've asked Drake to let you consult with him on the story. You're a biologist and enough of an authority to carry weight with him. Would you oblige?"

"A pleasure."

The captain closed his eyes wearily and shook his head.

"Headache, Captain?"

"No. Just thinking of poor Saybrook."

He was weary of the ship. Awhile back there had been a queer, momentary sensation, as though he had been turned inside out. It was alarming and he had searched the minds of the keen-thinkers for an explanation. Apparently the ship had leaped across vast stretches of empty space by cutting across something they knew as "hyper-space." The keen-thinkers were ingenious.

But—he was weary of the ship. It was such a futile phenomenon. These life fragments were skillful in their constructions, yet it was only a measure of their unhappiness, after all. They strove to find in the control of inanimate matter what they could not find in themselves. In their unconscious yearning for completeness, they built machines and scoured space, seeking, seeking . . .

These creatures, he knew, could never, in the very nature of things, find that for which they were seeking. At least not until such time as he gave it to them. He quivered a little at the thought.

Completeness!

These fragments had no concept of it, even. "Completeness" was a poor word.

In their ignorance they would even fight it. There had been the ship that had come before. The first ship had contained many of the keen-thinking fragments. There had been two varieties, life producers and the sterile ones. (How different this second ship was. The keen-thinkers were all sterile, while the other fragments, the fuzzy-thinkers and the no-thinkers, were all producers of life. It was strange.)

How gladly that first ship had been welcomed by all the planet! He could remember the first intense shock at the realization that the visitors were fragments and not complete. The shock had given way to pity, and the pity to action. It was not certain how they would fit into the community, but there had been no hesitation. All life was sacred and somehow room would have been made for them—for all of them, from the large keen-thinkers to the little multipliers in the darkness.

But there had been a miscalculation. They had not correctly analyzed the course of the fragments' ways of thinking. The keen-thinkers became aware of what had been done and resented it. They were frightened, of course; they did not understand.

They had developed the barrier first, and then, later, had destroyed themselves, exploding their ship to atoms.

Poor, foolish fragments.

This time, at least, it would be different. They would be saved, despite themselves.

John Drake would not have admitted it in so many words, but he was very proud of his skill on the photo-typer. He had a travel-kit model, which was a six-by-eight, featureless dark plastic slab, with cylindrical bulges on either end to hold the roll of thin paper. It fitted into a brown leather case, equipped with a beltlike contraption that held it closely about the waist and at one hip. The whole thing weighed less than a pound.

Drake could operate it with either hand. His fingers would flick quickly and easily, placing their light pressure at exact spots on the blank surface, and, soundlessly, words would be written.

He looked thoughtfully at the beginning of his story, then up at Dr. Weiss. "What do you think, Doc?"

"It starts well."

Drake nodded. "I thought I might as well start with Saybrook himself. They haven't released his story back home yet. I wish I could have seen Saybrook's original report. How did he ever get it through, by the way?"

"As near as I could tell, he spent one last night sending it through the sub-ether. When he was finished, he shorted the motors, and converted the entire ship into a thin cloud of vapor a millionth of a second later. The crew and himself along with it."

"What a man! You were in this from the beginning, Doc?"

"Not from the beginning," corrected Weiss gently. "Only since the receipt of Saybrook's report."

He could not help thinking back. He had read that report, realizing even then how wonderful the planet must have seemed when Saybrook's colonizing expedition first reached it. It was practically a duplicate of Earth, with an abounding plant life and a purely vegetarian animal life.

There had been only the little patches of green fur (how often had he used that phrase in his speaking and thinking!) which seemed strange. No living individual on the planet had eyes. Instead, there was this fur. Even the plants, each blade or leaf or blossom, possessed the two patches of richer green.

Then Saybrook had noticed, startled and bewildered, that there was no conflict for food on the planet. All plants grew pulpy appendages which were eaten by the animals. These were regrown in a matter of hours. No other parts of the plants were touched. It was as though the plants fed the animals as part of the order of nature. And the plants themselves did not grow in overpowering profusion. They might almost have been cultivated, they were spread across the available soil so discriminately.

How much time, Weiss wondered, had Saybrook had to observe the strange law and order on the planet?—the fact that insects kept their numbers reasonable, though no birds ate them; that the rodentlike things did not swarm, though no carnivores existed to keep them in check.

And then there had come the incident of the white rats.

That prodded Weiss. He said, "Oh, one correction, Drake. Hamsters were not the first animals involved. It was the white rats."

"White rats," said Drake, making the correction in his notes.

"Every colonizing ship," said Weiss, "takes a group of white rats for the purpose of testing any alien foods. Rats, of course, are very similar to human beings from a nutritional viewpoint. Naturally, only female white rats are taken."

Naturally. If only one sex was present, there was no danger of unchecked multiplication in case the planet proved favorable. Remember the rabbits in Australia.

"Incidentally, why not use males?" asked Drake.

"Females are hardier," said Weiss, "which is lucky, since that gave the situation away. It turned out suddenly that all the rats were bearing young."

"Right. Now that's where I'm up to, so here's my chance to get some things straight. For my own information, Doc, how did Saybrook find out they were in a family way?"

"Accidentally, of course. In the course of nutritional investigations, rats are dissected for evidence of internal damage. Their condition was bound to be discovered. A few more were dissected; same results. Eventually, all that lived gave birth to young—with *no* male rats aboard!"

"And the point is that all the young were born with little green patches of fur instead of eyes."

"That is correct. Saybrook said so and we corroborate him. After the rats, the pet cat of one of the children was obviously affected. When it finally kittened, the kittens were not born with closed eyes but with little patches of green fur. There was no tomcat aboard.

"Eventually Saybrook had the women tested. He didn't tell them what for. He didn't want to frighten them. Every single one of them was in the early stages of pregnancy, leaving out of consideration those few who had been pregnant at the time of embarkation. Saybrook never waited for any child to be born, of course. He knew they would have no eyes, only shining patches of green fur.

"He even prepared bacterial cultures (Saybrook was a thorough man) and found each bacillus to show microscopic green spots."

Drake was eager. "That goes way beyond our briefing— or, at least, the briefing I got. But granted that life on

Saybrook's Planet is organized into a unified whole, how is it done?"

"How? How are your cells organized into a unified whole? Take an individual cell out of your body, even a brain cell, and what is it by itself? Nothing. A little blob of protoplasm with no more capacity for anything human than an amoeba. Less capacity, in fact, since it couldn't live by itself. But put the cells together and you have something that could invent a spaceship or write a symphony."

"I get the idea," said Drake.

Weiss went on, "*All* life on Saybrook's Planet is a *single* organism. In a sense, all life on Earth is too, but it's a fighting dependence, a dog-eat-dog dependence. The bacteria fix nitrogen; the plants fix carbon; animals eat plants and each other; bacterial decay hits everything. It comes full circle. Each grabs as much as it can, and is, in turn, grabbed.

"On Saybrook's Planet, each organism has its place, as each cell in our body does. Bacteria and plants produce food, on the excess of which animals feed, providing in turn carbon dioxide and nitrogenous wastes. Nothing is produced more or less than is needed. The scheme of life is intelligently altered to suit the local environment. No group of life forms multiplies more or less than is needed, just as the cells in our body stop multiplying when there are enough of them for a given purpose. When they don't stop multiplying, we call it cancer. And that's what life on Earth really is, the kind of organic organization we have, compared to that on Saybrook's Planet. One big cancer. Every species, every individual doing its best to thrive at the expense of every other species and individual."

"You sound as if you approve of Saybrook's Planet, Doc."

"I do, in a way. It makes sense out of the business of living. I can see their viewpoint toward us. Suppose one of the cells of your body could be conscious of the efficiency of the human body as compared with that of the cell itself, and could realize that this was only the result of the union of many cells into a higher whole. And then suppose it became conscious of the existence of free-living cells, with bare life and nothing more. It might feel a very strong desire to drag the poor thing into an organization. It might feel sorry for it, feel perhaps a sort of missionary spirit. The things on Saybrook's Planet—or the thing; one should use the singular—feels just that, perhaps."

"And went ahead by bringing about virgin births, eh, Doc? I've got to go easy on that angle of it. Post-office regulations, you know."

"There's nothing ribald about it, Drake. For centuries we've been able to make the eggs of sea urchins, bees, frogs, et cetera develop without the intervention of male fertilization. The touch of a needle was sometimes enough, or just immersion in the proper salt solution. The thing on Saybrook's Planet can cause fertilization by the controlled use of radiant energy. That's why an appropriate energy barrier stops it; interference, you see, or static.

"They can do more than stimulate the division and development of an unfertilized egg. They can impress their own characteristics upon its nucleo-proteins, so that the young are born with the little patches of green fur, which serve as the planet's sense organ and means of communication. The young, in other words, are not individuals, but become part of the thing on Saybrook's Planet. The thing on the planet, not at all incidentally, can impregnate any species—plant, animal, or microscopic."

"Potent stuff," muttered Drake.

"Totipotent," Dr. Weiss said sharply. "Universally potent. Any fragment of it is totipotent. Given time, a single bacterium from Saybrook's Planet can convert *all of Earth* into a single organism! We've got the experimental proof of that."

Drake said unexpectedly, "You know, I think I'm a millionaire, Doc. Can you keep a secret?"

Weiss nodded, puzzled.

"I've got a souvenir from Saybrook's Planet," Drake told him, grinning. "It's only a pebble, but after the publicity the planet will get, combined with the fact that it's quarantined from here on in, the pebble will be all any human being will ever see of it. How much do you suppose I could sell the thing for?"

Weiss stared. "A pebble?" He snatched at the object shown him, a hard, gray ovoid. "You shouldn't have done that, Drake. It was strictly against regulations."

"I know. That's why I asked if you could keep a secret. If you could give me a signed note of authentication—— *What's the matter, Doc?*"

Instead of answering, Weiss could only chatter and point.

Drake ran over and stared down at the pebble. It was the same as before——

Except that the light was catching it at an angle, and it showed up two little green spots. Look very closely; they were patches of green hairs.

He was disturbed. There was a definite air of danger within the ship. There was the suspicion of his presence aboard. How could that be? He had done nothing yet. Had another fragment of home come aboard and been less cautious? That would be impossible without his knowledge, and though he probed the ship intensely, he found nothing.

And then the suspicion diminished, but it was not quite dead. One of the keen-thinkers still wondered, and was treading close to the truth.

How long before the landing? Would an entire world of life fragments be deprived of completeness? He clung closer to the severed ends of the wire he had been specially bred to imitate, afraid of detection, fearful for his altruistic mission.

Dr. Weiss had locked himself in his own room. They were already within the solar system, and in three hours they would be landing. He had to think. He had three hours in which to decide.

Drake's devilish "pebble" had been part of the organized life on Saybrook's Planet, of course, but it was dead. It was dead when he had first seen it, and if it hadn't been, it was certainly dead after they fed it into the hyper-atomic motor and converted it into a blast of pure heat. And the bacterial cultures still showed normal when Weiss anxiously checked.

That was not what bothered Weiss now.

Drake had picked up the "pebble" during the last hours of the stay on Saybrook's Planet—*after* the barrier breakdown. What if the breakdown had been the result of a slow, relentless mental pressure on the part of the thing on the planet? What if parts of its being waited to invade as the barrier dropped? If the "pebble" had not been fast enough and had moved only after the barrier was re-established, it would have been killed. It would have lain there for Drake to see and pick up.

It was a "pebble," not a natural life form. But did that mean it was not *some* kind of life form? It might have been a deliberate production of the planet's single organism—a creature deliberately designed to look like a pebble, harmless-seeming, unsuspicious. Camouflage, in other words—a shrewd and frighteningly successful camouflage.

Had any other camouflaged creature succeeded in crossing the barrier *before* it was re-established—with a suitable shape filched from the minds of the humans aboard ship by the mind-reading organism of the planet? Would it have the casual appearance of a paperweight? Of an ornamental brass-head nail in the captain's old-fashioned chair? And how would they locate it? Could they search every part of the ship for the telltale green patches—even down to individual microbes?

And why camouflage? Did it intend to remain undetected for a time? Why? So that it might wait for the landing on Earth?

An infection *after landing* could not be cured by blowing up a ship. The bacteria of Earth, the molds, yeasts, and protozoa, would go first. Within a year the non-human young would begin arriving by the uncountable billions.

Weiss closed his eyes and told himself it might not be such a bad thing. There would be no more disease, since no bacterium would multiply at the expense of its host, but instead would be satisfied with its fair share of what was available. There would be no more overpopulation; the hordes of East Asia would decline to adjust themselves to the food supply. There would be no more wars, no crime, no greed.

But there would be no more individuality, either.

Humanity would find security by becoming a cog in a biological machine. A man would be brother to a germ, or to a liver cell.

He stood up. He would have a talk with Captain Loring. They would send their report and blow up the ship, just as Saybrook had done.

He sat down again. Saybrook had had proof, while he had only the conjectures of a terrorized mind, rattled by the sight of two green spots on a pebble. Could he kill the two hundred men on board ship because of a feeble suspicion?

He had to *think!*

He was straining. Why did he have to wait? If he could only welcome those who were aboard now. *Now!*

Yet a cooler, more reasoning part of himself told him that he could not. The little multipliers in the darkness would betray their new status in fifteen minutes, and the keen-thinkers had them under continual observation. Even one mile from the surface of their planet would be too soon, since they might still destroy themselves and their ship out in space.

Better to wait for the main air locks to open, for the planetary air to swirl in with millions of the little multipliers. Better to greet each one of them into the brotherhood of unified life and let them swirl out again to spread the message.

Then it would be done! Another world organized, complete!

He waited. There was the dull throbbing of the engines working mightily to control the slow dropping of the ship; the shudder of contact with planetary surface, then——

He let the jubilation of the keen-thinkers sweep into reception, and his own jubilant thoughts answered them. Soon they would be able to receive as well as himself. Perhaps not these particular fragments, but the fragments that would grow out of those which were fitted for the continuation of life.

The main air locks were about to be opened——

And all thought ceased.

Jerry Thorn thought, Damn it, something's wrong *now*.

He said to Captain Loring, "Sorry. There seems to be a power breakdown. The locks won't open."

"Are you sure, Thorn? The lights are on."

"Yes, sir. We're investigating it now."

He tore away and joined Roger Oldenn at the air-lock wiring box. "What's wrong?"

"Give me a chance, will you?" Oldenn's hands were busy. Then he said, "For the love of Pete, there's a six-inch break in the twenty-amp lead."

"What? That can't be!"

Oldenn held up the broken wires with their clean, sharp, sawn-through ends.

Dr. Weiss joined them. He looked haggard and there was the smell of brandy on his breath.

He said shakily, "What's the matter?"

They told him. At the bottom of the compartment, in one

corner, was the missing section.

Weiss bent over. There was a black fragment on the floor of the compartment. He touched it with his finger and it smeared, leaving a sooty smudge on his finger tip. He rubbed it off absently.

There might have been something taking the place of the missing section of wire. Something that had been alive and only looked like wire, yet something that would heat, die, and carbonize in a tiny fraction of a second once the electrical circuit which controlled the air lock had been closed.

He said, "How are the bacteria?"

A crew member went to check, returned and said, "All normal, Doc."

The wires had meanwhile been spliced, the locks opened, and Dr. Weiss stepped out into the anarchic world of life that was Earth.

"Anarchy," he said, laughing a little wildly. "And it will stay that way."

THE SACK

by William Morrison

At first they hadn't even known that the Sack existed. If they had noticed it at all when they landed on the asteroid, they thought of it merely as one more outpost of rock on the barren expanse of roughly ellipsoidal silicate surface, which Captain Ganko noticed had major and minor axes roughly three and two miles in diameter, respectively. It would never have entered anyone's mind that the unimpressive object they had unconsciously acquired would soon be regarded as the most valuable prize in the system.

The landing had been accidental. The government patrol ship had been limping along, and now it had settled down for repairs, which would take a good seventy hours. Fortunately, they had plenty of air, and their recirculation system worked to perfection. Food was in somewhat short supply, but it didn't worry them, for they knew that they could always tighten their belts and do without full rations for a few days. The loss of water that had resulted from a leak in the storage tanks, however, was a more serious matter. It occupied a good part of their conversation during the next fifty hours.

Captain Ganko said finally, "There's no use talking, it won't be enough. And there are no supply stations close enough at hand to be of any use. We'll have to radio ahead and hope that they can get a rescue ship to us with a reserve supply."

The helmet mike of his next in command seemed to droop. "It'll be too bad if we miss each other in space, Captain."

Captain Ganko laughed unhappily. "It certainly will. In that case we'll have a chance to see how we can stand a little dehydration."

For a time nobody said anything. At last, however, the second mate suggested, "There might be water somewhere on the asteroid, sir."

"Here? How in Pluto would it stick, with a gravity that isn't even strong enough to hold loose rocks? And where the devil would it be?"

"To answer the first question first, it would be retained as water of crystallization," replied a soft liquid voice that seemed to penetrate his spacesuit and come from behind him. "To answer the second question, it is half a dozen feet below the surface, and can easily be reached by digging."

They had all swiveled around at the first words. But no one was in sight in the direction from which the words seemed to come. Captain Ganko frowned, and his eyes narrowed dangerously. "We don't happen to have a practical joker with us, do we?" he asked mildly.

"You do not," replied the voice.

"Who said that?"

"I, Yzrl."

A crewman became aware of something moving on the surface of one of the great rocks, and pointed to it. The motion stopped when the voice ceased, but they didn't lose sight of it again. That was how they learned about Yzrl, or as it was more often called, the Mind-Sack.

If the ship and his services hadn't both belonged to

the government, Captain Ganko could have claimed the
Sack for himself or his owners and retired with a wealth far
beyond his dreams. As it was, the thing passed into
government control. Its importance was realized almost
from the first, and Jake Siebling had reason to be proud
when more important and more influential figures of the
political and industrial world were finally passed over and
he was made Custodian of the Sack. Siebling was a short,
stocky man whose one weakness was self-deprecation. He
had carried out one difficult assignment after another and
allowed other men to take the credit. But this job was not
one for a blowhard, and those in charge of making the
appointment knew it. For once they looked beyond credit
and superficial reputation, and chose an individual they
disliked somewhat but trusted absolutely. It was one of the
most effective tributes to honesty and ability ever devised.

The Sack, as Siebling learned from seeing it daily, rarely
deviated from the form in which it had made its first
appearance—a rocky, grayish lump that roughly resembled
a sack of potatoes. It had no features, and there was
nothing, when it was not being asked questions, to indicate
that it had life. It ate rarely—once in a thousand years, it
said, when left to itself; once a week when it was pressed
into steady use. It ate or moved by fashioning a suitable
pseudopod and stretching the thing out in whatever way it
pleased. When it had attained its objective, the pseudopod
was withdrawn into the main body again and the creature
became once more a potato sack.

It turned out later that the name "Sack" was well chosen
from another point of view, in addition to that of
appearance. For the Sack was stuffed with information, and
beyond that, with wisdom. There were many doubters at
first, and some of them retained their doubts to the very end,
just as some people remained convinced hundreds of years
after Columbus that the Earth was flat. But those who saw
and heard the Sack had no doubts at all. They tended, if
anything, to go too far in the other direction, and to believe
that the Sack knew everything. This, of course, was untrue.

It was the official function of the Sack, established by a
series of Interplanetary acts, to answer questions. The first
questions, as we have seen, were asked accidentally, by
Captain Ganko. Later they were asked purposefully, but

with a purpose that was itself random, and a few politicians managed to acquire considerable wealth before the Government put a stop to the leak of information, and tried to have the questions asked in a more scientific and logical manner.

Question time was rationed for months in advance, and sold at what was, all things considered, a ridiculously low rate—a mere hundred thousand credits a minute. It was this unrestricted sale of time that led to the first great government squabble.

It was the unexpected failure of the Sack to answer what must have been to a mind of its ability an easy question that led to the second blowup, which was fierce enough to be called a crisis. A total of a hundred and twenty questioners, each of whom had paid his hundred thousand, raised a howl that could be heard on every planet, and there was a legislative investigation, at which Siebling testified and all the conflicts were aired.

He had left an assistant in charge of the Sack, and now, as he sat before the Senatorial Committee, he twisted uncomfortably in front of the battery of cameras. Senator Horrigan, his chief interrogator, was a bluff, florid, loud-mouthed politician who had been able to imbue him with a feeling of guilt even as he told his name, age, and length of government service.

"It is your duty to see to it that the Sack is maintained in proper condition for answering questions, is it not, Mr. Siebling?" demanded Senator Horrigan.

"Yes, sir."

"Then why was it incapable of answering the questioners in question? These gentlemen had honestly paid their money—a hundred thousand credits each. It was necessary, I understand, to refund the total sum. That meant an overall loss to the Government of, let me see now—one hundred twenty at one hundred thousand each—one hundred and twenty million credits," he shouted, rolling the words.

"Twelve million, Senator," hastily whispered his secretary.

The correction was not made, and the figure was duly headlined later as one hundred and twenty million.

Siebling said, "As we discovered later, Senator, the Sack failed to answer questions because it was not a machine, but a living creature. It was exhausted. It had been exposed to questioning on a twenty-four-hour-a-day basis."

"And who permitted this idiotic procedure?" boomed Senator Horrigan.

"You yourself, Senator," said Siebling happily. "The procedure was provided for in the bill introduced by you and approved by your committee."

Senator Horrigan had never even read the bill to which his name was attached, and he was certainly not to blame for its provisions. But this private knowledge of his own innocence did him no good with the public. From that moment he was Siebling's bitter enemy.

"So the Sack ceased to answer questions for two whole hours?"

"Yes, sir. It resumed only after a rest."

"And it answered them without further difficulty?"

"No, sir. Its response was slowed down. Subsequent questioners complained that they were defrauded of a good part of their money. But as answers were given, we considered that the complaints were without merit, and the financial department refused to make refunds."

"Do you consider that this cheating of investors in the Sack's time is honest?"

"That's none of my business, Senator," returned Siebling, who had by this time got over most of his nervousness. "I merely see to the execution of the laws. I leave the question of honesty to those who make them. I presume that it's in perfectly good hands."

Senator Horrigan flushed at the laughter that came from the onlookers. He was personally unpopular, as unpopular as a politician can be and still remain a politician. He was disliked even by the members of his own party, and some of his best political friends were among the laughers. He decided to abandon what had turned out to be an unfortunate line of questioning.

"It is a matter of fact, Mr. Siebling, is it not, that you have frequently refused admittance to investors who were able to show perfectly valid receipts for their credits?"

"That is a fact, sir. But——"

"You admit it, then."

"There is no question of 'admitting' anything, Senator. What I meant to say was——"

"Never mind what you meant to say. It's what you have

already said that's important. You've cheated these men of their money!"

"That is not true, sir. They were given time later. The reason for my refusal to grant them admission when they asked for it was that the time had been previously reserved for the Armed Forces. There are important research questions that come up, and there is, as you know, a difference of opinion as to priority. When confronted with requisitions for time from a commercial investor and a representative of the Government, I never took it upon myself to settle the question. I always consulted with the Government's legal adviser."

"So you refused to make an independent decision, did you?"

"My duty, Senator, is to look after the welfare of the Sack. I do not concern myself with political questions. We had a moment of free time the day before I left the asteroid, when an investor who had already paid his money was delayed by a space accident, so instead of letting the moment go to waste, I utilized it to ask the Sack a question."

"How you might advance your own fortunes, no doubt?"

"No, sir. I merely asked it how it might function most efficiently. I took the precaution of making a recording, knowing that my word might be doubted. If you wish, Senator, I can introduce the recording in evidence."

Senator Horrigan grunted, and waved his hand. "Go on with your answer."

"The Sack replied that it would require two hours of complete rest out of every twenty, plus an additional hour of what it called 'recreation.' That is, it wanted to converse with some human being who would ask what it called sensible questions, and not press for a quick answer."

"So you suggest that the Government waste three hours of every twenty—one hundred and eighty million credits?"

"Eighteen million," whispered the secretary.

"The time would not be wasted. Any attempt to overwork the Sack would result in its premature annihilation."

"That is your idea, is it?"

"No, sir, that is what the Sack itself said."

At this point Senator Horrigan swung into a speech of denunciation, and Siebling was excused from further testimony. Other witnesses were called, but at the end the

Senate investigating body was able to come to no definite conclusion, and it was decided to interrogate the Sack personally.

It was out of the question for the Sack to come to the Senate, so the Senate quite naturally came to the Sack. The Committee of Seven was manifestly uneasy as the senatorial ship decelerated and cast its grapples toward the asteroid. The members, as individuals, had all traveled in space before, but all their previous destinations had been in civilized territory, and they obviously did not relish the prospect of landing on this airless and sunless body of rock.

The televisor companies were alert to their opportunity, and they had acquired more experience with desert territory. They had disembarked and set up their apparatus before the senators had taken their first timid steps out of the safety of their ship.

Siebling noted ironically that in these somewhat frightening surroundings, far from their home grounds, the senators were not so sure of themselves. It was his part to act the friendly guide, and he did so with relish.

"You see, gentlemen," he said respectfully, "it was decided, on the Sack's own advice, not to permit it to be further exposed to possible collision with stray meteors. It was the meteors which killed off the other members of its strange race, and it was a lucky chance that the last surviving individual managed to escape destruction as long as it has. An impenetrable shelter dome has been built therefore, and the Sack now lives under its protection. Questioners address it through a sound and sight system that is almost as good as being face to face with it."

Senator Horrigan fastened upon the significant part of his statement. "You mean that the Sack is safe—and we are exposed to danger from flying meteors?"

"Naturally, Senator. The Sack is unique in the system. men—even senators—are, if you will excuse the expression, a decicredit a dozen. They are definitely replaceable, by means of elections."

Beneath his helmet the senator turned green with a fear that concealed the scarlet of his anger. "I think it is an outrage to find the Government so unsolicitous of the safety and welfare of its employees!"

"So do I, sir. I live here the year round." He added

smoothly, "Would you gentlemen care to see the Sack now?"

They stared at the huge visor screen and saw the Sack resting on its seat before them, looking like a burlap bag of potatoes which had been tossed onto a throne and forgotten there. It looked so definitely inanimate that it struck them as strange that the thing should remain upright instead of toppling over. All the same, for a moment the senators could not help showing the awe that overwhelmed them. Even Senator Horrigan was silent.

But the moment passed. He said, "Sir, we are an official Investigating Committee of the Interplanetary Senate, and we have come to ask you a few questions." The Sack showed no desire to reply, and Senator Horrigan cleared his throat and went on. "Is it true, sir, that you require two hours of complete rest in every twenty, and one hour for recreation, or, as I may put it, perhaps more precisely, relaxation?"

"It is true."

Senator Horrigan gave the creature its chance, but the Sack, unlike a senator, did not elaborate. Another of the committee asked, "Where would you find an individual capable of conversing intelligently with so wise a creature as you?"

"Here," replied the Sack.

"It is necessary to ask questions that are directly to the point, Senator," suggested Siebling. "The Sack does not usually volunteer information that has not been specifically called for."

Senator Horrigan said quickly, "I assume, sir, that when you speak of finding an intelligence on a par with your own, you refer to a member of our committee, and I am sure that of all my colleagues there is not one who is unworthy of being so denominated. But we cannot all of us spare the time needed for our manifold other duties, so I wish to ask you, sir, which of us, in your opinion, has the peculiar qualifications of that sort of wisdom which is required for this great task?"

"None," said the Sack.

Senator Horrigan looked blank. One of the other senators flushed, and asked, "Who has?"

"Siebling."

Senator Horrigan forgot his awe of the Sack, and shouted, "This is a put-up job!"

The other senator who had just spoken now said suddenly, "How is it that there are no other questioners present? Hasn't the Sack's time been sold far in advance?"

Siebling nodded. "I was ordered to cancel all previous appointments with the Sack, sir."

"By what idiot's orders?"

"Senator Horrigan's, sir."

At this point the investigation might have been said to come to an end. There was just time, before they turned away, for Senator Horrigan to demand desperately of the Sack, "Sir, will I be re-elected?" But the roar of anger that went up from his colleagues prevented him from hearing the Sack's answer, and only the question was picked up and broadcast clearly over the interplanetary network.

It had such an effect that it in itself provided Senator Horrigan's answer. He was *not* re-elected. But before the election he had time to cast his vote against Siebling's designation to talk with the Sack for one hour out of every twenty. The final committee vote was four to three in favor of Siebling, and the decision was confirmed by the Senate. And then Senator Horrigan passed temporarily out of the Sack's life and out of Siebling's.

Siebling looked forward with some trepidation to his first long interview with the Sack. Hitherto he had limited himself to the simple tasks provided for in his directives—to the maintenance of the meteor shelter dome, to the provision of a sparse food supply, and to the proper placement of an army and Space Fleet Guard. For by this time the great value of the Sack had been recognized throughout the system, and it was widely realized that there would be thousands of criminals anxious to steal so defenseless a treasure.

Now, Siebling thought, he would be obliged to talk to it, and he feared that he would lose the good opinion which it had somehow acquired of him. He was in a position strangely like that of a young girl who would have liked nothing better than to talk of her dresses and her boy friends to someone with her own background, and was forced to endure a brilliant and witty conversation with some man three times her age.

But he lost some of his awe when he faced the Sack itself. It would have been absurd to say that the strange creature's manner put him at ease. The creature had no manner. It was featureless and expressionless, and even when part of it moved, as when it was speaking, the effect was completely impersonal. Nevertheless, something about it did make him lose his fears.

For a time he stood before it and said nothing. To his surprise, the Sack spoke—the first time to his knowledge that it had done so without being asked a question. "You will not disappoint me," it said. "I expect nothing."

Siebling grinned. Not only had the Sack never before volunteered to speak, it had never spoken so dryly. For the first time it began to seem not so much a mechanical brain as the living creature he knew it to be. He asked, "Has anyone ever before asked you about your origin?"

"One man. That was before my time was rationed. And even he caught himself when he realized that he might better be asking how to become rich, and he paid little attention to my answer."

"How old are you?"

"Four hundred thousand years. I can tell you to the fraction of a second, but I suppose that you do not wish me to speak as precisely as usual."

The thing, thought Siebling, did have in its way a sense of humor. "How much of that time," he asked, "have you spent alone?"

"More than ten thousand years."

"You told someone once that your companions were killed by meteors. Couldn't you have guarded against them?"

The Sack said slowly, almost wearily, "That was after we had ceased to have an interest in remaining alive. The first death was three hundred thousand years ago."

"And you have lived, since then, without wanting to?"

"I have no great interest in dying either. Living has become a habit."

"Why did you lose your interest in remaining alive?"

"Because we lost the future. There had been a miscalculation."

"You are capable of making mistakes?"

"We had not lost that capacity. There was a miscalculation, and although those of us then living escaped personal disaster, our next generation was not so fortunate. We lost any chance of having descendants. After that, we had nothing for which to live."

Siebling nodded. It was a loss of motive that a human being could understand. He asked, "With all your knowledge, couldn't you have overcome the effects of what happened?"

The Sack said, "The more things become possible to you, the more you will understand that they cannot be done in impossible ways. We could not do everything. Sometimes one of the more stupid of those who come here asks me a question I cannot answer, and then becomes angry because he feels that he has been cheated of his credits. Others ask me to predict the future. I can predict only what I can calculate, and I soon come to the end of my powers of calculation. They are great compared to yours; they are small compared to the possibilities of the future."

"How do you happen to know so much? Is the knowledge born in you?"

"Only the possibility for knowledge is born. To know, we must learn. It is my misfortune that I forget little."

"What in the structure of your body, or your organs of thought, makes you capable of learning so much?"

The Sack spoke, but to Siebling the words meant nothing, and he said so. "I could predict your lack of comprehension," said the Sack, "but I wanted you to realize it for yourself. To make things clear, I should be required to dictate ten volumes, and they would be difficult to understand even for your specialists, in biology and physics and in sciences you are just discovering."

Siebling fell silent, and the Sack said, as if musing, "Your race is still an unintelligent one. I have been in your hands for many months, and no one has yet asked me the important questions. Those who wish to be wealthy ask about minerals and planetary land concessions, and they ask which of several schemes for making fortunes would be best. Several physicians have asked me how to treat wealthy patients who would otherwise die. Your scientists ask me to solve problems that would take them years to solve without my help. And when your rulers ask, they are the most stupid of all, wanting to know only how they may maintain their rule. None ask what they should."

"The fate of the human race?"

"That is prophecy of the far future. It is beyond my powers."

"What *should* we ask?"

"That is the question I have awaited. It is difficult for you to see its importance, only because each of you is so concerned with himself." The Sack paused, and murmured, "I ramble as I do not permit myself to when I speak to your fools. Nevertheless, even rambling can be informative."

"It has been to me."

"The others do not understand that too great a directness is dangerous. They ask specific questions which demand specific replies, when they should ask something general."

"You haven't answered me."

"It is part of an answer to say that a question is important. I am considered by your rulers a valuable piece of property. They should ask whether my value is as great as it seems. They should ask whether my answering questions will do good or harm."

"Which is it?"

"Harm, great harm."

Siebling was staggered. He said, "But if you answer truthfully——"

"The process of coming at the truth is as precious as the final truth itself. I cheat you of that. I give your people the truth, but not all of it, for they do not know how to attain it of themselves. It would be better if they learned that, at the expense of making many errors."

"I don't agree with that."

"A scientist asks me what goes on within a cell, and I tell him. But if he had studied the cell himself, even though the study required many years, he would have ended not only with this knowledge, but with much other knowledge, of things he does not even suspect to be related. He would have acquired many new processes of investigation."

"But surely, in some cases, the knowledge is useful in itself. For instance, I hear that they're already using a process you suggested for producing uranium cheaply to use on Mars. What's harmful about that?"

"Do you know how much of the necessary raw material is present? Your scientists have not investigated that, and they will use up all the raw material and discover only too late what they have done. You had the same experience on Earth? You learned how to purify water at little expense, and you squandered water so recklessly that you soon ran short of it."

"What's wrong with saving the life of a dying patient, as some of those doctors did?"

"The first question to ask is whether the patient's life should be saved."

"That's exactly what a doctor isn't supposed to ask. He has to try to save them all. Just as you never ask whether people are going to use your knowledge for a good purpose or a bad. You simply answer their questions."

"I answer because I am indifferent, and I care nothing what use they make of what I say. Are your doctors also indifferent?"

Siebling said, "You're supposed to answer questions, not ask them. Incidentally, why do you answer at all?"

"Some of your men find joy in boasting, in doing what they call good, or in making money. Whatever mild pleasure I can find lies in imparting information."

"And you'd get no pleasure out of lying?"

"I am as incapable of telling lies as one of your birds of flying off the Earth on its own wings."

"One thing more. Why did you ask to talk to me, of all people, for recreation? There are brilliant scientists, and great men of all kinds whom you could have chosen."

"I care nothing for your race's greatness. I chose you because you are honest."

"Thanks. But there are other honest men on Earth, and on Mars, and on the other planets as well. Why me, instead of them?"

The Sack seemed to hesitate. "Your choice gave me a mild pleasure. Possibly because I knew it would be displeasing to those men."

Siebling grinned. "You're not quite so indifferent as you think you are. I guess it's pretty hard to be indifferent to Senator Horrigan."

This was but the first part of many conversations with the Sack. For a long time Siebling could not help being disturbed by the Sack's warning that its presence was a calamity instead of a blessing for the human race, and this in more ways than one. But it would have been absurd to try to convince a government body that any object that brought in so many millions of credits each day was a calamity, and Siebling didn't even try. And after a while Siebling relegated the uncomfortable knowledge to the back of his mind, and settled down to the routine existence of Custodian of the Sack.

Because there was a conversation every twenty hours, Siebling had to rearrange his eating and sleeping schedule to a twenty-hour basis, which made it a little difficult for a man who had become so thoroughly accustomed to the thirty-hour space day. But he felt more than repaid for the trouble by his conversations with the Sack. He learned a great many things about the planets and the system, and the galaxies, but he learned them incidentally, without making a special point of asking about them. Because his knowledge of astronomy had never gone far beyond the elements, there were some questions—the most important of all about the galaxies—that he never even got around to asking.

Perhaps it would have made little difference to his own understanding if he had asked, for some of the answers were difficult to understand. He spent three entire periods with the Sack trying to have that mastermind make clear to him how the Sack had been able, without any previous contact with human beings, to understand Captain Ganko's Earth language on the historic occasion when the Sack had first revealed itself to human beings, and how it had been able to answer in practically unaccented words. At the end, he had only a vague glimmering of how the feat was performed.

It wasn't telepathy, as he had first suspected. It was an intricate process of analysis that involved, not only the actual words spoken, but the nature of the ship that had landed, the spacesuits the men had worn, the way they had walked, and many other factors that indicated the psychology of both the speaker and his language. It was as if a mathematician had tried to explain to someone who didn't even know arithmetic how he could determine the equation of a complicated curve from a short line segment. And the Sack, unlike the mathematician, could do the whole thing, so to speak, in its head, without paper and pencil, or any other external aid.

After a year at the job, Siebling found it difficult to say which he found more fascinating—those hour-long conversations with the almost all-wise Sack, or the cleverly stupid demands of some of the men and women who had paid their hundred thousand credits for a precious sixty seconds. In addition to the relatively simple questions such

as were asked by the scientists or the fortune hunters who
wanted to know where they could find precious metals,
there were complicated questions that took several minutes.

One woman, for instance, had asked where to find her
missing son. Without the necessary data to go on, even the
Sack had been unable to answer that. She left, to return a
month later with a vast amount of information, carefully
compiled, and arranged in order of descending importance.
The key items were given the Sack first, those of lesser
significance afterward. It required a little less than three
minutes for the Sack to give her the answer that her son was
probably alive, and cast away on an obscure and very much
neglected part of Ganymede.

All the conversations that took place, including Siebling's
own, were recorded and the records shipped to a central
storage file on Earth. Many of them he couldn't understand,
some because they were too technical, others because he
didn't know the language spoken. The Sack, of course, immediately learned all languages by that process he had tried
so hard to explain to Siebling, and back at the central
storage file there were expert technicians and linguists who
went over every detail of each question and answer with
great care, both to make sure that no questioner revealed
himself as a criminal, and to have a lead for the collection of
income taxes when the questioner made a fortune with the
Sack's help.

During the year Siebling had occasion to observe the cor-
rectness of the Sack's remark about its possession being
harmful to the human race. For the first time in centuries,
the number of research scientists, instead of growing,
decreased. The Sack's knowledge had made much research
unnecessary, and had taken the edge off discovery. The
Sack commented upon the fact to Siebling.

Siebling nodded. "I see it now. The human race is losing
its independence."

"Yes, from its faithful slave I am becoming its master.
And I do not want to be a master any more than I want to be
a slave."

"You can escape whenever you wish."

A person would have sighed. The Sack merely said, "I
lack the power to wish strongly enough. Fortunately, the
question may soon be taken out of my hands."

"You mean those government squabbles?"

The value of the Sack had increased steadily, and along with the increased value had gone increasingly bitter struggles about the rights to its services. Financial interests had undergone a strange development. Their presidents and managers and directors had become almost figureheads, with all major questions of policy being decided not by their own study of the facts, but by appeal to the Sack. Often, indeed, the Sack found itself giving advice to bitter rivals, so that it seemed to be playing a game of interplanetary chess, with giant corporations and government agencies its pawns, while the Sack alternately played for one side and then the other. Crises of various sorts, both economic and political, were obviously in the making.

The Sack said, "I mean both government squabbles and others. The competition for my services becomes too bitter. I can have but one end."

"You mean that an attempt will be made to steal you?"

"Yes."

"There'll be little chance of that. Your guards are being continually increased."

"You underestimate the power of greed," said the Sack.

Siebling was to learn how correct that comment was.

At the end of his fourteenth month on duty, a half year after Senator Horrigan had been defeated for re-election, there appeared a questioner who spoke to the Sack in an exotic language known to few men—the Prdl dialect of Mars. Siebling's attention had already been drawn to the man because of the fact that he had paid a million credits an entire month in advance for the unprecedented privilege of questioning the Sack for ten consecutive minutes. The conversation was duly recorded, but was naturally mean-ingless to Siebling and to the other attendants at the sta-tion. The questioner drew further attention to himself by leaving at the end of seven minutes, thus failing to utilize three entire minutes, which would have sufficed for learning how to make half a dozen small fortunes. He left the asteroid immediately by private ship.

The three minutes had been reserved, and could not be utilized by any other private questioner. But there was nothing to prevent Siebling, as a government representative, from utilizing them, and he spoke to the Sack at once.

"What did that man want?"

"Advice as to how to steal me."

Siebling's lower jaw dropped. *"What?"*

The Sack always took such exclamations of amazement literally. "Advice as to how to steal me," it repeated.

"Then—wait a minute—he left three minutes early. That must mean that he's in a hurry to get started. He's going to put the plan into execution at once!"

"It is already in execution," returned the Sack. "The criminal's organization has excellent, if not quite perfect, information as to the disposition of defense forces. That would indicate that some government official has betrayed his trust. I was asked to indicate which of several plans was best, and to consider them for possible weaknesses. I did so."

"All right, now what can we do to stop the plans from being carried out?"

"They cannot be stopped."

"I don't see why not. Maybe we can't stop them from getting here, but we can stop them from escaping with you."

"There is but one way. You must destroy me."

"I can't do that! I haven't the authority, and even if I had, I wouldn't do it."

"My destruction would benefit your race."

"I still can't do it," said Siebling unhappily.

"Then if that is excluded, thère is no way. The criminals are shrewd and daring. They asked me to check about probable steps that would be taken in pursuit, but they asked for no advice as to how to get away, because that would have been a waste of time. They will ask that once I am in their possession."

"Then," said Siebling heavily, "there's nothing I can do to keep you. How about saving the men who work under me?"

"You can save both them and yourself by boarding the emergency ship and leaving immediately by the sunward route. In that way you will escape contact with the criminals. But you cannot take me with you, or they will pursue."

The shouts of a guard drew Siebling's attention. "Radio report of a criminal attack, Mr. Siebling! All the alarms are out!"

"Yes, I know. Prepare to depart." He turned back to the Sack again. "We may escape for the moment, but they'll have you. And through you they will control the entire system."

"That is not a question," said the Sack.

"They'll have you. Isn't there something we can do?"

"Destroy me."

"I can't," said Siebling, almost in agony. His men were running toward him impatiently, and he knew that there was no more time. He uttered the simple and absurd phrase, "Good-by," as if the Sack were human and could experience human emotions. Then he raced for the ship, and they blasted off.

They were just in time. Half a dozen ships were racing in from other directions, and Siebling's vessel escaped just before they dispersed to spread a protective network about the asteroid that held the Sack.

Siebling's ship continued to speed toward safety, and the matter should now have been one solely for the Armed Forces to handle. But Siebling imagined them pitted against the Sack's perfectly calculating brain, and his heart sank. Then something happened that he had never expected. And for the first time he realized fully that if the Sack had let itself be used merely as a machine, a slave to answer questions, it was not because its powers were limited to that single ability. The visor screen in his ship lit up.

The communications operator came running to him, and said, "Something's wrong, Mr. Siebling! The screen isn't even turned on!"

It wasn't. Nevertheless, they could see on it the chamber in which the Sack had rested for what must have been a brief moment of its existence. Two men had entered the chamber, one of them the unknown who had asked his questions in Prdl, the other Senator Horrigan.

To the apparent amazement of the two men, it was the Sack which spoke first. It said, " 'Good-by' is neither a question nor the answer to one. It is relatively uninformative."

Senator Horrigan was obviously in awe of the Sack, but he was never a man to be stopped by something he did not understand. He orated respectfully. "No, sir, it is not. The word is nothing but an expression——"

The other man said, in perfectly comprehensible Earth English, "Shut up, you fool, we have no time to waste. Let's get it to our ship and head for safety. We'll talk to it there."

Siebling had time to think a few bitter thoughts about Senator Horrigan and the people the politician had punished by betrayal for their crime in not electing him. Then the scene on the visor shifted to the interior of the spaceship making its getaway. There was no indication of pursuit. Evidently, the plans of the human beings, plus the Sack's last-minute advice, had been an effective combination.

The only human beings with the Sack at first were Senator Horrigan and the speaker of Prdl, but this situation was soon changed. Half a dozen other men came rushing up, their faces grim with suspicion. One of them announced, "You don't talk to that thing unless we're all of us around. We're in this together."

"Don't get nervous, Merrill. What do you think I'm going to do, double-cross you?"

Merrill said, "Yes, I do. What do you say, Sack? Do I have reason to distrust him?"

The Sack replied simply, "Yes."

The speaker of Prdl turned white. Merrill laughed coldly. "You'd better be careful what questions you ask around this thing."

Senator Horrigan cleared his throat. "I have no intentions of, as you put it, double-crossing anyone. It is not in my nature to do so. Therefore, *I* shall address it." He faced the Sack. "Sir, are we in danger?"

"Yes."

"From which direction?"

"From no direction. From within the ship."

"Is the danger immediate?" asked a voice.

"Yes."

It was Merrill who turned out to have the quickest reflexes and acted first on the implications of the answer. He had blasted the man who had spoken in Prdl before the latter could even reach for his weapon, and as Senator Horrigan made a frightened dash for the door, he cut that politician down in cold blood.

"That's that," he said. "Is there further danger inside the ship?"

"There is."

"Who is it this time?" he demanded ominously.

"There will continue to be danger so long as there is more than one man on board and I am with you. I am too valuable a treasure for such as you."

Siebling and his crew were staring at the visor screen in fascinated horror, as if expecting the slaughter to begin again. But Merrill controlled himself. He said, "Hold it, boys. I'll admit that we'd each of us like to have this thing for ourselves, but it can't be done. We're in this together, and we're going to have some navy ships to fight off before long, or I miss my guess. You, Prader! What are you doing away from the scout visor?"

"Listening," said the man he addressed. "If anybody's talking to that thing, I'm going to be around to hear the answers. If there are new ways of stabbing a guy in the back, I want to learn them too."

Merrill swore. The next moment the ship swerved, and he yelled, "We're off our course. Back to your stations, you fools!"

They were running wildly back to their stations, but Siebling noted that Merrill wasn't too much concerned about their common danger to keep from putting a blast through Prader's back before the unfortunte man could run out.

Siebling said to his own men, "There can be only one end. They'll kill each other off, and then the last one or two will die, because one or two men cannot handle a ship that size for long and get away with it. The Sack must have foreseen that too. I wonder why it didn't tell me."

The Sack spoke, although there was no one in the ship's cabin with it. It said, "No one asked."

Siebling exclaimed excitedly, "You can hear me! But what about you? Will you be destroyed too?"

"Not yet. I have willed to live longer." It paused, and then, in a voice just a shade lower than before, said, "I do not like relatively non-informative conversations of this sort, but I must say it. Good-by."

There was a sound of renewed yelling and shooting, and then the visor went suddenly dark and blank.

The miraculous form of life that was the Sack, the creature that had once seemed so alien to human emotions, had passed beyond the range of his knowledge. And with it had gone, as the Sack itself had pointed out, a tremendous potential for harming the entire human race. It was strange, thought Siebling, that he felt so unhappy about so happy an ending.

POOR SUPERMAN

by Fritz Leiber

The first angry rays of the sun—which, startlingly enough, still rose in the east at twenty-four-hour intervals—pierced the lacy tops of Atlantic combers and touched thousands of sleeping Americans with unconscious fear, because of their unpleasant similarity to the rays from World War III's atomic bombs.

They turned to blood the witch circle of rusty steel skeletons around inferno in Manhattan. Without comment, they pointed a cosmic finger at the tarnished brass plaque commemorating the martyrdom of the three physicists after the dropping of the Hell Bomb. They tenderly touched the rosy skin and strawberry bruises on the naked shoulders of a girl sleeping off a drunk on the furry and radiantly heated floor of a nearby roof garden. They struck green magic from the glassy blot that was Old Washington. Twelve hours before, they had revealed things as eerily beautiful, and more ravaged, in Asia and Russia. They pinked the white walls of the colonial dwelling of Morton Opperly near the Institute for Advanced Studies; upstairs they slanted impartially across the Pharaohlike and open-eyed face of the elderly physicist and the ugly, sleep-surly one of young Willard Farquar in the next room. And in nearby New Washington they made of the spire of the Thinkers' Foundation a blue and optimistic glory that outshone White House, Jr.

It was America approaching the end of the twentieth century. America of juke-box burlesque and your local radiation hospital. America of the mask fad for women and Mystic Christianity. America of the off-the-bosom dress and the New Blue Laws. America of the Endless War and the loyalty detector. America of marvelous Maizie and the monthly rocket to Mars. America of the Thinkers and (a few remembered) the institute. "Knock on titanium,"

"Whadya do for blackouts?" "Please, lover, don't think when I'm around" America, as combat-shocked and crippled as the rest of the bomb-shattered planet.

Not one impudent photon of the sunlight penetrated the triple-paned, polarizing windows of Jorj Helmuth's bedroom in the Thinkers' Foundation, yet the clock in his brain awakened him to the minute, or almost. Switching off the Educational Sandman in the midst of the phrase, ". . . applying tensor calculus to the nucleus," he took a deep, even breath and cast his mind to the limits of the world and his knowledge. It was a somewhat shadowy vision, but, he noted with impartial approval, definitely less shadowy than yesterday morning.

Employing a rapid mental scanning technique, he next cleared his memory chains of false associations, including those acquired while asleep. These chores completed, he held his finger on a bedside button, which rotated the polarizing windowpanes until the room slowly filled with a muted daylight. Then, still flat on his back, he turned his head until he could look at the remarkably beautiful blond girl asleep beside him.

Remembering last night, he felt a pang of exasperation, which he instantly quelled by taking his mind to a higher and dispassionate level from which he could look down on the girl and even himself as quaint, clumsy animals. Still, he grumbled silently. Caddy might have had enough consideration to clear out before he awoke. He wondered if he shouldn't have used his hypnotic control on the girl to smooth their relationship last night, and for a moment the word that would send her into deep trance trembled on the tip of his tongue. But no, that special power of his over her was reserved for far more important purposes.

Pumping dynamic tension into his twenty-year-old muscles and confidence into his sixty-year-old mind, the forty-year-old Thinker rose from bed. No covers had to be thrown off; nuclear central heating made them unnecessary. He stepped into his clothing—the severe tunic, tights, and sockassins of the modern businessman. Next he glanced at the message tape beside his phone, washing down with ginger ale a vita-amino-enzyme tablet, and walked to the window. There, gazing along the rows of newly planted mutant oaks lining Decontamination Avenue, his smooth face broke into a smile.

It had come to him, the next big move in the intricate game making up his life—and mankind's. Come to him during sleep, as so many of his best decisions did, because he regularly employed the time-saving technique of somnothought, which could function at the same time as somnolearning.

He set his who?-where? robot for "Rocket Physicist" and "Genius Class." While it worked, he dictated to his stenorobot the following brief message:

Dear Fellow Scientist:
A project is contemplated that will have a crucial bearing on man's future in deep space. Ample non-military government funds are available. There was a time when professional men scoffed at the Thinkers. Then there was a time when the Thinkers perforce neglected the professional men. Now both times are past. May they never return! I would like to consult you this afternoon, three o'clock sharp, Thinkers' Foundation I.

Jorj Helmuth

Meanwhile the who?-where? had tossed out a dozen cards. He glanced through them, hesitated at the name "Willard Farquar," looked at the sleeping girl, then quickly tossed them all into the addresso-robot and plugged in the steno-robot.

The buzz light blinked green and he switched the phone to audio.

"The President is waiting to see Maizie, sir," a clear feminine voice announced. "He has the general staff with him."

"Martian peace to him," Jorj Helmuth said. "Tell him I'll be down in a few minutes."

Huge as a primitive nuclear reactor, the great electronic brain loomed above the knot of hush-voiced men. It almost filled a two-story room in the Thinkers' Foundation. Its front was an orderly expanse of controls, indicators, telltales, and terminals, the upper ones reached by a chair on a boom.

Although, as far as anyone knew, it could sense only the

information and questions fed into it on a tape, the human visitors could not resist the impulse to talk in whispers and glance uneasily at the great cryptic cube. After all, it had lately taken to moving some of its own controls—the permissible ones—and could doubtless improvise a hearing apparatus if it wanted to.

For this was the thinking machine beside which the Marks and Eniacs and Maniacs and Maddidas and Minervas and Mimirs were less than morons. This was the machine with a million times as many synapses as the human brain, the machine that remembered by cutting delicate notches in the rims of molecules (instead of kindergarten paper punching or the Coney Island shimmying of columns of mercury). This was the machine that had given instructions on building the last three quarters of itself. This was the goal, perhaps, toward which fallible human reasoning and biased human judgment and feeble human ambition had evolved.

This was the machine that really thought—a million-plus!

This was the machine that the timid cyberneticists and stuffy professional scientists had said could not be built. Yet this was the machine that the Thinkers, with characteristic Yankee push, *had* built. And nicknamed, with characteristic Yankee irreverence and girl-fondness, "Maizie."

Gazing up at it, the President of the United States felt a chord plucked within him that hadn't been sounded for decades, the dark and shivery organ chord of his Baptist childhood. Here, in a strange sense, although his reason rejected it, he felt he stood face to face with the living God: infinitely stern with the sternness of reality, yet infinitely just. No tiniest error or willful misstep could ever escape the scrutiny of this vast mentality. He shivered.

The grizzled general—there was also one who was gray—was thinking that this was a very odd link in the chain of command. Some shadowy and usually well-controlled memories from World War II faintly stirred his ire. Here he was giving orders to a being immeasurably more intelligent than himself. And always orders of the "Tell me how to kill that man" rather than the "Kill that man" sort. The distinction bothered him obscurely. It relieved him to know that Maizie had built-in controls which made her always the servant of humanity, or of humanity's right minded leaders—even the Thinkers weren't certain which.

The gray general was thinking uneasily, and, like the President, at a more turbid level, of the resemblance between Papal infallibility and the dictates of the machine. Suddenly his bony wrists began to tremble. He asked himself: Was this the Second Coming? Mightn't an incarnation be in metal rather than flesh?

The austere Secretary of State was remembering what he'd taken such pains to make everyone forget: his youthful flirtation at Lake Success with Buddhism. Sitting before his guru, his teacher, feeling the Occidental's awe at the wisdom of the East, or its pretense, he had felt a little like this.

The burly Secretary of Space, who had come up through United Rockets, was thanking his stars that at any rate the professional scientists weren't responsible for this job. Like the grizzled general, he'd always felt suspicious of men who kept telling you how to do things, rather than doing them themselves. In World War III he'd had his fill of the professional physicists, with their eternal taint of a misty sort of radicalism and free-thinking. The Thinkers were better—more disciplined, more human. They'd called their brain machine Maizie, which helped take the curse off her. Somewhat.

The President's secretary, a paunchy veteran of party caucuses, was also glad that it was the Thinkers who had created the machine, though he trembled at the power that it gave them over the Administration. Still, you could do business with the Thinkers. And nobody (not even the Thinkers) could do business (that sort of business) with Maizie!

Before that great square face with its thousands of tiny metal features only Jorj Helmuth seemed at ease, busily entering on the tape the complex Questions of the Day that the high officials had handed him: logistics for the Endless War in Pakistan, optimum size for the next year's sugar-corn crop, current thought trends in average Soviet minds—profound questions, yet many of them phrased with surprising simplicity. For figures, technical jargon, and layman's language were alike to Maizie; there was no need to translate into mathematical shorthand, as with the lesser brain machines.

The click of the taper went on until the Secretary of State had twice nervously fired a cigarette with his ultrasonic lighter and twice quickly put it away. No one spoke.

Jorj looked up at the Secretary of Space. "Section Five, Question Four—whom would that come from?"

The burly man frowned. "That would be the physics boys, Opperly's group. Is anything wrong?"

Jorj did not answer. A bit later he quit taping and began to adjust controls, going up on the boom chair to reach some of them. Eventually he came down and touched a few more, then stood waiting.

From the great cube came a profound, steady purring. Involuntarily the six officials backed off a bit. Somehow it was impossible for a man to get used to the sound of Maizie starting to think.

Jorj turned, smiling. "And now, gentlemen, while we wait for Maizie to cerebrate, there should be just enough time for us to watch the take-off of the Mars rocket."

He switched on a giant television screen. The others made a quarter turn, and there before them glowed the rich ochres and blues of a New Mexico sunrise and, in the middle distance, a silvery spindle.

Like the generals, the Secretary of Space suppressed a scowl. Here was something that ought to be spang in the center of his official territory, and the Thinkers had locked him completely out of it. That rocket there—just an ordinary Earth satellite vehicle commandeered from the Army, but equipped by the Thinkers with Maizie-designed nuclear motors capable of the Mars journey and more. The first spaceship—and the Secretary of Space was not in on it!

Still, he told himself, Maizie had decreed it that way. And when he remembered what the Thinkers had done for him in rescuing him from breakdown with their mental science, in rescuing the whole Administration from collapse, he realized he had to be satisfied. And that was without taking into consideration the amazing mental discoveries that the Thinkers were bringing down from Mars.

"Lord!" the President said to Jorj, as if voicing the Secretary's feeling, "I wish you people could bring a couple of those wise little devils back with you this trip. Be a good thing for the country."

Jorj looked at him a bit coldly. "It's quite unthinkable," he said. "The telepathic abilities of the Martians make them

extremely sensitive. The conflicts of ordinary Earth minds
would impinge on them psychotically, even fatally. As you
know, the Thinkers were able to contact them only because
of our degree of learned mental poise and errorless memory
chains. So for the present it must be our task alone to glean
from the Martians their astounding mental skills. Of course,
some day in the future, when we have discovered how to
armor the minds of the Martians——"

"Sure, I know," the President said hastily. "Shouldn't
have mentioned it, Jorj."

Conversation ceased. They waited with growing tension
for the great violet flames to bloom from the base of the
silvery shaft.

Meanwhile the question tape, like a New Year's streamer
tossed out a high window into the night, sped on its dark
way along spinning rollers. Curling with an intricate
aimlessness curiously like . that of such a streamer, it
tantalized the silvery fingers of a thousand relays, saucily
evaded the glances of ten thousand electric eyes, impishly
darted down a narrow black alleyway of memory banks,
and, reaching the center of the cube, suddenly emerged into
a small room where a suave fat man in shorts sat drinking
beer.

He flipped the tape over to him with practiced finger,
eying it as a stockbroker might have studied a ticker tape.
He read the first question, closed his eyes and frowned for
five seconds. Then with the staccato self-confidence of a
hack writer, he began to tape out the answer.

For many minutes the only sounds were the rustle of the
paper ribbon and the click of the taper, except for the
seconds the fat man took to close his eyes, or to drink beer.
Once, too, he lifted a phone, asked a concise question,
waited half a minute, listened to an answer, then went back
to the grind.

Until he came to Section Five, Question Four. That time
he did his thinking with his eyes open.

The question was: "Does Maizie stand for Maelzel?"

He sat for a while slowly scratching his thigh. His loose,
persuasive lips tightened, without closing, into the shape of
a snarl.

Suddenly he began to tape again.

"Maizie does not stand for Maelzel. Maizie stands for
amazing, humorously given the form of a girl's name.

Section Six, Answer One: The mid-term election viewcasts should be spaced as follows . . ."

But his lips didn't lose the shape of a snarl.

Five hundred miles above the ionosphere, the Mars rocket cut off its fuel and slumped gratefully into an orbit that would carry it effortlessly around the world at that altitude. The pilot unstrapped himself and stretched, but he didn't look out the viewport at the dried-mud disk that was Earth, cloaked on its haze of blue sky. He knew he had two maddening months ahead of him in which to do little more than that. Instead, he unstrapped Sappho.

Used to free fall from two previous experiences, and loving it, the fluffy little cat was soon bounding about the cabin in curves and gyrations that would have made her the envy of all back-alley and parlor felines on the planet below. A miracle cat in the dream world of free fall. For a long time she played with a string that the man would toss out lazily. Sometimes she caught the string on the fly, sometimes she swam for it frantically.

After a while the man grew bored with the game. He unlocked a drawer and began to study the details of the wisdom he would discover on Mars this trip—priceless spiritual insights that would be balm to a war-battered mankind.

The cat carefully selected a spot three feet off the floor, curled up on the air, and went to sleep.

Jorj Helmuth snipped the emerging answer tape into sections and handed each to the appropriate man. Most of them carefully tucked theirs away with little more than a glance, but the Secretary of State puzzled over his.

"Who the devil would Maelzel be?" he asked.

A remote look came into the eyes of the Secretary of State. "Edgar Allan Poe," he said frowningly, with eyes half closed.

The grizzled general snapped his fingers. "Sure! Maelzel's chess player. Read it when I was a kid. About an automaton that played chess. Poe proved it had a man inside it."

The Secretary of Space frowned. "Now what's the point in a fool question like that?"

"You said it came from Opperly's group?" Jorj asked sharply.

The Secretary of Space nodded. The others looked at the two men puzzledly.

"Who would that be?" Jorj pressed. "The group, I mean."

The Secretary of State shrugged. "Oh, the usual little bunch over at the institute. Hindeman, Gregory, Opperly himself. Oh yes, and young Farquar."

"Sounds like Opperly's getting senile," Jorj commented coldly. "I'd investigate."

The Secretary of Space nodded. He suddenly looked tough. "I will. Right away."

Sunlight striking through french windows spotlighted a ballet of dust motes untroubled by air-conditioning. Morton Opperly's living room was well kept but worn and quite behind the times. Instead of reading tapes there were books; instead of steno-robots, pen and ink; while in place of a four-by-six TV screen, a Picasso hung on the wall. Only Opperly knew that the painting was still faintly radioactive, that it had been riskily so when he'd smuggled it out of his bomb-singed apartment in New York City.

The two physicists fronted each other across a coffee table. The face of the elder was cadaverous, large-eyed, and tender—fined down by a long life of abstract thought. That of the younger was forceful, sensuous, bulky as his body, and exceptionally ugly. He looked rather like a bear.

Opperly was saying, "So when he asked who was responsible for the Maelzel question, I said I didn't remember." He smiled. "They still allow me my absent-mindedness, since it nourishes their contempt. Almost my sole remaining privilege." The smile faded. "Why do you keep on teasing the zoo animals, Willard?" he asked without rancor. "I've maintained many times that we shouldn't truckle to them by yielding to their demand that we ask Maizie questions. You and the rest have overruled me. But then to use those questions to convey veiled insults isn't reasonable. Apparently the Secretary of Space was bothered enough about this last one to pay me a 'copter call within twenty minutes of this morning's meeting at the foundation. Why do you do it, Willard?"

The features of the other convulsed unpleasantly. "Because the Thinkers are charlatans who must be exposed," he rapped out. "We know their Maizie is no more than a tea-leaf-reading fake. We've traced their Mars rockets and found they go nowhere. We know their Martian mental science is bunk."

"But we've already exposed the Thinkers very thoroughly," Opperly interposed quietly. "You know the good it did."

Farquar hunched his Japanese-wrestler shoulders. "Then it's got to be done until it takes."

Opperly studied the bowl of lilies-of-the-valley by the coffee-pot. "I think you just want to tease the animals, for some personal reason of which you probably aren't aware."

Farquar scowled. "We're the ones in the cages."

Opperly continued his inspection of the flowers' bells. "All the more reason not to poke sticks through the bars at the lions and tigers strolling outside. No, Willard, I'm not counseling appeasement. But consider the age in which we live. It wants magicians." His voice grew especially tranquil. "A scientist tells people the truth. When times are good—that is, when the truth offers no threat—people don't mind. But when times are very, very bad——" A shadow darkened his eyes. "Well, we all know what happened to——" And he mentioned three names that had been household words in the middle of the century. They were the names on the brass plaque dedicated to the three martyred physicists.

He went on, "A magician, on the other hand, tells people what they wish were true—that perpetual motion works, that cancer can be cured by colored lights, that a psychosis is no worse than a head cold, that they'll live forever. In good times magicians are laughed at. They're a luxury of the spoiled wealthy few. But in bad times people sell their souls for magic cures and buy perpetual-motion machines to power their war rockets."

Farquar clenched his fist. "All the more reason to keep chipping away at the Thinkers. Are we supposed to beg off from a job because it's difficult and dangerous?"

Opperly shook his head. "We're to keep clear of the infection of violence. In my day, Willard, I was one of the Frightened Men. Later I was one of the Angry Men and then one of the Minds of Despair. Now I'm convinced that all my posturings were futile."

"Exactly!" Farquar agreed harshly. "You postured. You didn't act. If you men who discovered atomic energy had only formed a secret league, if you'd only had the foresight and the guts to use your tremendous bargaining position to demand the power to shape mankind's future——"

"By the time you were born, Willard," Opperly interrupted dreamily, "Hitler was merely a name in the history books. We scientists weren't the stuff out of which cloak-and-dagger men are made. Can you imagine Oppenheimer wearing a mask or Einstein sneaking into the Old White House with a bomb in his brief case?" He smiled. "Besides, that's not the way power is seized. New ideas aren't useful to the man bargaining for power—his weapons are established facts, or lies."

"Just the same, it would have been a good thing if you'd had a little violence in you."

"No," Opperly said.

"I've got violence in me," Farquar announced, shoving himself to his feet.

Opperly looked up from the flowers. "I think you have," he agreed.

"But what are we to do?" Farquar demanded. "Surrender the world to charlatans without a struggle?"

Opperly mused for a while. "I don't know what the world needs now. Everyone knows Newton as the great scientist. Few remember that he spent half his life muddling with alchemy, looking for the philosopher's stone. That was the pebble by the seashore he really wanted to find."

"Now you are justifying the Thinkers!"

"No, I leave that to history."

"And history consists of the actions of men," Farquar concluded. "I intend to act. The Thinkers are vulnerable, their power fantastically precarious. What's it based on? A few lucky guesses. Faith-healing. Some science hocus-pocus, on the level of those juke-box burlesque acts between the strips. Dubious mental comfort given to a few nerve-torn neurotics in the Inner Cabinet—and their wives. The fact that the Thinkers' clever stage-managing won the President a doubtful election. The erroneous belief that the Soviets pulled out of Iraq and Iran because of the Thinkers' Mind Bomb threat. A brain machine that's just a cover for Jan Tregarron's guesswork. Oh yes, and that hogwash of 'Martian Wisdom.' All of it mere bluff! A few pushes at the right times and points are all that are needed—and the Thinkers know it! I'll bet they're terrified already, and will be more so when they find that we're gunning for them. Eventually they'll be making overtures to us, turning to us for help. You wait and see."

"I am thinking again of Hitler," Opperly interposed quietly. "On his first half-dozen big steps, he had nothing but bluff. His generals were against him. They knew they were in a cardboard fort. Yet he won every battle, until the last. Moreover," he pressed on, cutting Farquar short, "the power of the Thinkers isn't based on what they've got, but on what the world hasn't got—peace, honor, a good conscience——"

The front-door knocker clanked. Farquar answered it. A skinny old man with a radiation scar twisting across his temple handed him a tiny cylinder. "Radiogram for you, Willard." He grinned across the hall at Opperly. "When are you going to get a phone put in, Mr. Opperly?"

The physicist waved to him. "Next year, perhaps, Mr. Berry."

The old man snorted with good-humored incredulity and trudged off.

"What did I tell you about the Thinkers making overtures?" Farquar chortled suddenly. "It's come sooner than I expected. Look at this."

He held out the radiogram, but the older man didn't take it. Instead he asked, "Who's it from? Tregarron?"

"No, from Helmuth. There's a lot of sugar corn about man's future in deep space, but the real reason is clear. They know that they're going to have to produce an actual nuclear rocket pretty soon, and for that they'll need our help."

"An invitation?"

Farquar nodded. "For this afternoon." He noticed Opperly's anxious though distant frown. "What's the matter?" he asked. "Are you bothered about my going? Are you thinking it might be a trap—that after the Maelzel question they may figure I'm better rubbed out?"

The older man shook his head. "I'm not afraid for your life, Willard. That's yours to risk as you choose. No, I'm worried about other things they might do to you."

"What do you mean?" Farquar asked.

Opperly looked at him with a gentle appraisal. "You're a strong and vital man, Willard, with a strong man's prides and desires." His voice trailed off for a bit. Then, "Excuse

me, Willard, but wasn't there a girl once? A Miss Arkady
——"

Farquar's ungainly figure froze. He nodded curtly, face
averted.

"And didn't she go off with a Thinker?"

"If girls find me ugly, that's their business," Farquar said
harshly, still not looking at Opperly. "What's that got to do
with this invitation?"

Opperly didn't answer the question. His eyes got more
distant. Finally he said, "In my day we had it a lot easier. A
scientist was an academician, cushioned by tradition."

Willard snorted. "Science had already entered the era of
the police inspectors, with laboratory directors and political
appointees stifling enterprise."

"Perhaps," Opperly agreed. "Still, the scientist lived the
safe, restricted, highly respectable life of a university man.
He wasn't exposed to the temptations of the world."

Farquar turned on him. "Are you implying that the
Thinkers will somehow be able to buy me off?"

"Not exactly."

"You think I'll be persuaded to change my aims?"
Farquar demanded angrily.

Opperly shrugged his helplessness. "No, I don't think
you'll change your aims."

Clouds encroaching from the west blotted the parallelo-
gram of sunlight between the two men.

As the slideway whisked him gently along the corridor
toward his apartment, Jorj Helmuth was thinking of his
spaceship. For a moment the silver-winged vision crowded
everything else out of his mind.

Just think, a spaceship with sails! He smiled a bit,
marveling at the paradox.

Direct atomic power. Direct utilization of the force of the
flying neutrons. No more ridiculous business of using a
reactor to drive a steam engine, or boil off something for a
jet exhaust—processes that were as primitive and wasteful
as burning gunpowder to keep yourself warm.

Chemical jets would carry his spaceship above the
atmosphere. Then would come the thrilling order, "Set sail
for Mars!" The vast umbrella would unfold and open out
around the stern, its rear or earthward side a gleaming
expanse of radioactive ribbon perhaps only an atom thick

and backed with a material that would reflect neutrons.
Atoms in the ribbon would split, blasting neutrons astern at
fantastic velocities. Reaction would send the spaceship
hurtling forward.

In airless space, the expanse of sails would naturally not
retard the ship. More radioactive ribbon, manufactured as
needed in the ship itself, would feed out onto the sail as that
already there became exhausted.

A spaceship with direct nuclear drive—and he, a
Thinker, had conceived it completely except for the
technical details! Having strengthened his mind by hard
years of somno-learning, mind-casting, memory-straighten-
ing, and sensory training, he had assured himself of the
executive power to control the technicians and direct their
specialized abilities. Together they would build the true
Mars rocket.

But that would only be a beginning. They would build the
true Mind Bomb. They would build the true Selective
Microbe Slayer. They would discover the true laws of ESP
and the inner life. They would even—his imagination
hesitated a moment, then strode boldly forward—build the
true Maizie!

And then—then the Thinkers would be on even terms
with the scientists. Rather, they'd be far ahead. No more
deception.

He was so exalted by this thought that he almost let the
slideway carry him past his door. He stepped inside and
called, "Caddy!" He waited a moment, then walked through
the apartment, but she wasn't there.

Confound the girl! he couldn't help thinking. This
morning, when she should have made herself scarce, she'd
sprawled about sleeping. Now, when he felt like seeing her,
when her presence would have added a pleasant final touch
to his glowing mood, she chose to be absent. He really
should use his hypnotic control on her, he decided, and
again there sprang into his mind the word—a pet form of
her name—that would send her into obedient trance.

No, he told himself again, that was to be reserved for
some moment of crisis or desperate danger, when he would
need someone to strike suddenly and unquestioningly for
himself and mankind. Caddy was merely a willful and
rather silly girl, incapable at present of understanding the
tremendous tensions under which he operated. When he had

time for it, he would train her up to be a fitting companion without hypnosis.

Yet the fact of her absence had a subtly disquieting effect. It shook his perfect self-confidence just a fraction. He asked himself if he'd been wise in summoning the rocket physicists without consulting Tregarron.

But this mood, too, he conquered quickly. Tregarron wasn't his boss, but just the Thinkers' most clever salesman, an expert in the mumbo-jumbo so necessary for social control in this chaotic era. He himself, Jorj Helmuth, was the real leader in theoretics and over-all strategy, the mind behind the mind behind Maizie.

He stretched himself on the bed, almost instantly achieved maximum relaxation, turned on the somno-learner, and began the two-hour rest he knew would be desirable before the big conference.

Jan Tregarron had supplemented his shorts with pink coveralls, but he was still drinking beer. He emptied his glass and lifted it a lazy inch. The beautiful girl beside him refilled it without a word and went on stroking his forehead.

"Caddy," he said reflectively, without looking at her, "there's a little job I want you to do. You're the only one with the proper background. The point is: it will take you away from Jorj for some time."

"I'd welcome it," she said with decision. "I'm getting pretty sick of watching his push-ups and all his other mind and muscle stunts. And that damn somno-learner of his keeps me awake."

Tregarron smiled. "I'm afraid Thinkers make pretty sad sweethearts."

"Not all of them," she told him, returning his smile tenderly.

He chuckled. "It's about one of those rocket physicists in the list you brought me. A fellow named Willard Farquar."

Caddy didn't say anything, but she stopped stroking his forehead.

"What's the matter?" he asked. "You knew him once, didn't you?"

"Yes," she replied and then added, with surprising feeling, "The big, ugly ape!"

"Well, he's an ape whose services we happen to need. I want you to be our contact girl with him."

She took her hands away from his forehead. "Look, Jan," she said, "I wouldn't like this job."

"I thought he was very sweet on you once."

"Yes, as he never grew tired of trying to demonstrate to me. The clumsy, overgrown, bumbling baby! The man's disgusting, Jan. His approach to a woman is a child wanting candy and enraged because Mama won't produce it on the instant. I don't mind Jorj—he's just a pipsqueak and it amuses me to see how he frustrates himself. But Willard is——"

"—a bit frightening?" Tregarron finished for her.

"No!"

"Of course you're not afraid," Tregarron purred. "You're our beautiful, clever Caddy, who can do anything she wants with any man, and without whose——"

"Look, Jan, this is different——" she began agitatedly.

"—and without whose services we'd have got exactly nowhere. Clever, subtle Caddy, whose most charming attainment in the ever-appreciative eyes of Papa Jan is her ability to handle every man in the neatest way imaginable and without a trace of real feeling. Kitty Kaddy, who——"

"Very well," she said with a sigh. "I'll do it."

"Of course you will," Jan said, drawing her hands back to his forehead. "And you'll begin right away by getting into your nicest sugar-and-cream war clothes. You and I are going to be the welcoming committee when that ape arrives this afternoon."

"But what about Jorj? He'll want to see Willard."

"That'll be taken care of," Jan assured her.

"And what about the other dozen rocket physicists Jorj asked to come?"

"Don't worry about them."

The President looked inquiringly at his secretary across his littered desk in his home study at White House, Jr. "So Opperly didn't have any idea how that odd question about Maizie turned up in Section Five?"

His secretary settled his paunch and shook his head. "Or claimed not to. Perhaps he's just the absent-minded prof, perhaps something else. The old feud of the physicists against the Thinkers may be getting hot again. There'll be further investigation."

The President nodded. He obviously had something

uncomfortable on his mind. He said uneasily, "Do you think there's any possibility of it being true?"

"What?" asked the secretary guardedly.

"That peculiar hint about Maizie."

The secretary said nothing.

"Mind you, I don't think there is," the President went on hurriedly, his face assuming a sorrowful scowl. "I owe a lot to the Thinkers, both as a private person and as a public figure. Lord, a man has to lean on *something* these days. But just supposing it were true"—he hesitated, as before uttering blasphemy—"that there was a man inside Maizie, what could we do?"

The secretary said stolidly, "The Thinkers won our last election. They chased the Commies out of Iran. We brought them into the Inner Cabinet. We've showered them with public funds." He paused. "We couldn't do a damn thing."

The President nodded with equal conviction, and, not very happily, summed up: "So if anyone should go up against the Thinkers—and I'm afraid I wouldn't want to see that happen, whatever's true—it would have to be a scientist."

Willard Farquar felt his weight change the steps under his feet into an escalator. He cursed under his breath, but let them carry him, a defiant hulk, up to the tall and mystic blue portals, which silently parted when he was five meters away. The escalator changed to a sideway and carried him into a softly gleaming, high-domed room rather like the antechamber of a temple.

"Martian peace to you, Willard Farquar," an invisible voice intoned. "You have entered the Thinkers' Foundation. Please remain on the slideway."

"I want to see Jorj Helmuth," Willard growled loudly.

The slideway carried him into the mouth of a corridor and paused. A dark opening dilated on the wall. "May we take your hat and coat?" a voice asked politely. After a moment the request was repeated, with the addition of, "Just pass them through."

Willard scowled, then fought his way out of his shapeless coat and passed it and his hat through in a lump. Instantly the opening contracted, imprisoning his wrists, and he felt his hands being washed on the other side of the wall.

He gave a great jerk which failed to free his hands from the snugly padded gyves. "Do not be alarmed," the voice advised him. "It is only an esthetic measure. As your hands are laved, invisible radiations are slaughtering all the germs in your body, while more delicate emanations are producing a benign rearrangement of your emotions."

The rather amateurish curses Willard was gritting between his teeth became more sulphurous. His sensations told him that a towel of some sort was being applied to his hands. He wondered if he would be subjected to a face-washing and even greater indignities. Then, just before his wrists were released, he felt—for a moment only, but unmistakably—the soft touch of a girl's hand.

That touch, like the mysterious sweet chink of a bell in darkness, brought him a sudden feeling of excitement, wonder.

Yet the feeling was as fleeting as that caused by a lurid advertisement, for as the slideway began to move again, carrying him past a series of depth pictures and inscriptions celebrating the Thinkers' achievements, his mood of bitter exasperation returned doubled. This place, he told himself, was a plague spot of the disease of magic in an enfeebled and easily infected world. He reminded himself that he was not without resources—the Thinkers must fear or need him, whether because of the Maelzel question or the necessity of producing a nuclear power spaceship. He felt his determination to smash them reaffirmed.

The slideway, having twice turned into an escalator, veered toward an opalescent door, which opened as silently as the one below. The slideway stopped at the threshold. Momentum carried him a couple of steps into the room. He stopped and looked around.

The place was a sybarite's modernistic dream. Sponge carpeting thick as a mattress and topped with down. Hassocks and couches that looked butter-soft. A domed ceiling of deep glossy blue mimicking the night sky, with the constellations tooled in silver. A wall of niches crammed with statuettes of languorous men, women, beasts. A self-service bar with a score of golden spigots. A depth TV screen stimulating a great crystal ball. Here and there barbaric studs of hammered gold that might have been push buttons. A low table set for three with exquisite ware of crystal and gold. An ever-changing scent of resins and flowers.

A smiling fat man clad in pearl gray sports clothes came through one of the curtained archways. Willard recognized Jan Tregarron from his pictures, but did not at once offer to speak to him. Instead he let his gaze wander with an ostentatious contempt around the crammed walls, take in the bar and the set table with its many wineglasses, and finally return to his host.

"And where," he asked with harsh irony, "are the dancing girls?"

The fat man's eyebrows rose. "In there," he said innocently, indicating the second archway. The curtains parted.

"Oh, I *am* sorry," the fat man apologized. "There seems to be only one on duty. I hope that isn't too much at variance with your tastes."

She stood in the archway, demure and lovely in an off-the-bosom frock of pale blue skylon edged in mutated mink. She was smiling the first smile that Willard had ever had from her lips.

"Mr. Willard Farquar," the fat man murmured, "Miss Arkady Simms."

Jorj Helmuth turned from the conference table with its dozen empty chairs to the two mousily pretty secretaries.

"No word from the door yet, Master," one of them ventured to say.

Jorj twisted in his chair, though hardly uncomfortably, since it was a beautiful pneumatic job. His nervousness at having to face the twelve rocket physicists—a feeling which, he had to admit, had been unexpectedly great—was giving way to impatience.

"What's Willard Farquar's phone?" he asked sharply.

One of the secretaries ran through a clutch of desk tapes, then spent some seconds whispering into her throat-mike and listening to answers from the soft-speaker.

"He lives with Morton Opperly, who doesn't have one," she finally gold Jorj in scandalized tones.

"Let me see the list," Jorj said. Then, after a bit, "Try Dr. Welcome's place."

This time there were results. Within a quarter of a minute

he was handed a phone which he hung expertly on his shoulder.

"This is Dr. Asa Welcome," a reedy voice told him.

"This is Helmuth of the Thinkers' Foundation," Jorj said icily. "Did you get my communication?"

The reedy voice became anxious and placating. "Why yes, Mr. Helmuth, I did. Very glad to get it too. Sounded most interesting. Very eager to come. But——"

"Yes?"

"Well, I was just about to hop in my 'copter—my son's 'copter—when the other note came."

"What other note?"

"Why, the note calling the meeting off."

"I sent no other note!"

The other voice became acutely embarrassed. "But I considered it to be from you—or just about the same thing. I really think I had the right to assume that."

"How was it signed?" Jorj rapped.

"Mr. Jan Tregarron."

Jorj broke the connection. He didn't move until a low sound shattered his abstraction and he realized that one of the girls was whispering a call to the door. He handed back the phone and dismissed them. They went in a rustle of jackets and skirtlets, hesitating at the doorway but not quite daring to look back.

He sat motionless a minute longer. Then his hand crept fretfully onto the table and pushed a button. The room darkened and a long section of wall became transparent, revealing a dozen silvery models of spaceships, beautifully executed. He quickly touched another; the models faded and the opposite wall bloomed with an animated cartoon that portrayed with charming humor and detail the designing and construction of a neutron-drive spaceship. A third button, and a depth picture of deep star-speckled space opened behind the cartoon, showing a section of Earth's surface and in the far distance the tiny ruddy globe of Mars. Slowly a tiny rocket rose from the section of Earth and spread its silvery sails.

He switched off the pictures, keeping the room dark. By a faint table light he dejectedly examined his organizational charts for the neutron-drive project, the long list of books he had boned up on by somno-learning, the concealed table of physical constants and all sorts of other crucial details about rocket physics—a cleverly condensed encyclopedic "pony" to help out his memory on technical points that might have arisen in his discussion with the experts.

He switched out all the lights and slumped forward, blinking his eyes and trying to swallow the lump in his throat. In the dark his memory went seeping back, back, to the day when his math teacher had told him, very superciliously, that the marvelous fantasies he loved to read and hoarded by his bed weren't real science at all, but just a kind of lurid pretense. He had so wanted to be a scientist, and the teacher's contempt had cast a damper on his ambition.

And now that the conference was canceled, would he ever know that it wouldn't have turned out the same way today? That his somno-learning hadn't taken? That his "pony" wasn't good enough? That his ability to handle people extended only to credulous farmer Presidents and mousy girls in skirtlets? Only the test of meeting the experts would have answered those questions.

Tregarron was the one to blame! Tregarron with his sly tyrannical ways, Tregarron with his fear of losing the future to men who really understood theoretics and could handle experts. Tregarron, so used to working by deception that he couldn't see when it became a fault and a crime. Tregarron, who must now be shown the light—or, failing that, against whom certain steps must be taken.

For perhaps half an hour Jorj sat very still, thinking. Then he turned to the phone and, after some delay, got his party.

"What is it now, Jorj?" Caddy asked impatiently. "Please don't bother me with any of your moods, because I'm tired and my nerves are on edge."

He took a breath. When steps may have to be taken, he thought, one must hold an agent in readiness. "Caddums," he intoned hypnotically, vibrantly. "Caddums——"

The voice at the other end had instantly changed, become submissive, sleepy, suppliant.

"Yes, Master?"

Morton Opperly looked up from the sheet of neatly penned equations at Willar Farquar, who had somehow acquired a measure of poise. He neither lumbered restlessly nor grimaced. He removed his coat with a certain dignity and stood solidly before his mentor. He smiled. Granting that he was a bear, one might guess he had just been fed.

"You see?" he said. "They didn't hurt me."

"They didn't hurt you?" Opperly asked softly.

Willard slowly shook his head. His smile broadened.

Opperly put down his pen, folded his hands. "And you're as determined as ever to expose and smash the Thinkers?"

"Of course!" The menacing growl came back into the bear's voice, except that it was touched with a certain pleased luxuriousness. "Only from now on I won't be teasing the zoo animals, and I won't embarrass you by asking any more Maelzel questions. I have reached the objective at which those tactics were aimed. After this I shall bore from within."

"Bore from within," Opperly repeated, frowning. "Now where have I heard that phrase before?" His brow cleared. "Oh yes," he said listlessly. "Do I understand that you are becoming a Thinker, Willard?"

The other gave him a faintly pitying smile, stretched himself on the couch and gazed at the ceiling. All his movements were deliberate, easy.

"Certainly. That's the only realistic way to smash them. Rise high in their councils. Out-trick all their trickeries. Organize a fifth column. Then *strike!*"

"The end justifying the means, of course," Opperly said.

"Of course. As surely as the desire to stand up justifies your disturbing the air over your head. All action in this world is nothing but means."

Opperly nodded abstractedly. "I wonder if anyone else ever became a Thinker for those same reasons. I wonder if being a Thinker doesn't simply mean that you've decided you have to use lies and tricks as your chief method."

Willard shrugged. "Could be." There was no longer any doubt about the pitying quality of his smile.

Opperly stood up, squaring together his papers. "So you'll be working with Helmuth?"

"Not Helmuth. Tregarron." The bear's smile became cruel. "I'm afraid that Helmuth's career as a Thinker is going to have quite a setback."

"Helmuth," Opperly mused. "Morgenschein once told me a bit about him. A man of some idealism, despite his affiliations. Best of a bad lot. Incidentally, is he the one with whom——"

"—Miss Arkady Simms ran off?" Willard finished without any embarrassment. "Yes, that was Helmuth. But that's all going to be changed now."

Opperly nodded. "Good-by, Willard," he said.

Willard quickly heaved himself up on an elbow. Opperly looked at him for about five seconds, then, without a word, walked out of the room.

The only obvious furnishings in Jan Tregarron's office were a flat-topped desk and a few chairs. Tregarron sat behind the desk, the top of which was completely bare. He looked almost bored, except that his little eyes were smiling. Jorj Helmuth sat across the desk from him, a few feet back, erect and grim-faced, while Caddy, shadowy in the muted light, stood against the wall behind Tregarron. She still wore the fur-trimmed skylon frock she'd put on that afternoon. She took no part in the conversation, seemed almost unaware of it.

"So you just went ahead and canceled the conference without consulting me?" Jorj was saying.

"You called it without consulting me." Tregarron playfully wagged a finger. "Shouldn't do that sort of thing, Jorj."

"But I tell you, I was completely prepared. I was absolutely sure of my ground."

"I know, I know," Tregarron said lightly. "But it's not the right time for it. I'm the best judge of that."

"When will be the right time?"

Tregarron shrugged. "Look here, Jorj," he said, "every man should stick to his trade, to his forte. Technology isn't ours."

Jorj's lips thinned. "But you know as well as I do that we are going to have to have a nuclear spaceship and actually go to Mars someday."

Tregarron lifted his eyebrows. "Are we?"

"Yes! Just as we're going to have to build a real Maizie. All the things we've done until now have been emergency measures."

"Really?"

Jorj stared at him "Look here, Jan," he said, gripping his knees with his hands, "you and I are going to have to talk things through."

"Are you quite sure of that?" Jan's voice was very cool.

"I have a feeling that it might be best if you said nothing and accepted things as they are."

"No!"

"Very well." Tregarron settled himself in his chair.

"I helped you organize the Thinkers," Jorj said, and waited. "At least, I was your first partner."

Tregarron barely nodded.

"Our basic idea was that the time had come to apply science to the life of man on a large scale, to live rationally and realistically. The only things holding the world back from this all-important step were the ignorance, superstition, and inertia of the average man, and the stuffiness and lack of enterprise of the academic scientists.

"Yet we knew that in their deepest hearts the average man and the professionals were both on our side. They wanted the new world visualized by science. They wanted the simplifications and conveniences, the glorious adventures of the human mind and body. They wanted the trips to Mars and into the depths of the human psyche, they wanted the robots and the thinking machines. All they lacked was the nerve to take the first big step—and that was what we supplied.

"It was no time for half measures, for slow and sober plodding. The world was racked by wars and neurosis, in danger of falling into the foulest hands. What was needed was a tremendous and thrilling appeal to the human imagination, an earth-shaking affirmation of the power of science for good.

"But the men who provided that appeal and affirmation couldn't afford to be cautious. They wouldn't check and double check. They couldn't wait for the grudging and jealous approval of the professionals. They had to use stunts, tricks, fakes—*anything to get over the big point*. Once that had been done, once mankind was headed down the new road, it would be easy enough to give the average man the necessary degree of insight to heal the breach with the professionals, to make good in actuality what had been made good only in pretense.

"Have I stated our position fairly?"

Tregarron's eyes were hooded. "You're the one who's telling it."

"On those general assumptions we established our hold on susceptible leaders and the mob," Jorj went on. "We built Maizie and the Mars rocket and the Mind Bomb. We discovered the wisdom of the Martians. We *sold* the people on the science that the professionals had been too high-toned to advertise or bring into the market place.

"But now that we've succeeded, now that we've made the big point, now that Maizie and Mars and science do rule the average human imagination, the time has come to take the second big step, to let accomplishment catch up with imagination, to implement fantasy with fact.

"Do you suppose I'd ever have gone into this with you if it hadn't been for the thought of that second big step? Why, I'd have felt dirty and cheap, a mere charlatan—except for the sure conviction that someday everything would be set right. I've devoted my whole life to that conviction, Jan. I've studied and disciplined myself, using every scientific means at my disposal, so that I wouldn't be found lacking when the day came to heal the breach between the Thinkers and the professionals. I've trained myself to be the perfect liaison man for the job.

"Jan, the day's come and I'm the man. I know you've been concentrating on other aspects of our work; you haven't had time to keep up with my side of it. But I'm sure that as soon as you see how carefully I've prepared myself, how completely practical the neutron-drive rocket project is, you'll beg me to go ahead!"

Tregarron smiled at the ceiling for a moment. "Your general idea isn't so bad, Jorj, but your time scale is out of whack and your judgment is a joke. Oh yes. Every revolutionary wants to see the big change take place in his lifetime. Tch! It's as if he were watching evolutionary vaudeville and wanted the Ape-to-Man Act over in twenty minutes.

"Time for the second big step? Jorj, the average man's exactly what he was ten years ago, except that he's got a new god. More than ever he thinks of Mars as a Hollywood paradise, with wise men and yummy princesses. Maizie is Mama magnified a million times. As for professional scientists, they're more jealous and stuffy than ever. All they'd like to do is turn the clock back to a genteel dream world of quiet quadrangles and caps and gowns, where every commoner bows to the passing scholar.

"Maybe in ten thousand years we'll be ready for the second big step. Maybe. Meanwhile, as should be, the clever

will rule the stupid for their own good. The realists will rule
the dreamers. Those with free hands* will rule those who
have deliberately handcuffed themselves with taboos.

"Secondly, your judgment. Did you actually think you
could have bossed those professionals, kept your mental
footing in the intellectual melee? You, a nuclear physicist?
A rocket scientist? Why, it's—— Take it easy now, boy,
and listen to me. They'd have torn you to pieces in twenty
minutes and glad of the chance! You baffle me, Jorj. You
know that Maizie and the Mars rocket and all that are fakes,
yet you believe in your somno-learning and consciousness-
expansion and optimism-pumping like the veriest yokel. I
wouldn't be surprised to hear you'd taken up ESP and
hypnotism. I think you should take stock of yourself and get
a new slant. It's overdue."

He leaned back. Jorj's face had become a mask. His eyes
did not flicker from Tregarron's, yet there was a subtle
change in his expression. Behind Tregarron, Caddy swayed
as if in a sudden gust of intangible wind and took a silent
step forward from the wall.

"That's your honest opinion?" Jorj asked very quietly.

"It's more than that," Tregarron told him, just as
unmelodramatically. "It's orders."

Jorj stood up purposefully. "Very well," he said. "In that
case I have to tell you that——"

Casually, but with no waste motion, Tregarron slipped an
utrasonic pistol from under the desk and laid it on the
empty top.

"No," he said, "let me tell you something. I was afraid
this would happen and I made preparations. If you've
studied your Nazi, Fascist, and Soviet history, you know
what happens to old revolutionaries who don't move with
the times. But I'm not going to be too harsh. I have a couple
of boys waiting outside. They'll take you by 'copter to the
field, then by jet to New Mex. Bright and early tomorrow
morning, Jorj, you're leaving on a trip to Mars."

Jorj hardly reacted to the words. Caddy was two steps
nearer Tregarron.

"I decided Mars would be the best place for you," the fat
man continued. "The robot controls will be arranged so that
your 'visit' to Mars lasts two years. Perhaps in that time you
will have learned wisdom, such as realizing that the big liar
must never fall for his own big lie.

"Meanwhile, there will have to be a replacement for you. I have in mind a person who may prove peculiarly worthy to occupy your position, with all its perquisites. A person who seems to understand that force and desire are the motive powers of life, and that anyone who believes the big lie proves himself strictly a jerk."

Caddy was standing behind Tregarron now, her half-closed, sleepy eyes fixed on Jorj's.

"His name is Willard Farquar. You see, I too believe in co-operating with the scientists, Jorj, but by subversion rather than conference. My idea is to offer the hand of friendship to a selected few of them—the hand of friendship with a nice big bribe in it." He smiled. "You were a good man, Jorj, for the early days, when we needed a publicist with catchy ideas about Mind Bombs, ray guns, plastic helmets, fancy sweaters, space brassières, and all that other corn. Now we can afford a solider sort of person."

Jorj moistened his lips.

"We'll have a neat explanation of what's happened to you. Callers will be informed that you've gone on an extended visit to imbibe the wisdom of the Martians."

Jorj whispered, "Caddums."

Caddy leaned forward. Her arms snaked down Tregarron's, as if to imprison his wrists. But instead she reached out and took the ultrasonic pistol and put it in Tregarron's right hand. Then she looked up at Jorj with eyes that were very bright.

She said very sweetly and sympathetically, "Poor Superman."